The Jordon Journals: Book Two

TWICE in a BLUE MOON

a novel

Derek Bullard

Brenda
Stay warm
while you
read this one!

Derek Bullard

James Kay Publishing

Tulsa, Oklahoma

TWICE in a BLUE MOON
ISBN 978-0-9728288-8-8

For Mom... I Love You
& For Dad... I Miss You

SPECIAL THANKS!

There are so many folks to thank in
the writing of this book.
First of all and always – wife LaDonna (my best friend),
to the Whiteside Gang (you know who you are),
to Carolyn Steele for the hours of editing & advice
(and her husband Carl for his support),
to Jane Hallman for being my champion of unwavering
encouragement (and for her curiosity as to what came after
"to be continued" in Mayan Moon),
all those guys in the oil fields
so many years ago
and of course to all of you who support
these efforts by purchasing and reading my wild tales!

I can do all things through Christ who strengthens me.
Phil 4:13 (NKJV)

also by

Derek Bullard

(Fiction)

Mayan Moon

Moon Ridge

Twist

(Non-Fiction)

Being the Best Employee You Can Be!

Scan this code to order:

or visit:

http://www.jameskaypublishing.com/BookStore.html

Personae

Sen. Ryan Scott Monarch

Sen. Simpson Jacks

Mitch Jordon

Tyler Kincade

Darius "Mr. Detail" Cabrettii

Alan Dover

Veronda Winston

Caxton Grant

Caesar Hamilton

Clifford Foard

Tate Smullins

Kerry Jordon/Lana Turner

"Ox" Oxenthall

Gina Wellingham

Miguel Cortez

Marcel Gatreux

Meg Mordel

A. J. Crandell

Calvin Bellaire

Gen. Antony Stone

Lincoln Bucksaw

Annabelle Jacks

P. T. "Theo" Shay

The following letter obtained through the Freedom of Information Act. Selected portions deemed sensitive and deleted in the interest of national security......

THE WHITE HOUSE

WASHINGTON

5 February 1943

The Honorable Ryan Scott Monarch
United States Senate
Washington D.C.

Dear Senator Monarch:

My apologies for the delay in this correspondence. I have just returned from a conference with the Allied leaders in Morocco and wanted to consider your proposal carefully.

After great deliberation and careful consideration, I have consulted with my security advisers, Mr. ████ and Mr. D█████. It is under their recommendation we implement Special Executive Order # ███ in accordance with all established procedures. (With the exception of █████.) It is with great reservation I agree to this stipulation.

As you and Senator Jacks advised, we will put into place your plan to conceal the following from the enemy with all due haste.

1) ███████   2) ████████

3) ███████   4) ████████

I have also consulted with Major General ██████ and he advises the "Manhattan Project" is on schedule and a prototype will be available. The following three locations have been recommended to me pending your final evaluation of the operation.

1)   Near Cody, W█████

2)   Near Wildwood, O██████

3)   Near Sioux City, I███

The project will be labeled TOP SECRET and designated "Project Liberty Hole" to be administered by yourself and Senator Jacks.

I need not remind you of the consequences of our actions should you fail at your mission.

(signature)

Franklin D. Roosevelt
cc/MS/KD/SJ/LG

PROLOGUE_____

April 13, 1945

Ryan Scott Monarch puffed his cigar, sipped his brandy and concentrated on the centerline of the two lane blacktop. Life had taken a sudden and unexpected ninety degree swing for the better.

He nudged the accelerator and felt the air swim through his hair while his '37 supercharged convertible took advantage of the lonely road. "Yessiree," he said and poked his passenger with the flask. "Life is good! Wake up, Jacky boy. F.D.R. is dead."

Monarch's business partner and Senate crony, Simpson Jacks, rubbed his lips and accepted the flask. "Watcha say?" Too much booze on the train the night before left him lethargic.

"I said, Jacky boy, old man Roos-e-velt is dead. It's been all over the radio."

"Where? When?" Jacks sloshed the brandy onto his tie.

"Warm Springs. Sometime yesterday. Was havin' his picture painted and..." Monarch whistled and pantomimed his cigar dive bombing, like a plane he'd seen in the newsreels. Ash scattered across the seat when it slammed into the dash.

Jacks sat upright. "Thash awful."

Monarch eased the fast car back into his lane and glanced at the speedometer. One hundred ten. *What a car!* "You hated the old man."

"No, I mean how you just wasted a good cigar."

"Not to worry, Jacky boy. We've got so much money, we can trash a thousand cigars and not bat an eye."

"That means..." Jacks stared ahead. "That means, Truman's preshhident nooww. I'm not liking that, I'll tell you right (hic) right now. I'll tell you right now, I'm not liking that."

"Don't you mind Harry. He's got enough worries without sniffin' around in our business. It'll be years before anyone gets a chance to read

1

the old man's private papers. I tell ya' Jacky boy, you had a brainstorm and a half when you dreamed this scheme up. A stroke of genius, absolute stroke of genius."

"I am, I am, I am." Jacks guzzled more brandy. "You laughed at me."

"Maybe so, but no longer." Monarch pulled another cigar from his pocket, bit off the end and spit it over his head into the wind. "You suckered those idiots Dupree and Stuart into convincing the old man we had the patriotic plan of a lifetime." He grabbed the flask and enjoyed the fire as it rolled down his throat. "Here's to the good ol' U.S.A. and Project Liberty Hole."

A grin centered on Jacks' face. "Here, here, Shenator Monarch. And to Rocky Grazzzzzshiano while we're at it! Hey and wash the tree, will ya?"

Ryan Scott Monarch looked forward in time to see the hood of his Cord engulf the large cottonwood. In a matter of seconds, life had taken a one-eighty.

- PART I: OLD WOUNDS -

"Well meant are the wounds
a friend
inflicts, but profuse are the kisses of
an enemy."

Proverbs 27:6

ONE_____

The Day After Tomorrow:

A faint noise echoed through the peaks and faded away.
"Wonder what...?" Mitch Jordon glanced over his shoulder and shrugged. "Probably nothing." Satisfied, he slipped his supply laden canoe into the gentle water and searched under a pile of blankets for his paddle. Soon he knifed his way toward the far shore.

The ripples from his strokes grew larger, then swept away in the current formed by the graceful movement of his sleek canoe. A flock of black-billed magpies argued overhead as a strong wind knocked them from the air.

"What--"

A loud roar, produced by the rotors of a helicopter, assaulted his ears as it dropped from above.

"What is he doing?" Jordon paddled faster and felt his breath echo the rhythm of each stroke. He calculated his time to shore. "Maybe I can get to cover."

The copter hovered and hesitated before it dropped to within a few feet above. Escape appeared futile and Jordon held up a hand to keep the spray from his eyes while he slipped the other under the blankets. His finger curled around the trigger of his rifle.

A man with a bandaged head struggled in the door of the huge unmarked, military craft to steady a mounted M6O-D machine gun. He peered down the site and the first burst from the weapon sliced through the bow of the canoe.

When the man looked down to view the damage, Jordon saw his face. Treacherous eyes smoldered in the folds of scar tissue. Clenched teeth spoke revenge.

"Kincade!" Jordon braced himself as the canoe took on icy cold water. *How'd he get a helicopter?* The questions multiplied in inverse proportion to the amount of time he felt he had left to live.

The flying menace swept through the air for another attack.

Something doesn't pan out here. Markings. They're all wrong. It's not ASTRO and it's not military either.

Mist spiraled upward from the cold Colorado lake when the craft shot past.

Jordon's fingers located the butt plate of his rifle, but he recoiled as bullets peppered the pile of blankets like hailstones on fire.

"Now, this is getting serious!" Jordon peeled back shredded cloth. "Thought I'd seen the last of you. But, no. You can't leave well enough alone." He uncovered his rifle, yanked it to his shoulder and tried to steady the canoe with his knees. A single shot, intended for wild game, waited in the barrel. This one round of lead needed to take out the tail rotor of a hostile helicopter... From a rocking, sinking platform... In poor visibility...

"When they lock someone up in the nut house, they're supposed to stay locked up. Not allowed out for joy rides." *Especially not with heavy artillery.*

He held his breath and focused. Flame spit from the end of the barrel as the canoe jerked aft.

Way off... He struggled to steady himself without losing his weapon and watched the .50 caliber ball strike the copter wide of the spinning blade. Seconds later a shower of sparks revealed damage to something important.

"...and maybe not."

Jordon scrambled to reload but an interruption of machine gun fire splattered in the water and ramped up the difficulty of the task. A second blast split the ramrod above the barrel. Wood splinters sliced into Jordon's shoulder and pain raced down his arm like molten steel.

The helicopter circled wide and descended for the final kill.

Jordon abandoned his useless weapon and crawled toward the front of his sinking craft in hopes of finding the small caliber pistol hid in his bedroll.

A bullet penetrated his shoulder, inches from the ramrod wound, and slapped him back with the force of a charging bull. He felt blood splatter across his cheek. A glance down revealed torn flesh and a flow of crimson.

The water swirled around him, beat into a frenzied froth by the hovering helicopter.

Not good. Jordon gripped the lip of the canoe with the hand of his uninjured arm and rocked from side to side until he capsized.

From inside the icy cold air pocket, he heard more bullets pop and zing as they attacked the surface like a swarm of mad bees. He peered through a jagged hole in the hull and saw smoke. It billowed around

Kincade in the open door a few yards above the scuttled craft.

The smoke thickened and without warning, the front of the vehicle exploded. The force of the blast sent the pilot like a cannonball through the windshield and the human projectile landed with an unceremonious splash fifty yards away. Hot debris sizzled and rained from the air onto the bottom of the capsized canoe as the main fuselage hesitated as if unsure of when to give up.

Jordon struggled to swim with his one good arm. Fearful the remains of the craft might drop out of the sky on top of him, he pushed away from the fiery boat with his feet. When his head broke the surface of the numbing water he saw the remaining fuselage explode again and cartwheel in slow motion toward the shore, trailing thick, oily smoke like a medieval fire-spitting dragon. The tail rotor of the beheaded beast chewed through the tops of pine trees with a vengeance and an orange fireball surrounded everything else. Nothing but the ground promised to stop the deadly descent, except...

No, not the...

He closed his eyes as the twisted carnage crashed and exploded for the last time.

...roof of my cabin!

TWO

D arius Cabrettii concentrated on his mental clock. *Two minutes until Moonrise.* When it appeared over the top of the chalk white rampart as if scheduled by him, he smiled and watched a long shadow crawl across the roadway.

"That's why they call me, 'Mr. Detail'," he whispered and thought of his brother's death during the botched heist in D.C. *Never again. From now on, 'Mr. Detail' makes all the plans.* He championed himself a lone wolf, meticulous and exact in every phase.

"I'll show 'em I'm not crazy. Ain't a joint in the world I can't break into." He watched the movement of the prison lights. "Breakin' in is easy. They don't expect it, especially with the Moon so bright. They're too busy playin' nursemaid to all them maximum security birds. Too busy to notice the master at work."

The hard preparation completed weeks earlier, Cabrettii mentally reviewed his plan one final time. *Plastic surgery, dental work, voice lessons.* "Yeah, tough part's over." *Now, the final act.* Break into the fed's most secure rock without gadgets or gizmos. No infrared night scopes, no computerized code breakers, nothing to trace if found. *Doin' it the old fashioned way: Like Papa usta.*

He pulled the black ski mask over his face and slipped into the shadows as a humorous thought came to mind. *What was it they called Papa in the old days? Cat burglar! Ain't no cat cooler than me.*

A half hour later Cabrettii stared up through the scum-covered grate at the yellowed ceiling of the shower next to the guard's locker room. At this hour, he expected no shift changes. *'Mr. Detail' is on the job.* With effort he pushed up on the drain, careful to avoid the scrape of metal on tile, and squeezed through the hole. He wrinkled his nose as the reek of mildew and deodorant soap wafted over him.

He stripped from his black attire, pulled a wallet from the pocket and dropped the bundle of garments into the sewer before he lowered the grill back to the floor.

A quick shower, then a search for a certain locker produced the necessary replacement wardrobe. After dressing, he buckled his nylon 'utility belt', adjusted his badge, pocketed the wallet and walked into the weapons room with a mock yawn. The sharp-resistant vest under his shirt felt a bit tight, but otherwise everything fit fine.

He waved at the duty officer, leaning against the wall reading the sports page. "Mornin', Lou," he said in a voice an octave lower than his own. "How's it goin'?"

Lou McLanathan barely glanced up. "Can't complain, Billy." He took a sip from the mug he held in his other hand. "Didn't see you come in. What'd you do, sleep in there last night?" His attention remained on the scores. "'Fraid all those little Halloween rug rats will bite you?"

Cabrettii stroked his fake mustache and thought of Bill Morgan's body sinking to the bottom of the river a few hours earlier. "You seen the teeth on some of those kiddies?" He pantomimed a shiver. "Chew right through a man's ankle in no time flat, tie a rock around his neck and throw him off a bridge. Ain't no night to be out."

McLanathan guffawed like a bull moose, rolled up his paper and slapped Cabrettii on the shoulder with it. "That's what I like about you, Billy. Always quick with the cracks early in the morning. Don't know how you do it. I ain't even awake yet." He rubbed a bit of sleep crud from the corner of his eye, set his mug on a desk and moved to a cabinet on the wall. He unlocked a panel and extracted Morgan's sidearm. "Here, don't shoot yourself."

Cabrettii holstered the Glock. "Don't know, Lou. Might be good for a worker's comp claim."

"Naw, you'd get writer's cramp from filling out all the forms." McLanathan opened the door into the main corridor and laughed until he bumped into the desk and sloshed his coffee on the floor. "See ya later, Billy. Maybe someday we'll have ourselves a quick draw contest. See who gets the blue ribbon at the fair."

Not likely. "Yeah, maybe. See ya, Lou." *How about that? 'Mr. Detail' fools the senior duty officer. Anybody surprised? I can picture him tomorrow. 'Whata ya mean, Billy's dead? Just saw him yesterday mornin'. Yeah, he was alive. He weren't no Halloween spook, if that's what ya mean.'*

Next stop, M-Block, maximum solitaire. The Hole. Punk guard's name is Clarkson. Goofy car buff, girlfriend named... Cabrettii spooled off the details in his mind as he walked.

Clarkson lounged behind his desk next to the sallyport, a copy of *MUFFLER ILLUSTRATED* in his hands and his feet propped on a filing cabinet.

"Clarkson!"

The young guard spilled from his chair and ripped the cover off his magazine as he tried to right himself. "Lieutenant Morgan! Good morning, sir!"

"Wipe the jelly doughnut off your tie, Mister!" Cabrettii barked the command in his best 'Billy Morgan' military style. "Get me the clipboard on number eight."

"Right away, sir." Clarkson fumbled with his tie, wet his thumb and rubbed at the stain.

"Now!"

"Yes, sir. Now, sir!"

When the file hit his hand, Cabrettii hesitated for a moment, stared Clarkson back into his chair and lowered his gaze to the papers to study information he already knew. But, by their very nature, details always needed to be updated. "I'll be escorting the prisoner up to Warden Quinn's office. Open up."

The stunned guard scavenged his desk for the daily log. "Warden... Uh..." He scanned the list of names and pursed his lips. "Uh, I'm sorry, sir, but you're not... Uh, and besides, it's kinda early, isn't it? I thought the warden didn't come in... You know? Until seven. That's a few hours away. And anyway--"

"Look," Cabrettii put his knuckles on the desk and moved nose-to-nose with the younger man, "number eight is not your run-of-the-mill prisoner. He's a guest here of the brass in D.C. If the warden wants to keep going to those brandy and cigar dinners, he hops when they ask favors. He hops high. You getting my drift here, son?"

"Yes, sir." Clarkson held up the list and pointed to the names. "But I still have to have proper authorization."

"Very well." Cabrettii lifted the receiver on the phone and held it at arm's length while he leaned back against the bars. "You call Quinn in his office and get your authorization. He's probably through his first cup of coffee by now. Usually not a bit social until after his fourth, but you can take your chances."

The guard reached for the receiver as if it'd been decorated with razor blades, glanced at the clock on the wall and bit his lip.

Seconds ticked like thunder.

"Maybe he'll be on his fourth cup by the time you get there with the prisoner." Clarkson dropped the list and pulled his keys to unlock the gate control box. "Your weapon, sir. Anything happens to you and Quinn will have my neck. The guy in number eight is a sneaky so-and-so."

The Glock went into the desk drawer.

Cabrettii retrieved the magazine from the floor and slapped it into

Clarkson's hand. "Son, you have made a wise decision." On the way through the outer cell door he turned. "I'll remind the warden of your good work."

"Thank you, sir."

The bars clanked shut. Cabrettii proceeded through and waited for the second gate. *Piece of cake--*

"Hold it right there!" Clarkson yelled.

Cabrettii turned.

"Your hand, sir. Place it under the black light."

Cabrettii flinched. A detail missed. *Bad sign.* "Why of course. Good work, Clarkson. Glad to see you're paying attention. You'll go far here." He passed the back of his hand under the ultraviolet bulb and the word-of-the-day, normally ink stamped when a guard arrived for work at the main entrance, lit up for Clarkson to read. The outer gate of the sallyport opened and Cabrettii walked to number eight, mentally kicking himself with every step.

Arrival at his destination refocused him to the mission. A survey of his surroundings confirmed the trek almost complete. Damp, musty. Hole described the cell before him to a fault.

He peeked through the slotted opening in the steel door and a light flashed on inside the small room, activated by Clarkson at the far end of the corridor.

A lone prisoner lay asleep on a lumpy bunk.

"So, this is the famous Alan Dover." Darius Cabrettii whispered. *Time to introduce myself.*

THREE

S omeone pounds on the door.
A man in a spacesuit.
He wants to open the escape hatch.
He wants to pull all the air from the room.
A face.
Reflected sunlight distorts the features.
Who is he?
Is it Jordon?
It is!
He haunts me.
He stalks me.
He must...
...die!
"Wake up, Dover!"
The voice isn't Jordon's.
A dream? No, this nightmare will end like all the others. When I open my eyes, I'll still be in a stinking hole. And Jordon will still be...
Another distraction.
Why are the lights on? Is this the day? Wake up. He's here. He's come for me. No, he's still out there. Free. But not for long.
"Get up, Dover! Move your sorry self against the back wall."
Dover rolled over on the lumpy bunk and shielded his eyes from the light. *It's that sadistic Morgan. I'd recognize his cheesy mustache anywhere.* "W-Wha? W-What do you w-want?"
"You do as you're told. Now, mister!"
The floor felt cold on Dover's bare feet as he reached for the sink and pulled himself upright. Two bottles of liquid soap toppled from the basin and rolled on the floor. "I'm up. What t-time is it?"
The guard's face disappeared from the portal in the door. "Open it, Clarkson."
"Keep quiet!" a muffled voice yelled from a cell down the way.
"You'll think 'keep quiet' when my night stick is rattling on your

skull." The door slid open with a whine and Morgan stepped across the threshold. He surveyed the rock cubical. "I think you've been expecting me."

The door complained again as it shut.

"N-No, I had hoped you'd found th-the valet who has my car keys. What do you want, Mor-Morgan?"

"You'll be pleased with what I've got to show you." The guard removed his hat.

Isn't Morgan taller than me? Dover cocked his head to the side and studied the man.

The guard tugged on his eyebrow. It peeled away like the skin of an orange. Next came plastic teeth and a false nose. The cheesy mustache disappeared and revealed the last of the transformation.

"No..." Dover tried to take a step back and flinched when the cold edge of the sink prevented his retreat.

The man moved forward into what better light the bulb overhead offered.

Dover stared into a mirror image of himself. "Remarkable!"

"Satisfied?"

So, this is the guy they call, 'Mr. Detail'. "You're earlier than I expected. How about the scar?" Dover grabbed at the imposter's tie.

"No, I'm right on time." He glanced at his watch. "To the second." He removed his shirt to reveal a healed wound. A perfect match. "I'm your twin."

"How did you g-get it?"

"Little lady down in Mexico bit me."

"W-What's your deal?"

'Mr. Detail' turned, examined the corridor through the portal, then sat on the bunk. He kicked off his shoes and tested the mattress. "I've already deposited t-ten million into a bank in the Caymans." His voice pitched higher. "I swap p-places with you here in 'Club Fed', get a master's degree at the ta-taxpayer's expense, wait two years, then escape. Meanwhile I'll be racking up mucho dinero as my interest c-compounds daily and you'll be settled into your new life."

This guy is good, but I don't stutter that bad. Dover scratched his ear and sat next to his reflection on the bunk. "What about d-dental?"

"Every cavity has been c-completely duplicated. Didn't spend three months in a hospital for nothing. The plastic surgery is a work of art. Our voices are so sim-similar, your own mother couldn't tell us apart. Matter-of-fact, she can't. I called her last week. You've been a bad boy. She said you hadn't called her since you got in. Anyway, lower it a bit to get past Clarkson. Bully him and he'll melt."

Dover continued to admire his twin while they exchanged clothes. While they did so, 'Mr. Detail' outlined his entrance, which in turn represented the escape route.

"G-Got a cigarette on you?" said Dover.

His liberator's expression went blank. Something in his eyes conveyed a sort of bewildered terror.

"They told me you didn't smoke," he said in his own voice. "They were supposed ta tell me everythin'." He stood, stared at the ceiling, and rocked back and forth on his heels. "Not good, not good at all. What else did they forget?"

Dover pulled at the man's sleeve. "C-Calm d-down. They didn't know. I just started."

"Bad plan." His eyes drew Dover in.

The overwhelming sensation of staring into a mirror gave Dover cold chills. "Look, smoke for a week or so, then g-give it up if you don't like it. Who's t-to say I wouldn't do the sa-same?" He reached under the bunk and pulled out a carton. "This stuff is like cash in this place."

"Everything okay down there?" Clarkson's voice echoed in the corridor.

"Shut up, punk!" yelled the disgruntled inmate down the way.

'Mr. Detail' put his face to the opening. "Everything's fine," he said in Billy Morgan's voice.

"Yell when you're ready, sir."

"One more minute."

Dover pressed the fake eyebrows over his own and inserted the plastic teeth. They tasted stale. Morgan's cap completed the transferred disguise. "Y-You bring the powder?"

'Mr. Detail' pointed to the guard's pants. "In the wal-wallet."

Dover pulled the billfold from his pocket, searched the compartments and extracted a folded slip of wax paper. He handed it to his twin. "C-Crawl into bed and take this. It'll make you sick enough to convince that idiot Clarkson you're in no shape to visit the warden."

"Yeah, yeah I know... I've been over it and over it." The substitute gulped down the yellow powder without water. "Here's to ten m-million dollars."

"Compounded d-daily."

"Yeah, comp..." 'Mr. Detail's' eyes glazed over and he clutched his stomach. "You--"

Dover checked the man's pulse. "Guess you missed a c-crucial one there, pal." He reached for the two bottles of liquid soap on the floor, selected the brown one and unscrewed the cap. An oily smell wafted out.

He poured the bogus soap over his victim's face and shoulders, then lit an unfiltered cigarette and wedged it between the dead man's teeth. He gazed at the dial on his new watch, supplied by his rescuer. "This will burn for ten minutes, j-just in case you wanted th-that trivial little tid-bit of detail for your scrapbook. Then, whoosh! You're a crispy cr-critter and everybody thinks the world is rid of Alan Dover."

FOUR

"**N**ice office." Veronda Winston eased the door shut and kicked off her high heels. The plush carpet felt good between her toes. "So, this is where the fat man sang his last song." She wrinkled her nose. "Smells like my grandfather's den."

A dozen feet away, a large oak desk dominated a fair portion at the room. Behind it, an oversized chair confessed the girth of its previous occupant. A brass plate still announced his name:

CAXTON GRANT - Executive Director
American Space Technical Research Organization

Big title for a big man. Winston plucked the plaque from the desk, polished its bronze surface with the sleeve of her jacket, and dropped it into the wastepaper basket. She dusted her hands against each other and surveyed the rest of the office. "This stuffy old macho codger decor has got to go." With a purse of her lips, she placed an immaculate sculptured fingernail to her chin. "I think maybe a Dalí or Picasso. No. This place needs some cheering up. Warhol. That's the ticket." She plunked into the chair and felt like Goldilocks. "This papa bear chair is definitely on its way to the dumper."

The doorknob rattled.

She leaned back, folded her arms across her chest and waited for the door to open.

"What are you doing in my chair, Winston?"

She pushed away from the desk and spun around. "Not yours anymore, Cax. You're gone, I'm in charge." She toed the carpet and continued the spin.

"Temporarily," Grant approached, a bit of bull elephant in his gait, "until the President appoints a new director."

"Whatever." *How dare he? I should order the old fossil to vacate the premises.*

"Out!" Grant rounded the corner and stopped her spin of the chair.

"Out this minute!"

"I beg your pardon?"

"You heard me, young lady. I may have resigned this office. But until six p.m. tonight, by George, it's still mine!"

"I suppose I'll let you clean out your debris." Winston stood, then perched on the edge at the desk as she crossed her legs and admired their firmness. *Not bad for a forty-plus career minded woman. Pays to work out.* "Mind if I get rid of the old globe and move a stair-stepper in here?" She smiled. "Why, I bet those are words never spoken from behind your desk."

The big man dropped into the chair so hard, Winston expected the wheels to snap off.

"You must have some heavy duty shock absorbers." She ran a finger over her knee. "Industrial even."

Grant huffed.

The intercom buzzed and Winston reached to activate the speaker.

"Do you mind?" Grant said through a glare.

"Not at all. Maybe it's the moving van." *Hope it's equipped with a crane.*

The secretary's voice filled the room. "Mr. Grant, there's a Mr. Caesar Hamilton to see you. He says he's ASTRO's new Director of Lunar Exploration, but I haven't seen a memo to that effect."

"He's--"

Winston cleared her throat. "Send him in."

Grant looked as if an egg fried under his collar when a short man stormed into the office and waved an overstuffed folder in the air.

"Ah, my first bit of important business." Winston intercepted a photo out of the fidgety newcomer's hand and studied it care-fully.

Grant came out his chair, mad as an elephant, and grabbed at the pho-to. "Perhaps, young man, if we introduce ourselves first we can ascertain if we've any business to attend to at all."

"Name's Hamilton." He cocked an eyebrow at Winston. "Caesar Hamilton. I'm in charge of the new lunar exploration project on the dark side."

Grant pointed at the picture. "And does this have something to do with that?"

"Naw, I was killing time and introducing myself around when one of the boys down in the Geo section brought it to my attention. Strangest thing I ever came across."

Winston snagged the photo and bobbed it over the shorter Grant's head like a carrot on a stick. "What is this? An amoeba?"

"No ma'am," Hamilton said. "Satellite recon. S-SMC."

"Which is?"

"I'm sorry, ma'am. I didn't catch your name." He glanced at Grant. "Should we be letting her see these?"

"My name is Veronda Winston, bucko. And at six o'clock this evening, I'm your new boss."

Hamilton blushed. "Sorry, ma'am, no offense. Anyway this is a S-SMC's of--"

"Slow the geek speak, acronym boy." Winston held up her hand, palm out. "I'll ask again. What's an S-SMC?"

Grant cleared his throat. "Sub-Surface Mapping Computer. You've got to learn the alphabet. They use it quite a bit around here."

"Yeah? Well here's some more letters; PhD, UCLA, MIT. That's me. AARP, that's you."

Grant erupted from his chair a second time.

The intercom buzzed, stopping him halfway in and halfway out.

Hamilton took a step back, one eye on the red-faced Grant, the other on Winston.

"Careful little Caesar, you're going to go cross-eyed if you keep making such a face."

Grant huffed at the intercom. "Yes."

"Sir--"

"I gotta see the Chief!" The door burst open and bent a hinge as a huge bald man, with a foul cigar, planted himself in front of the desk. "I'm here to tell you, it's all broke loose out there."

FIVE_____

G rant closed his eyes, then opened them again. *Wishing doesn't make her go away.* He moved his stare to the huge bald man. Former pro football player, great physical shape. *Why does Foard smoke those blasted cigars?* "Welcome, Clifford," he said. "I hadn't expected a going away party, but it appears a convention has been scheduled in lieu of any festivities. I find the chaos invigorating on my last day."

Winston slid from the top of the desk and offered ASTRO's new Security Director her hand. "I'm Veronda Winston. Your new boss."

Foard ignored the offer, but nodded. "Pleased to meet you, lady."

Grant allowed himself a broad smile. *I knew I liked Clifford for a reason.* "So, what's so important, you had to break my door?"

Foard started to speak, then glanced from Winston to the smaller Hamilton. "Sorry, Chief. For your ears only. Security level eight."

Winston recovered her high heels and worked them back onto her feet. With the added height, she managed to stand toe-to-toe with Foard and look him in the chest. "Hey, fella! I'm talking to you. If you have level eight information, we're cleared to hear it."

Grant sensed Foard's need for a response and wiggled his index finger from side-to-side.

"Sorry, lady. I'm mistaken. They boosted this to level nine. I don't recall if you, or shorty over there, have level nine clearance? I know I do. I know the Chief does. Your status remains in great doubt at the moment."

Winston pointed her dagger nail at Foard's chin. "Matter-of-fact--"

Grant cleared his throat. "As a matter-of-fact, she doesn't. Not until six p.m."

Winston turned to glare, narrowed her eyes and moved to grab Hamilton by the collar. "Come on, geo man. We'll go discuss your amoeba photos over a cappuccino."

Hamilton shrugged and offered little resistance. He left the office with Winston in a flurry of, "Yes, ma'ams," and "No, ma'ams."

Foard pulled up a wingback chair and dropped his stout two hundred and eighty pound body into it. "What say, I turn in my resignation and go fishing with you, Chief?"

Grant leaned back in his chair until it creaked. *Nice to have at least one friend to say good-bye to.* "Now, Clifford. You've been here a mere couple of weeks. Why in the world leave so soon?"

"Queen Veronda for a start. How'd she get appointed to the number two position? Didn't anyone realize she'd be in charge once you stepped down?"

Even though Grant knew full well her educational background, he wondered the same thing himself. "I'm in the dark as much as you. She's got more degrees than a thermometer, but no common sense to back them up." He rubbed his eyes and inventoried the top of the desk. "Where in blazes is my nameplate? Enough regarding her, what brought you in such a roar?"

"This." Foard glanced over his shoulder at the door which, because of the damaged hinge, didn't quite close all the way. He slid an Infopak across the blotter with a photo on the wide-screen. "Came in on my little box a few minutes ago. If you've eaten breakfast, don't study it too long."

Grant raised the graphic color image to arm's length. His stomach churned and bile crept up into his throat. He lowered the gruesome photo and swallowed hard. "What is this, Clifford? Somebody's idea of a sick joke?"

Foard retrieved the Infopak and studied the photo in detail by zooming it in and out.

"This slab of barbecue used to be Alan Dover."

A cold chill ran along Grant's spine. "I don't believe it."

"Believe it," said Foard. "Warden Quinn ordered an autopsy almost immediately after they found the body. M.E. gave a positive I.D. within the hour."

"DNA?"

"No need. Dental records. Besides it happened while locked in his cell."

"But how did it happen?"

"At first they thought he fell asleep with a cigarette in his mouth and managed to set himself on fire." Foard started to relight his huge cigar, examined the flame on the match, then blew it out.

Is it possible? Is the crazed killer responsible for my downfall dead? Images swirled through Grant's mind and slammed into freeze frame. He focused on the blackened tip of Foard's match. "Dover didn't smoke."

"He'd just started. Guess he felt one more bad habit didn't make much difference."

Grant cleared the thoughts from his mind. "You said 'at first'..."

"After the photo came in, I got a call. They've changed their minds after going over the cell. Dover may have been murdered."

"What! By whom?"

"Don't know." Foard moved his soggy cigar over to the other side of his mouth. "Apparently he had an unauthorized visitor earlier in the morning. Seems a senior guard named Morgan waltzed right in. Rookie guard fouled up. Some farmer found Morgan's body a couple of hours later, floating downriver."

"An inside job? Why did the guard visit?"

"They're checking it out." Foard stood and moved for the door. "Oh, by the way, my men have a lead on Kincade."

Grant closed his eyes. "And?"

"They're certain he's still in the States, southwestern region."

"Any idea where he's going?"

Foard lit his cigar. "Now, this is speculation, Chief, but I'd guess the mountains. Maybe New Mexico, Utah. Who knows?"

Grant felt all the energy drain from his body. *Mitch. He's going after Mitch.* "Kincade's on his way to Colorado." He felt the quiver in his own voice.

"How can you be certain?"

"It all makes sense. He's after Mitch Jordon."

"On a good day Kincade's in a dangerous state of mind, Chief. Right now..? You better get in touch with Jordon and warn him to be ready. I'll have my men concentrate their search in the Rockies."

"I wish it were so simple. Jordon's a loner. There's no way to get in touch with him, except through personal contact. His cabin is almost inaccessible. Far as I know, there are no roads anywhere near Burns' Lake."

"E-mail?"

Grant shook his head.

"Cell phone?"

"Afraid not. He absolutely detests any form of technology."

"We talking about the same guy? Walked on the Moon? Flies jets?" Foard ran a hand over his hairless head. "I guess Carrier Pigeons are out too."

"Jordon is an odd sort; an eccentric and quintessential pain." Grant lowered his head and studied the carpet. "Wish I'd had ten more like him in the program."

"Hey!" Foard slapped his hands together. "I bet he's got a short wave radio."

"Unlikely, but if he did he'd use it to transmit only during an emergency. And it takes a lot for him to consider something an emergency."

Foard exhaled a puff of smoke and headed for the wounded door. "It's worth a try."

Grant rose from his chair, walked across the office and put his hand on Foard's shoulder. "Clifford, I'd be most grateful if you'd attend to it yourself. Consider it my final instruction as Executive Director. Go up to Jordon's cabin. See if he's okay. Find him, and you'll find Kincade."

Another puff rolled to the ceiling. "Sure, Chief. Be glad to. What about Dover?"

Grant patted Foard on the back. "I'll believe it when I see his body."

"I'll bring the coleslaw." The big security man pulled his cell phone from his pocket, punched numbers and spoke into the receiver. "This is Foard. Have the Lear standing by to take me to Denver. Pack some mountain gear and clothing. Yes. Have it waiting on the plane. I'll be driving over to the airstrip direct. Oh, and arrange a chopper..."

"Mr. Grant, your call to California is on line one."

The director removed his jacket and draped it over the back of his chair, wiped his brow and lifted the receiver. *This is a call I never thought I'd have to make.* The connection crackled in his ear. "Hello?"

"Smullins here. What do you want?"

A certain air of animosity filtered through the line. Tate Smullins, Director of Flight Training, had no trouble displaying his dislike at every opportunity.

Grant took a breath. *Can't say I blame him.* "Good morning, Tate. Sorry to bother you, but I didn't know who else to call. Can you be in Houston by late tonight?"

"Not unless you insist. What's going on?"

Grant looked around his office, or to be more precise, soon to be ex-office. "On second thought, I'll come to you. Maybe tomorrow. This is very sensitive."

"Guess I'll wait. I don't mind telling you, I don't feel real comfortable being in the same zip code with you after all that's taken place. I suppose you want Kelly along?"

Grant pictured Smullins biting through his ever present toothpick and considered whether or not to invite his new bride into the mess. *She might keep Tate in check.* Yet... "I don't want anyone to know we're meeting." *Not even your wife.* "As I said, this is quite sensitive. I'll let you know when and where, after I arrive."

"Okay. It's a done deal. I'm teaching a class, but I can meet you afterwards."

"Thank you, Tate. I know I can count on you." He cradled the receiver gently, leaned over to his credenza and opened a lower drawer with a key from his vest pocket. A spin of a small dial opened the safe inside. He extracted a sheaf of personal papers, shuffled through them and discarded the majority into the shredder next to the wastepaper basket. Near the back of the safe he found the leather document case he'd placed there during a crisis best forgotten.

Time to open old wounds.

"One final obligation to complete."

His fat fingers worked the tiny six digit lock and released the clasp. From the case he pulled a sealed folder. Stamped across the front of the file cautioned the words:

CLASSIFIED - TOP SECRET

The folder contained a single manila envelope with a name typed on the flap:

<u>Kerry Stone Jordon</u>

Grant felt a tear roll down his cheek and he watched it drip onto the inked-in word beneath:

DECEASED

"Forgive me, Mitch. After all this time, how can I tell you she might still be alive?"

He ripped open the envelope and peered inside.

"Empty!"

SIX

A chill breeze danced across the rippled surface of Burns' Lake and tickled the hair on Jordon's neck. He opened his eyes, released his hug on the driftwood and rolled onto his back. Cold water lapped at his ankles and sent electric shivers through his body.

The sun, shielded by low clouds, had moved since he'd clutched at the log and lost consciousness.

I've been out for quite awhile, he thought and tried to inventory his surroundings. *Where am I?* Another spasm bent him in half.

He tried to lie still and stared up into the green needles of a small group of pinion where a pair of chipmunks played tag in the branches and bounced from limb to limb until they stopped to stare back. Nearby, naked aspen and twin ponderosa pine finally provided him the benchmark he needed.

"The cabin!"

The furry creatures scurried at the sound of his voice.

The exclamation sent enough pain through his shoulder to indicate his arm remained attached and although he had no recollection of doing so, the blood soaked tatters of his shirt indicated he'd somehow managed to tie a makeshift bandage about the wounds.

A quarter of a mile down the shore, he focused on the ruins of his home.

Flames still crawled inside the fuselage of the twisted helicopter. The tail section stood on end and leaned against the smooth stone chimney of what had once been the great room.

The chill assaulted him again and he sat upright. A familiar smell lingered with the pine needles. *Snow.* Not now, but soon.

Aware his damp clothes absorbed the cold like a sponge, he struggled to his knees and felt an awkward tenderness in his right ankle. "I've got to get warm." A breath of fog rolled from his lips and disappeared into the gray sky. The timbers of the cabin smoldered and invited him to seek comfort in their demise.

Jordon snapped a limb from the driftwood and fashioned it into a rudimentary crutch. A shaft of pain racked his arm and he forced himself to stand on the injured ankle. "I'll not freeze to death this close to a fire," he said and summoned the last of his strength to take a step.

"So far, so good." He tore more of his shirt to rig a sling. "Now, all I have to do is make it off this mountain."

He trekked toward the cabin and gained more will with each step until he approached the front of the structure. The sight brought an overwhelming sense of defeat. The home he'd built for Kerry, the one she'd never spent a night in, destroyed.

He leaned on the crutch and pulled a smoke scarred piece of pine from the debris. A portion of the board still remained and he traced the wood burned letters with his finger.

PROSPECTOR'S CLAIM - Elevation 10,089 feet

"My home is gone."

He tucked the warm sign under his good arm and hobbled closer to the fire which still flickered inside the crashed vehicle. He held his breath to avoid the fuel smell, pushed around several burning logs with the makeshift crutch and placed them in a pile beside the undamaged picnic table, near the storage shed.

Claw marks across the top of the table reminded him of other dangers in the woods. "Old Scartooth's been here." He looked up toward the bluff. "Hope he's decided to go sleep off the winter."

A profound sense of sadness engulfed Jordon as he tossed the sign into the fire and warmed himself with its heat. Options seemed few and far between.

He sat on the bench and studied the copter. "What happened to Kincade?"

The sky became darker and the smell of snow less pronounced as it mingled with the blue spruce next to the table and the odor of campfire doused with jet fuel. "One thing's for sure. I can't stay here. If Kincade's still alive..."

A collapse of embers, in the area which had once been his study, caught his eye. *The firebox!*

Jordon arose from the bench and ignored the pains in his limbs even though the impact of the crutch under his arm drove another spike home with every step. A stick enabled him to rake the hot ashes aside and snag the handle of the small chest. He pushed it along the ground with his foot, away from the cabin and waited for the metal to cool.

A test of the surface with the tips of his fingers gauged it still warm to the touch, but in a fit of curious apprehension, he broke the hasp with a stone.

First inspection revealed most of the papers brittled by the intense heat. A tiny gold jewelry box lay in the blackened mess. He lifted the container and pried it open. Inside, his wedding ring encircled a rolled parchment.

"Kerry's poem." He whispered the words for fear his breath might blow the memento away. "It survived the heat." He slipped the band from the paper and unrolled the poem. Kerry had presented it to him a week after they'd met at the University of Colorado.

The parchment cracked as Jordon moved to the picnic table and cradled it in his hands. The snap of the fire punctuated the moment and he read the words aloud.

TWICE IN A BLUE MOON
for Mitch from Kerry

How do I love thee? Let me count the stars.
Tally up the Moonbeams, gather them in jars.
Hold thee in my arms so tight
to know thee under the blue Moonlight.
Love thee forever, this vow the heavens witness
till the end of time. Then a touch of a gentle kiss
from thy tender lips will ignite a common fire
in our hearts, our souls, 'til notes from an angelic choir
sing of joy. If parted by chance, to soon reunite.
To know each other once more under the blue Moonlight.

The paper disintegrated and the pieces flittered away in another cold burst of air from the lake.

He lowered his head to the table and rested it on the smooth pine surface. "I've lost my wife. My home. I feel..." *Angry?* "But what's the use?"

The breeze drifted across the nape of his neck and abruptly stopped. Jordon jerked to the side as the firebox smashed down on his hand. Oblivious to the sudden pain, he tumbled from the bench and kicked upward at Kincade's knee with his left foot.

"Not this time!" The madman's eyes blazed with fury like two hot coals embedded in the disfigured face. "I'm going to kill you if I have to do it barehanded."

26

Jordon scrambled for his makeshift crutch, but Kincade circled around the table, grabbed it first and pounded the blunt end of the wood into his wounded shoulder.

The picnic table overturned in the attack and Jordon stared at the claw marks left by Old Scartooth. *The tunnel! I've got to get to the tunnel.* He pictured the dark passage in his mind as he crawled over the bench and headed for the woods. *If I can just lead Kincade into the old bear's bedroom, I might have a chance.*

"Come back here, Jordon! I'm not finished killing you yet."

Jordon cradled his arm and peered back to see if Kincade followed, but the disfigured attacker stood firm for a moment, then headed for the storage shed.

"Man! Why didn't I think of looking in there?" Jordon scanned the ground for a rock to use as a weapon, but decided he didn't have the strength to lift it. *Best chance is the tunnel.*

It took a few minutes for him to locate the talus-covered trail which led up the ridge to the abandoned Denver & Central Grande narrow gauge tracks. The climb felt like a trip to the top of Everest. Every step required a supplemental grip of a tree or root. The thin air sapped him and each breath burned his throat.

The wind changed direction and chilled the sweat on his forehead. "Getting colder." He turned to look down the trail. "Where's Kincade?"

A voice echoed from the bluff. "I want... ant... You to feel... to feel... eel... The pain... pain... ain..."

Jordon kicked his way up the path with his good leg. "Got plenty to last for awhile, pal. Thanks to you."

"No way out of here, Jordon... here, Jordon... ordan... You'll either run out of mountain.., out of mountain... ntain... Or you'll run into me... into me... me... me..."

The railroad right-of-way appeared overhead. *Finally.* He looked to his right. The tunnel would be a few hundred yards up the rusty tracks. Open on one end and collapsed on the other, old Scartooth claimed it for his own many years ago.

He pulled himself over the lip of the embankment and steadied himself before he approached the dark hole. "Hey now! I forgot about this old piece of junk." Jordon hobbled toward the relic of railroad history parked on the side track inside the tunnel. *Never did figure out why the work gangs hauled it up here in the first place.* "Wonder if it still rolls or it's all frozen up?"

He shuffled through some small scrub brush which grew between the rough hewn ties. The passage still smelled of century old smoke and cinder. "Maybe the tracks down the line are still intact." He gulped deep breaths of cold air and checked the stub turnout to see if it switched closed.

Out of the corner of his eye, Jordon saw Kincade pull himself onto the right-of-way, stand between the rails and twirl a length of rope over his head. *Looks like he got into my shed.*

"Yee-haw." Kincade continued to spin the loop. "Time to have us same serious fun!" The sick enthusiasm foamed from his mouth like a rabid dog. "Come on out of there and let me rope your heels!" he yelled. "You're a dead man. Oh, it'll be slow and painful, but you'll be just as dead!"

As Kincade looked down to admire the loop at the end of the rope, Jordon turned and leaned on the back of the old handcar. Ancient and rusty, it refused to budge. He dug his heels into the gravel, ignored the pain, and forced again.

Movement.

The grade out of the tunnel proved enough to let gravity take over and as the handcar rolled, Jordon hopped backward onto its rough platform.

Kincade seemed so engrossed in his fantasy of revenge, he failed to hear the distinctive clickity-clack of the screechy wheels as they passed from rail to rail.

Jordon bobbed his head to avoid the T-bar as it pistoned up and down.

Kincade leapt to the side, twirled his coiled lariat and let the loop sail into the air.

It landed next to Jordon. The rope played out and jostled around as the handcar gained more speed. Jordon tried to kick it away but it caught on his right foot. Another ill-timed kick and it slipped up around his ankle and went taut. Pain ripped up his leg from knee to hip. He reached for the handle, wrapped his fingers around the T-bar and expected to feel his arm leave its socket. The levered handle pulled him off the platform and the bar caught him under the chin on the next pump.

With the other end of the rope now tied around his waist, Kincade made a sound like a deflated tire when the momentum jerked him forward and both feet left the ground.

Jordon felt as if his arm and leg came loose from their connecting joints as he fought to retain consciousness and hang on.

Kincade's body drug between the tracks, an unwilling anchor of flesh and bone.

The maintenance vehicle slowed but did not stop.

In anticipation of a steep four percent grade, Jordon took advantage of a bit of slack while Kincade struggled to regain his feet.

With a nauseous effort, Jordon pulled his knees into his chest, kicked out and managed to free the rope. He quickly looped it over a side pin and breathed a sigh of momentary relief.

The car found the grade and regained its speed.

Kincade fell back and sputtered while gravel and splintered ties tore the clothes from his legs.

Jordon released the T-bar, glanced down the tracks and through a haze of pain, realized the trestle ahead had long since collapsed. He eyed a wide spot in the right-of-way, before the end of the line, gauged his distance and tumbled over the side of the car onto the ground.

The runaway relic, Kincade in tow, sailed into the abyss. "Noooooo..."

Jordon coughed and rolled onto his back, exhausted. Wet spatters of snowflakes greeted his cheeks. He gulped lungfuls of air and tried to block out the sound of twisted metal which echoed from below.

He crawled to peer into the ravine. *Guess I better make sure he's dead this time.*

The chasm, deep and jagged, bottomed out a hundred feet below. Tyler Kincade's mangled body lay beneath the car.

"Yep. He's miserable no more." Jordon stood his weight on his left foot, cradled his arm and studied the long walk back up the right-a-way toward the tunnel. "Least wise not in this life. Good thing those rocks broke his fall."

Derek Bullard

SEVEN

Boxes of all size and shape lined the walls of the tiny office. In the middle of the cardboard sea stood a simple desk with a telephone. Behind the desk, Veronda Winston drummed her sculptured nails on the arm of her chair and yelled at someone on her cell phone.

"I don't care if they go home at five! I want all of these things moved into my new office at one minute after six. Sharp! Do you understand?" She listened for a moment. "No, I don't think you do." A movement in her periphery caught her attention. She glanced up. "Sit, geo man. I'll be with you in a moment. Did you bring your stuff?" Then to the unfortunate caller, "Buster, who is your supervisor?"

Caesar Hamilton glanced down at the folder in his hands. *What's she mean, 'Did I bring my stuff?* He'd been slighted on the promised cappuccino and ordered to her office the second they'd left Grant's office.

He sat and waited for her to finish the barrage.

"I thought you'd see it my way." She smiled and folded the phone as if she'd finished a conversation with an old friend. "Now, geo man. Let's see what you've got."

"Well, like I said, I came across some interesting remote sensing images sent down from Admiral Jay on the space station *Frontier*.

"Hold on a sec." She eyed the conglomeration of paper. "Didn't anyone issue you an Infopak when you came on board?"

"Don't trust 'em," he replied. "Not natural to keep everything on something small as your hand and dependent on batteries. Besides an electromatic pulse will..." *What's the word?* "Pffft!"

"Pffft?"

"Pffft," he agreed and broke eye contact with her incredulous stare. "These oilfield surveys sparked my interest." He pulled several glossy prints from a folder. "As you can see..." *without having to strain your eyes...* "to the untrained, these reverse topographic maps look like a collage of colors and shapes."

If Winston fielded the snub, she made no indication as she rotated the photos for a better angle."

"What's this blue spot? I don't see it in every picture."

Hamilton revised his opinion of her. Most of the men in the Geo section missed the anomaly on first inspection. "That's the odd part. The blue spot appears to be a pulse. It shows up and disappears every thirty seconds. You can set your watch by it."

"A flaw in the processing equipment?"

"No."

She held one of the images closer to her face. "Where is this?"

Hamilton rolled an aeronautical chart out next to a topographic map. He pointed to the area. "East central Oklahoma."

"Is it dangerous?"

"No way to tell."

She drummed her nails on the map. "Wait a sec." She leaned to study it closer. "According to this chart, there's a hundred square mile area designated PAS and if I'm reading this correctly, the pulse is right in the middle of it." She consulted the legend. "Let's see. Special use airspace, air defense identification zone, here it is. Prohibited airspace. But it doesn't make sense. Closest base is Tinker Field, over near the state capital."

Hamilton rotated the map to confirm her observations. "Why a no fly zone?"

"I don't know." She flipped open her cell and selected a number. "Let's find out." A few seconds later she leaned back in her chair and spoke into the phone. "Pentagon? Yes. Veronda Winston for General Brisbane please. Yes, I'll hold." Her nails drummed the rhythm of Rossini's *William Tell.* "Bris? How are you, darling? Great. Listen, Bris I need to know about a PAS near..." She located the area on the map. "Near Wildwood, Oklahoma. Know anything? Yes, I'll hold."

More *Lone Ranger.*

She nodded, thanked the general and flipped the cell shut.

Hamilton shrugged. "Well?"

Winston tapped a fingernail against her teeth. "Not a clue. Didn't seem too concerned either." She opened her phone again, perused more numbers and called the head of the FAA, then the Nuclear Regulatory Commission.

When she shook her head in defeat, Hamilton pointed to the phone. "Don't suppose you've got the President's number in there, do you?"

She thumbed through the organizer and stuck the little screen in his face. "I think it has his pager listed."

Another personnel folder joined the pile on the long conference table. Hamilton sat alone as he rubbed his eyes and reached for the next one. His earlier conversation with Winston still echoed in his aching head.

The audacity of the woman. "Has she no patience?"

The chewing out ended with his resignation. When she offered a raise, he refused. When she offered to keep her nose out of his business and let him run the expedition his way, he'd reconsidered. When she'd said 'Pretty please', he made her repeat it, then accepted the offer, the raise, and her guarantee to supply him all the resources he needed to conduct the investigation properly.

He'd suggested aerial recon. This launched her into another rage. "I want an eyewitness account from ground zero," she'd said. What she'd meant: "I intend to run this organization permanently and this will be the first feather in my cap, so get yourself up to Oklahoma and pluck me a bright one!"

Run it permanently into the ground. He selected the next file. "Not much to choose from on such short notice." To pull people off projects to take what amounted to a glorified field trip seemed ludicrous.

"Now, here's somebody I know." He flipped through the commendations and whistled to himself. "Alexander Phileas Oxenthall. Good ol' Ox. Geophysicist and sweaty hog." *He'll do.*

To the list he added three more names and made the calls.

Twenty minutes later, the first candidate to arrive crept into the room as if it contained hidden traps. Cautious to the point of paranoia, she selected the chair facing the door.

Hamilton peeked at the photo in her file and confirmed her identity. "Gina Wellingham, I presume?"

She played with a blond pigtail. It snaked from under her ball cap and made her look like Pippi Longstocking, escaped from the minor leagues. She adjusted her oversized glasses on her undersized nose. "Yes, sir. My supervisor said you had an assignment for me."

"You're a geologist?"

"Yes, sir." She scuffed her hiking boots on the carpet and examined the ceiling. "Colorado School of Mines. Class of last year."

A large, perspiration covered, redheaded man danced into the room and shut the door. The squawk from his portable MusiLink ground through the ear wigs. He tossed a bag of Gummi Bears on the table and saluted Hamilton in the style of a lax Roman soldier.

"Hail, Caesar. Good to see you, man. How you been?"

Hamilton waited for Oxenthall to pull the plugs from his ears. "Glad to see the best geophysicist in the room is still on the prowl."

Oxenthall pointed at Wellingham and stared at her hat, which read:

Geologists Rock and then at her shirt: *Trust No One.* "Love your ensemble. It's inconclusively definite. But, I take it, you're not a geophysicist."

She smiled a shy toothy grin. "Sorry, no."

The sweaty man slid into a chair opposite and gobbled Gummi Bears. "Ha, ha funny, little Caesar. You always offer such cruel kindness."

"Lest we forget the real reason we call you 'Ox'."

"Old news."

"Precisely."

"So, who else is coming to this somber party?"

Hamilton pushed the files across the conference table.

"Man, when are you gonna let Santa leave an Infopak in your stocking?"

Hamilton ignored the remark and pointed at the photos. "Miguel Cortez and Marcel Gatreux."

"The crawdad man!" Oxenthall slapped the table. "That ragin' Cajun is a gas. Met him last summer. Oh, man what a time we'll have! Who's this unknown amigo, Cortez?"

Wellingham cleared her throat. "Archaeoastronomy."

"No way?" Oxenthall ignored the files. "Where is this party, man? Mesa Verde? That's cliff city."

Hamilton rubbed his eyes and presented the two with S-SMC photos of east central Oklahoma.

Wellingham giggled. "Cortez's last project just finished. He was all packed and ready to ship off to SETI in Socorro."

"Dish City, sister." Oxenthall popped another Gummi. "Bummer."

"While we wait," said Hamilton, "we can discuss the data gathered so far."

"Smack pics from the *Frontier*." Wellingham flipped through the S-SMC photos and chose one. "What's this blue spot?"

Hamilton shrugged. "Beats me. That's what we're here to figure out."

"It's an alien homing beacon." Wellingham tilted the photo into the light. "Or a warped sensor array." She scratched her ear and adjusted her glasses. "Maybe a cloaking device for a secret stealth base?"

"Man, she fires 'em off like bullets. Got anything else, oh great Caesar?" Oxenthall fidgeted in his chair. "How about LANDSAT or ERBS? Gobs of platforms up there, any one of which can give us a better pic than this. These? They shot a close-up of some squashed bug or something."

Hamilton felt embarrassed and unprepared. Why hadn't he thought of collecting corroborating data before the meeting?

"Or how about my favorite? SPOT?"

Wellingham giggled again. "Are you referring to the pic or a remote sensing platform?"

"You know, the Frenchy's bird. *Satellite Pour l'Observation de la Terre*." He grinned. "Crawdad taught me that one. Sits up there in a sun-synchronous orbit and fires out eight hundred watts of pure active scans. Makes NIMBUS-7 look like a farm tractor. Then there's the Japanese JERS-11. Works in real time. You didn't check any of those?"

Hamilton shook his head. "Afraid not, Ox. I was a little pressed for time by Miss Winston."

"The self-elected queen of the universe? She's behind this?"

"Appears so."

Wellingham's eyes grew wider behind her thick lenses. "Is there something I need to know? About her, I mean?"

Oxenthall shook his head. "She's the most passive aggressive woman you'll ever meet."

Hamilton held up a hand. "Now, Ox. Don't draw any conclusions." A merciful sound in the form of a squeaky hinge saved him from further discussion.

Two men came through the door. One spotted Oxenthall and slapped him on the back. "Hey, *mon frère*. What's up?"

"Well if it isn't Marcel Gatreux, the pride of Westwego!" He gestured toward the Infopak in the Cajun's hand. "Glad to see you brought the old home office. Mighty Caesar has us idly working in the stone age here with all this paper."

Oxenthall introduced the man around the room, then offered a high-five to the other newcomer.

"Miguel Cortez."

What a pair, thought Hamilton. Cortez looked like someone who might still carry a slide rule. Even his corduroy jacket sported professor's patches. Gatreux on the other hand, with his ponytail and sandals, his polar opposite. *No wonder Ox connects with these guys.*

"Good to see you again for the first time, Miguel," said Oxenthall. "Ol' Crawdad here try to rope you into sampling his jambalaya again? He puts so much genuine imitation cayenne pepper in it, it'll eat the bottom out of your gut. Last batch gave me the bellyache for a week."

Cortez smiled and selected a seat next to Wellingham. "I prefer the *habanera* myself."

Hamilton cleared his throat and tapped his watch. "People, we can swap kitchen secrets on the road. Our chariot awaits."

Wellingham looked startled. "Not a field trip! Nobody mentioned a field trip."

"Afraid so. Miss Winston indicated our mode of transportation will be in the parking lot about ten minutes ago."

The chariot proved to be a cramped, family vehicle, called the Solar Wind. Hamilton closed his eyes and wished the camper-van back into a pumpkin. It didn't cooperate.

Oxenthall rummaged through a nearby trash can and walked toward the vehicle, an empty glass pop bottle in hand. "Let's send this land yacht off in style." He swung the flagon at the bumper. "I christen thee the *U.S.S. Queen Veronda.*"

Hamilton winced as the bottle glanced off the chrome and smashed into the headlight. "Way to go, Ox."

The van creaked as someone moved inside, then opened the door. "What in the world is going on out here?" Winston examined the broken lens. "I suppose you can explain this?"

Oxenthall tossed the bottle over his shoulder. "Uh, no ma'am. Don't think I can."

Winston pointed her finger. "Young man, your voice sounds very familiar. Do I know you?"

Hamilton put his arms out. "People, if you'll climb aboard." He gave Oxenthall a thumbs up behind Winston's back. "I think the sooner we leave, the sooner we'll be in Oklahoma."

Oxenthall ducked his head and bounded up the steps as he broke into an operatic chorus. "Sooner born and Sooner bred. And when I die. I'll be Sooner dead!"

Hamilton sighed. *This is going to be a long trip.*

EIGHT

Wet snow had fallen earlier in the night and covered the ground with a few inches of white. High winds whistled through the trees and echoed in the tunnel entrance like imagined ghosts in a haunted house. Eventually the clouds abandoned their hold on the mountain and swept away to reveal a clear, black sky.

The full Moon, its appearance altered by the thinner atmosphere, seemed larger than usual.

Jordon looked down the right-of-way and wondered how he'd managed to climb the grade. Now, inside the dark, abandoned passageway, he shivered against the cold, inhaled a deep breath and tasted the engine smoke which, after a hundred or so years, still reeked from the black walls and permeated the air with stories of a bygone era.

The shoulder felt better. Or maybe he felt nothing at all. "I know one thing," he said to the darkness, "my sixth sense is shot. A platoon of Marines could park a tank behind me and I'm not sure if I'd know it."

He shifted his weight a bit and leaned to gaze into the sky.

"Blue Moon, it's been a long time since I've seen you, old friend." Jordon whispered the words and watched them leave the tunnel on his breath. *Won't do to wake old Scartooth.* His numb mind focused on the bear, then drifted to the poem which crumbled in his hands. "What are the odds of a Blue Moon tonight? Have to stay awake," he told himself. "Can't go into shock. I'll freeze to death. Let's see now. What are the scientific reasons for a Blue Moon? Well, for starters... For starters there's..." He yawned. "Okay, so what are the romantic reasons behind a Blue Moon? Well, for starters..."

His mind sobered.

"There was Kerry." *Was? Is? She's really gone. Isn't she?* "Hey, Scartooth? Did you know I met Kerry during a Blue Moon?" Jordon heard his voice echo in the darkness. "They say it can only happen once." *Too bad.* "I lost you, Kerry, and you're never coming back to me."

His thoughts drifted for awhile as the cold forced him to brush against sleep. They wandered in a dreamlike state back to the first Blue Moon when he'd met her at a college party.

Kerry Stone, bright, beautiful astronomy major.

Mitch Jordon, senior on a quest for a degree in geology. He felt his head nod with a chuckle. "Who'd ever thought we'd both become astronauts, much less fall in love?"

Jordon remembered wandering away from the party with her and sitting on the cool spring grass. They'd leaned against a split-post fence and gazed into the sky.

"Is this your first Blue Moon?" she'd asked.

"Yes." Why had he felt so... shy?

"Mine, too." Kerry whispered the words as if afraid someone might hear. "Isn't it lovely?"

His courage slipped into a higher gear. "Tonight, it's the second loveliest thing I've seen."

In the shadows, he hadn't see her face, but he knew she'd blushed and turned away.

She reached for his hand and intertwined her fingers. "My friend Patricia says you've had an offer to work for ASTRO after graduation."

"Yeah. I don't know if I'll take it."

"Why not?"

"Oh, I guess because what I really want to do is move back up to a lake I know. Maybe build a little cabin."

"And just what is there for you do up there all day?"

"Why prospect for gold of course." He laughed and squeezed her hand. It felt soft like the breeze.

Kerry wriggled around to face him and stood on her knees. "Work for ASTRO and you'll be prospecting up there for Moonbeams."

"Me? On the Moon? You sound a lot like the recruiter." He reached out and caressed her cheek with the back of his hand.

She snuggled against the touch. "Why not, Mitchell Jordon?"

"You're the astronomy major. Why don't you join ASTRO and fly away to the Moon?"

She leaned to whisper in his ear. "I've already been accepted."

Clifford Foard adjusted his night vision goggles to peer through a green haze at the blackened skeleton of what appeared to be a cabin. He tapped the pilot of the Bell 489LD on the arm. "Hover closer. See if you can land."

The pilot held a hand to his headphones as if absorbing the instructions and nodded at Foard. "Weather's clear for the moment, sir. But a really bad storm is on the way. We've got an hour before this whole mountain is socked in for a week."

Foard nodded and continued to scan the area around the cabin. Bright green splotches of radiated heat flared in the viewfinder. "Man, there's pieces of chopper everywhere. I don't know what happened here, but whoever did it sure left a mess."

The Bell descended in a cloud of snow, blown outward from below. When the pilot gave him the thumbs up, Foard kneed his door open and stepped to the ground. The cold assaulted him as he reached to pull his parka from the rear seat. "Keep the heater on, son."

"Mind the rotors, sir."

"I hate these flying coffins." Foard ducked and moved toward the mountain cabin. "Should've hired a sled team." He inspected the crashed fuselage. Satisfied neither Jordon or Kincade lay in the wreckage, he pulled a cell phone and a cigar from his parka, lit up and spoke Caxton Grant's name for his private number.

"Grant here." The voice sounded agitated.

"Hello Chief." Foard checked his watch and calculated the time difference. "Sorry to wake you, Chief. I'm at the cabin... Or what's left of it."

Silence.

"No sign of Jordon yet," Foard continued. "Light snow came through and covered all the tracks. I'm going to look around."

"Very well, Clifford." Grant's voice seemed to have aged. "Continue the search and keep me informed. I want Mitch found alive or..." His voice faded. "I want some evidence." The connection ended abruptly.

Foard stared at the little phone in his enormous hand and puffed his cigar.

The Bell pilot had left the helicopter and circled around the cabin on foot. "Over here, sir." He waved and pulled the hood of his parka over his head to shield himself from a blast of wind. A high intensity xenon flashlight cut a swath of light up the ridge. "Somebody... or something... went this way."

Foard stepped around the toppled picnic table and studied the rocks. Protected by the evergreen canopy, little snow touched them. The dirt on top indicated a recent disturbance. "Good work, son. Let's see where this leads."

"The weather conditions are closing in pretty fast, sir." The pilot pulled on his gloves and headed up the trail. "Maybe twenty minutes."

"Well, what are we waiting for?" Foard took a breath of cold mountain air. "This can't be any worse than running bleachers." He grabbed at a tree limb, dug his boot into the bank and started his ascent.

Jordon stared down the right-of-way through the blowing snow. *Is that what I think it is?* The bright light approached with no sound. He rubbed his eyes with the balls of his hands. "Must be hallucinating. Can't be a train."

The beam cut the darkness like a sudden inspiration and lit each flake with a crystal sparkle. It hurt his eyes and he squinted to make out the form behind it.

Can't be a train.

Another puff wafted into the light.

Why is there smoke?

A voice. "Somebody's in the tunnel, sir."

A second voice. "Careful, son. He might be armed."

The first voice. "Watch it! There's a bear in here too!"

NINE

In the presidential suite of the Philippine Continental Park Hotel, Alan Dover scrolled through the information on the laptop with a sense of impatience. The need to move on overwhelmed him and refused to subside. He glanced at his watch. *Still set on U.S. time. One a.m.*

"You're s-sure of your findings?" He directed the question to the female across the room for the second time in as many minutes.

"Yes." The redhead filled her coffee mug from the carafe on the bar. "The woman you're looking for doesn't live far from here."

Dover adjusted the belt on his white, terrycloth bathrobe, worked his way deeper into the recliner and skimmed a portion of the first page. "You're absolutely s-sure?" He tilted his own glass mug, emptied the dark roast and stared through the bottom at the warped image of Meg Mordel as she pushed away from the bar and started toward him.

She stood slightly taller than himself, the fact more apparent when she stopped and stared down at him through the bottom of the mug. *A cheap detective with an expensive price.* His inside man at ASTRO recommended her highly.

"You hired me to find her, and I did," she said. "May have taken awhile, but things move slowly here. Had to work cautiously."

"I believe you, Meg." Still unaccustomed to his new found freedom, Dover shrunk back into the comforts of the chair. "Now, I have the ultimate weapon to use against J-J-Jordon. Providing that maniac Kincade doesn't k-kill him first." The thought mixed well with the caffeine rush he felt. "Besides, the information alone is enough to finish off G-G-Grant." He allowed himself a mirthless laugh. "My old buddy, G-Grant."

"From what I've heard, you'd prefer a root canal to Jordon and Grant." Mordel took his mug from him and refilled it.

The comment irritated him and he leapt from the chair to slap the carafe from her hand. "They're the ones who messed with my plans and railroaded me into prison. Yes, my dear. I hate them with a passion you cannot begin to imagine."

The sleeve of her blouse became a makeshift towel as she wiped the hot coffee from her face and picked the laptop up from the floor. She then extracted a crumpled pack of cigarettes and a disposable lighter from her purse on the desk. "I can imagine quite a bit." Her hand shook and she adjusted the flame.

"I'm sure you can." Dover plucked the cigarette from her lips.

"Hey, those cost money!"

"Don't smoke in here. I get an awful headache every time I'm around one of these th-things." He ground the cigarette out on the teakwood bar. "For what I'm paying, you can buy a b-box of good Cuban cigars."

"Sorry." She didn't sound like she meant it.

"Never mind." Claustrophobia set in. Dover pulled back the curtains and opened the French patio doors. "I need air." Beyond the rail he spotted the zoo, Roxas Boulevard and Manila Bay. The atmosphere felt wet and sultry, a product of the recent monsoons. A hint of sea salt mixed with the exhaust of a cafe on the street. The faint sun overhead reiterated the time difference. With another glance at his watch, he fought to suppress a yawn and the sudden craving for a fish sandwich.

He pulled a chair out from under the glass bistro, cinched his robe against the breeze and sat. "Let's get down to business. I've got some more w-work for you."

Mordel selected a chair across the table from him. "Still involve the woman?"

"It does." He propped his feet up on a wicker ottoman. "Tell me everything you know concerning th-this woman. Her past. Her p-present. What she likes. Who she knows. Any relationships. The whole enchilada."

"It's all in my report."

Dover wagered she'd either have a nicotine fit or throw herself over the rail. "I don't want j-just the facts. I want insight. I want a woman's point of view. Detective Meg Mordel's point of view."

"I don't think I understand what you're getting at." She glanced nervously back at the curtains.

"You can smoke out here. But keep it downwind from me."

"Thank you." She disappeared through the doors and returned with a fresh pack, her mug and the half-empty carafe. She lit up and inhaled like she hadn't had smoke in her lungs for years. "Where do I start?"

"At the b-beginning."

Mordel sat, drew her knees inward and clasped her hands together, then propped her chin up on an index finger. "Her name is Lana Turner, not her real name obviously, but one she chose after hearing English for the first time. An old black and white movie." A puff wafted into the sky.

41

"Turner was involved in a plane crash in the jungle at or near the time Kerry Jordon's own aircraft went missing. I can't pin down an exact time on it because of her injuries. Apparently she'd been nursed back to health by the *Infugao* hill people in a small village up in the Zambales Mountains."

"Yes, yes. On the northern part of this island. You've confirmed the report I had stolen from G-G-Grant's safe." Dover stood and moved to the rail. The honk of a jeepney filtered upward from the street. "Go on."

"Turner has no past as far as she knows. She remembers absolutely nothing of her life before the crash."

"T-Tell me about Lana Turner and the woman she's become since."

"Well, she's somewhat shy. Keeps to herself mostly. Works as a volunteer for room and board in a small Roman Catholic hospital north of the Pasig. That's where the *hilot* - the healer - brought her down from his *barrio*. I get a real sense of loneliness when I see her."

Dover slid his chair around the table, next to Mordel. "You've had personal c-contact?"

"Yes...to a small extent. Told her I'm a reporter, writing an article dealing with health care in Manila."

"Does she b-believe you?"

"She has no reason to doubt me."

"How soon c-can you introduce me to her?"

"Well..." Mordel pursed her lips and blew smoke straight up into the air. "Is that wise?"

"Kerry Jordon and I never met. G-G-Grant recruited me into ASTRO after her disappearance."

Mordel drained her coffee and refilled it from the carafe. "You said she used to be an astronaut?"

"Yes." Dover swirled the cold coffee in his own mug with his finger. "And?"

"She joined ASTRO soon after her graduation from college. A d-degree with honors. According to G-G-Grant's files, her second flight had been a scheduled Moonshot with J-J-Jordon, but G-G-Grant discovered they'd been secretly married several months before. Then, to top it off, during her preflight physical, they found out she was pregnant. What a d-deal. So G-G-Grant decided to take her off the mission and deep six her until the press got tired of snooping."

"Sounds like you've done your homework." Mordel lit a new cigarette off of her last.

Dover watched the smoke cloud drift over the rail. "What about a baby? Any information on a child?"

"No, she might have lost it in the crash. I'll check into it."

42

"Do that. And arrange a meeting. Perhaps the three of us over dinner tomorrow night. I m-must meet her. Tell her I'm a reporter friend of yours, just along for the ride. I'll take over from there."

"What's your game, Dover?"

He stared into her brown eyes. "A d-deadly one, my dear lady. A very deadly one."

TEN

"What do you suggest, sir?"
Clifford Foard tried to keep the bear in the blinding beam of his xenon flashlight. A large scar ran from the tip of its muzzle to the base of its neck. *Man, that beast stinks.* "Don't move." *Maybe not original, but for the moment, practical.*

"Then what?" The chopper pilot popped the snap on his sidearm.

"Forget it, son. You'll just irritate him." Foard stared at the snow covered rubble over the tunnel entrance. "Or bury us under this mountain."

The bear, appearing unsure of why his nap had been interrupted, scratched an ear with a massive paw, yawned and sniffed the air. One eye opened and then the other.

"If Jordon rolls over or yells out..." Foard held his breath and hoped the former astronaut didn't smell like a midnight snack.

"Maybe he'll go back to sleep, sir."

Foard clamped down on his soggy cigar. "And maybe I'll sprout wings and fly us out of here."

The bear lumbered to his feet and worked toward Jordon, nuzzled his side and rolled him over.

"I think he's dead, sir."

Jordon scuffed something in the gravel.

"No he's alive. Hears us, but doesn't dare move."

Curious, the huge animal perked its ears and stood upright on powerful hind legs. The massive paws flailed to block the light from his eyes.

Foard felt the stub of his cigar roll down his chin. "That beast must be seven feet tall," he whispered. He hadn't seen a bear so big since his last playoff game against... *Chicago. But their offensive tackles didn't have claws. This one does.* "Guess it's party time in the red zone. Fourth and goal. The quarterback is going down."

"Sir? "

Foard lowered his head and charged into the tunnel. "Time to BLITZ THE BEAR!"

First contact with the wild and woolly Goliath stunned him and he hoped, the beast as well.

Caught off guard by the surprise attack, the bear let loose a powerful howl, backed away, stumbled on the tracks and toppled over.

"Drag Jordon out of here! Now!" Foard waved his arms and kicked gravel in all directions.

The bear recovered his footing and attacked with an angry bellow.

The barrel of Foard's flashlight slammed into a wet, fleshy nose. The howl became a roar. The next blow connected with a sick crack. "Hope you got dental insurance, Yogi!"

The light went out.

Foard ducked away and groped in the darkness unable to pinpoint the location of the bear, despite the continued, maddened roar which reverberated off the rock walls.

Somehow, over the fracas, the pilot's voice filtered through. "I've pulled Jordon out, sir."

"Time to beat it for the lockers." Foard moved to the side of the tunnel and felt his way along the slick wall. His foot made contact with something firm. Muscles rippled under his boot. The odor of sweaty fur drifted into his nose. "Oh, man, Gentle Ben's got a roommate. What is this? Night of the stinking grizzlies? Lady, you snore like--"

Without warning, the flashlight snapped on and illuminated the tunnel and the first bear. Foard imitated the original hairy monster with a linebacker's yell likely to make any defensive coordinator proud.

The bear lunged at him, but landed in the middle of its sleeping companion.

The second bear woke and expressed its displeasure like a pit bull with a firecracker in its belly.

"I'll leave you two lovebirds to sort this out." Foard threw his parka into the fight and headed down the tracks. At the edge of the bluff, he overtook the pilot and transferred Jordon to his own shoulder. "Get to the chopper. Be ready to take off and hunt up that Thermos of soup for Jordon."

"What about the bear, sir?"

"Let him get his own soup."

✄   ✄   ✄

"By the way, thanks." Jordon eased into his seat behind the pilot and accepted the insulated mug. "Didn't expect any visitors until next spring."

"How serious are your wounds?" Foard broke the heat pack he'd retrieved from the first aid kit and slipped it behind Jordon's back.

"Took a couple of hits in the shoulder. Think they both went all the way through." He grimaced and lifted the mug to his lips. "Ankle's still a bit tender."

Foard examined the shredded sleeve and nodded a confirmation. "One's pretty bad, but the other's just a graze. Cold probably kept you from bleeding to death."

"Knew there had to be a reason I liked this weather." He moved his arm and pain telegraphed across his face.

Foard reached for the buckle and started to take the slack out of the seat belt in the rear compartment of the chopper. "Hang on, Chief. I'm going to cinch you in, but it's going to hurt a lot. I'm no trainer, so I better not give you any pain killers until we get to a doctor."

"Who are you? Not military." Jordon gritted his teeth. "F.B.Ayeee..!"

"Clifford Foard, head of security. Warned you about the hurt."

"ASTRO?"

"You got it, Chief. "What's the story on Kincade? Eaten by the bear?"

"Last I saw, he rearranged several rocks on his way to the bottom of a ravine. Happens when you bungee jump without a bridge."

"Dead?"

"If he's not, he had better survival training than I did."

"Hang on while I get aboard." Foard slammed the door and ducked under the gale of the spinning rotors. He remembered the pilot's warning about the rear of the copter, circled around the front and pulled himself into the copilot's seat. A hint of smoke still drifted from the ashes of the cabin. He glanced over his shoulder and gave Jordon the thumbs up. "We'll be off the ground in a few seconds."

"I've heard of you somewhere, but not with ASTRO. You're new."

The pilot increased the rotation of the blades. "I hate this weather up here." The dolphin shaped craft shimmied with a high frequency vibration. "The wind is blowing out of all different directions. The temperature keeps dropping and rising again. It's everything I can do to keep this bird from freezing up. I'm going to IMC."

"IMC? Speak English, son. Can you get us out of here?"

Facing backwards, behind the pilot, Jordon's raspy voice answered the question. "Instrument meteorological conditions. Used during night and poor visibility. Got any more soup?"

Foard unsleeved a cigar and bit the end off. "Hey, Chief. You sound pretty alert for a guy full of holes and covered with bear grease. I bet you can fly this thing unconscious."

"Maybe."

The pilot tapped his headset and pointed at Foard's. "Put those on please, sir. Mr. Jordon's are under your seat."

Foard reached back, slipped the third set over Jordon's head and plugged him in. "Much better. Gotta tell you, Chief, I'd rate bear wrestling an eight on things I never want to do."

Jordon cradled the mug in his arms and leaned his head back. "Storm's messing with communications, sir."

"Get this flying ice bucket out of here." Foard cinched his seat belt and looked through his window into the inky blackness." *This is number four on the list.* "Can't believe you love this weather, Chief. Not my idea of a fun Sunday afternoon."

"Now, I know where I've heard of you." Jordon's voice echoed in Foard's headset. "You played linebacker for Seattle a few years ago. They called you the Zookeeper. Way you handled Scartooth up there, I can see why."

"Always running into fans in the weirdest places." Foard chomped his cigar and rubbed his bald head. The copter left the ground with an unexpected lurch.

"Sorry to disappoint you." Another grimace of pain. "I... I always bet on Denver."

"Yeah. Figured you for an AFC man. Guess I'll have to throw you back out in the snow. How can you stand to live with this stuff?"

"Came up here to recalibrate. How'd you manage to trade a football for a job at ASTRO?"

"It's simple." Foard tensed as the copter shuddered, thankful Jordon seemed coherent enough to engage in small talk. It helped to keep his mind off the flight. "Brains, good looks and blind luck. After retirement, which for some reason comes early in pro ball, I opened a home security business with my brother. We catered to all those rich and famous people. Started with football players. That led to movie stars, politicians, other sports. Word got around to Grant."

"Good ol' Cax. He's a real charmer." The copter bucked again and sleet splattered against the fuselage. "Why are we flying in this mess?"

"To get you to a hospital, Chief. Before your arm rots off."

Jordon had turned his head to peer through his window. "If we keep on this course for long, we're all going to be in the hospital... Taken in ambulances with the sirens turned off."

Foard looked ahead and waved a hand at the pilot. "Flip on your landing lights."

"What?"

"Do it!"

The tips of pine tree tops stood in the foggy snowfall like soldiers guarding a palace. "Even I know those ain't supposed to be there! Get it up! Climb! Climb!"

The helicopter jumped and Foard felt his stomach in his throat. *Okay, this rockets to number one on the list.*

"Sorry, sir." Large hailstones pelted the window. This storm's a building fast. My instruments--"

A red warning flickered on the digital console, accompanied by a loud alarm which pierced Foard's brain. "What's that?"

"Chip detector."

"Chip what?" The craft shuddered.

"Little magnet on the tail rotor picked up a piece of metal. Hailstone might have dinked it."

"Bad?"

Jordon grunted in the headset. "It's bad. But, we're all right - long as this young man doesn't forget the two most important emergency rules."

The hail intensified.

Foard rotated his cigar and leaned toward the pilot. "Which are?"

"Step one, sir. Fly the aircraft."

"Very good," said Jordon. " And step two?"

"Don't forget step one."

"Great. Lousy aviator humor." Foard wiped the sweat from his bald head. "I suggest you proceed to step three. Land this crate. Now!"

Larger hail pelted the windshield and ruptured the Plexiglass. A second later, a softball size chunk of ice hit the instrument panel and exploded in the pilot's face.

Even I know this ain't good.

ELEVEN_____

"*My heart's sad. My lawyer's glad. How can I love you when you treat me so bad?*" The radio crooned the gloomy country and western ballad out of a cracked speaker.

"Blasted storm. How's a man supposed to sing his favorite songs with all this static?" A.J. Crandell scratched his beard and glanced at his watch. "Last load before going home and I'm running behind schedule again."

He squinted at the snow covered highway through the half fogged windshield of his Kenworth. "Matilda, will you please tell me, cold as it is here in the Rockies, why anyone wants ice cream?" A memory of his ex-wife, back in California, after whom he'd named the truck came to mind. *She could've eaten a barrel full of the stuff.* "Personally, I hate it. Makes my teeth hurt. Makes my brain hurt. But a load's a load, even if I'm the last man on this crooked old road."

Crandell whistled a tune to fit the words. "Hey, maybe I'll write me down one of these songs!"

The radio signal fuzzed in and out. "*...love me tomorrow or don't...*"

He pulled at the cuff of his fingerless leather glove with his teeth and switched stations. More static.

"...WSNB, your snow country radio. Here's the current forecast. Snuggle up with your snow bunny and get ready for..."

"Get ready for what?" Crandell pounded on the dash. "More snow?"

"...back to back hits and home of the snow bunny extravaganza!"

Crandell nodded at the empty seat next to him. "What snow bunny? You see a snow bunny in this truck, Mr. Radio Man?" He slapped his knee. "Maybe I'll write me down some of those commercials."

The wheel jerked in his free hand. "Whoa, Matilda. Don't go sliding off the road, 'less I say it's okay."

"...radar indicates a band of severe storms stalled in the area, but will move out of Colorado into the Great Plains within the next few days. It's stacking up to be the worst storm this century. BRRRRRR..."

The shifter shimmied and Crandell eased down a gear. "I'll get stuck.

Have to live off ice cream 'til spring." He punched the radio into the off position and reached for his CB mike. "Breaker one nine, this is The Chiller, anybody got his ears on?"

✗ ✗ ✗

"Foard, pay attention to me!"

The hometown crowd screamed a cheer. YOU CAN DO IT. YOU CAN DO IT. Echoes in the stadium. Instructions from the bench. TAKE CONTROL. TAKE CONTROL. YOU CAN DO IT. TAKE CONTROL.

"But my buddy's down. Call a time out. Somebody stop the clock. Somebody stop the game!" Foard fought to clear his eyes. "I can't see. Too much sweat." *No, something else.* "Snow! I've got snow in my eyes!"

"Don't worry about it. Take control of the aircraft."

A buzzer somewhere ahead. Two minute warning.

The sound of his brother's voice filtered into his helmet. Instructions from the bench. "Take control of the aircraft."

"But we're not playing the Jets." Time slowed. The echoes increased. *What's Jordon doing on the sidelines? Who died and made him coach?*

"Take the stick!"

"What sti... No a ball..." His eyes focused. "Dials? Gauges? "Where am... How long?"

Jordon sounded desperate. "Couple of seconds. Snap out of it. Take the stick in front of you." *YOU CAN DO IT. TAKE CONTROL.*

Something regarding rule number one. The young pilot joked about it right before he'd been knocked unconscious. *What is it? 'Rule number one, sir. Fly the aircraft.'* "But I can't fly this thing."

"No, but we can make a controlled crash."

"Controlled crash! Out of this spinning?" A flash of lightning to the left. To the right, unconscious, the pilot gripped the stick like his last hold on life.

Jordon yelled. "DO AS I SAY!"

Foard took a deep breath and grabbed the control in front of him. "Right, Chief."

"Down by your side. To your left. That's the collective. Ease the lever up and twist the throttle a bit. Rotate your knuckles toward your body. Push the left peddle gently with your foot."

The craft seemed to steady. Wet, cold wind whipped through the hole in front of the pilot.

"How's that?"

"Not bad. Read off the r.p.m.s on the tail rotor."

"Where?"

"Bottom row, last readout on the left."

Foard cleared his eyes by puffing air through pouted lips and browsed the indicators. "Radar altimeter, horizontal whatchamacallit, there it is." He blinked and the numbers fell to zero. Almost at once he felt the craft lurch to the right and another warning alarm sounded. "Reads--"

"Doesn't matter, we just lost it."

Foard reached to push the switch next to the master alarm, but the centrifugal force made his arm feel like lead.

"Don't touch anything!" Jordon sounded frantic. "You might shut down something important. Now, do this. Lower the collective all the way."

Foard thrust the control to the floor. "Done."

"Increase your throttle and push the stick forward. Put your foot hard into the left peddle."

The craft stopped vibrating and slowed rotation. "We're still spinning down," Foard said as he lost the feeling in his left foot. "I see trees in the lights!"

"We're gonna flare. Too low and too much velocity."

Foard wanted to do something. Pray. Cuss. Eject. "What now?"

"Tighten your seat belt. Brace your legs. Keep your eyes on the door handle. Cut the power and pull back on the stick with everything you've got. We'll auto rotate right into the ground."

"Where's the kill switch? Gotta be bright red or something... Here we go." He eyed all the toggles with off options as the engines sounded like a coughing motorboat. "I'll say one thing for you, Jordon." Foard tried to glance back at his passenger who'd curled himself into the semblance of a tucked position. "You're one bossy backseat driver."

✂ ✂ ✂

The glow of the useless radio lit the dash like a near dead firefly. "Who needs ya anyway? I can write tunes better than those sissy cowboys." *If you're outta cold beer, you're outta my life, dear.*

The beams of the rig's fog lights painted the road ahead of Crandell with two crescents of yellow. The snow ended, but the highway continued. "Oh boy! Black ice!" He pumped the brake with his toe and dropped a gear. "Bobsled time, Matilda. This stuff's slicker 'n oil."

The wheel moved freely in his hand. "There went my traction." He held his breath as the rig slipped from the road toward the rock embankment. Sparks flew as metal sheared away the side mirror and stack, then snagged the trailer as it bucked and fishtailed behind.

In the driver's side mirror he saw the running lights swerve into view as the trailer worked its way back into the road and jackknifed the eighteen wheeler around the next curve where the black ice ended abruptly.

Sideways, the rig plowed a path through the fresh snow drifts across the road.

"Matilda, you sweet thing. Hold together." Crandell gripped the wheel and closed his eyes until he sensed the truck come to a stop.

He kissed the wheel. "You are one fine lady." He thrust a thumb aver his shoulder toward the cargo. "Didn't spill a pint."

Crandell reached into his pocket for a dip of snuff and rolled down his frosty window. Over the chug of the engine through the mangled exhaust, he heard a roar and leaned to peer upward. He spotted a set of bright lights spinning in the air, the sight of which caused him to straighten in his seat. "Matilda, I've done gone and seen me a UFO!"

Another inspection out the window indicated the craft had dropped closer and the light stirred through the snow like a pinwheel.

Mike in hand, Crandell worked his CB to channel nine. "Anybody out there? A flying saucer is landing on top of my rig!" He kicked the door open and headed through the snow drift into the trees.

"Wait a second." Crandell stared at the mike in his hand while the end of the cord dangled at his feet. "That ain't no--"

The helicopter dropped onto the trailer, tail first and crushed it like a cheap cardboard box. Big gobs of ice cream blew out from the ruptured sides and streaked the snow with a rainbow of color and a splop-splap sound. In the blink of an eye, the cab of the truck looked like it'd rammed a paint factory.

The weight of the copter pulled the trailer over and away from the rocky mountainside. When the rotor struck the ground it shattered and bits of it shredded the trees all above Crandell.

Any snow and a few pine cones not already dislodged by the concussion of the impact pelted him on top of his head. "Tarnation! What have they done to you, Matilda?" He held his breath and waited for an explosion. "Pew!" The smell of fuel mixed with strawberry ice cream assaulted his nose.

Someone forced a door open.

"Hello!" Crandell shouted into the night, his voice echo chopped from the air as the helicopter and trailer creaked a complaint about their sudden union. "You folks okay?"

A big, bald man dropped to the slushy ground and reached back into the twisted cockpit. Over his shoulder he carried a wounded man in a green jump suit.

Crandell kicked his way through the goo and busted boxes toward the wreckage. "What a mess. Gonna blow me way off schedule. Miss my drop time. Hey, Matilda's totaled. Who's gonna pay for this?" He waved at the bald man. "Anybody else in there?"

"Yeah," said the giant. "Strapped into a rear seat. He's got two gun-shot wounds. Can you help?"

"Gunshot? Then crashed? Thought I was having a bad day. He a hi-jacker or a bank robber?" A country and western theme ran through Crandell's head. *I got me the makings of a song here somewheres.*

✗   ✗   ✗

Jordon woke in a dimly lit room. Next to him, in a bed with a shiny rail around it, he saw the helicopter pilot breathe into a plastic mask.

A scraggly man, hidden beneath a gray beard and a denim jacket, snored in a chair under the television.

"Where's Foard?" *And why am I craving ice cream?* Jordon groped for the switch to call the nurse's station when a loud, rude voice yelled in the hallway.

"I'm going in and you can't stop me."

A woman?

The scraggly man fidgeted and snorted as if ready to wake.

Foard's voice boomed through the door. "I'm afraid you can't, ma'am."

"Don't tell me what I can and cannot do. I'm in charge now. The man in there belongs to me."

Jordon glanced at the man under the television who sat bolt upright. "Who are you?"

"Name's, Crandell. A.J. Crandell." He clutched his hat in one hand and ran his fingers through his hair with the other. "I got me one bad headache from when you buggers fell outta the sky."

"Who's in the hall? Is she talking about you?"

"Don't think so. My old lady ran off years ago. She used to startle me awake like that too. But she done it just for fun."

The woman's voice grew louder. "Get out of my way, Foard. I can have you removed by the police."

"No need to get all cranky. I'll see if he's conscious."

The door opened and Foard eased into the room. "Please say you're not awake, Chief. Please say you're in a coma or something. You do not want her in here."

Jordon tried to lift his bandaged arm, but the sling prevented the move. "Sorry. Too hungry to sleep. Tell her she can come in if she brings me an Eskimo Pie."

"She comes in here," he threw a thumb over his shoulder, "and you'll lose what appetite you got. You'll never eat again."

"Hey, big feller?" Crandell rubbed his temples. "Who's doing all the yelling? Maybe it is my old lady."

Foard shook his head. "You know, I'd rather go back and wrestle a bear again. I'd even take another one of the Chief's budget flying lessons. I'm telling you, this lady gives me a reason to want to go up on the mountain again and shovel all the ice cream up..." He cracked the door and peered into the hallway. "...with one of those little sample spoons."

Jordon worked the bed control to raise himself, his curiosity overcoming his grogginess. "Well, let her in and introduce us. She can't be--"

Foard opened the door all the way. "Mitch Jordon, meet Veronda, the wicked witch of the west."

A young attractive woman in a fashionable parka stormed into the room. She removed her gloves, dropped them on the bed and pointed a long, slender finger at Crandell. "So, you're the famous Jordon. It's about time you got here!"

- PART II: PHANTOMS -

"...how frantic the pursuit, of that
treacherous phantom which men call
Liberty:
most treacherous, indeed, of all
phantoms..."

John Ruskin

TWELVE_____

Queen of diamonds. Hamilton surveyed the ten cards in his hand, the countess on the discard pile, and then Wellingham and Cortez across the table from him. A groan to his left broke his concentration. "What's the matter, Ox? You don't look so good."

He wheezed and mopped his brow with a handful of damp tissue. "Next time Marcel decides to cook us up some *etouffée*, promise me you'll make him cool it on the Louisiana hot sauce."

From the driver's seat, Gatreux turned his head and spoke over his shoulder. "*Laissez les bon temps roulez*! Let de good time roll!"

Through the windshield, Hamilton spied trees covered in ice, like fine crystal in his mother's china cabinet. The intermittent sun reflected a rainbow of colors into the mist rising from the highway.

"Just drive the land yacht. My gut feels like it's full of liquid ball bearings." Oxenthall staggered forward and rubbed his belly before he collapsed into the passenger seat. "I need to perform some relaxation exercises."

"You no like mah mudbug launch? Mah heart, she is broke. Perhaps dis rat cheer will settle de Fee Folay in you stomach. Ahm jus gon put dis een dare."

Gatreux shoved a CD into the deck and immediately the wheezing push-pull of an accordion tune blared from the overhead speakers. The rhythm of the music mimicked the sway of the van.

"Now, there's one of life's laughable tragedies and ultimate contradictions."

"What dat?"

"Zydeco music."

Cortez flexed his arm and flicked a card at Oxenthall. "Next time you take a hankering for thirds, I'll do my best to wave you off."

"Now, here's the thing." Oxenthall swiveled in his seat. "Why do people say 'past due'? Is it the Cajun influence of their word *'deux'* on our--"

"We get the picture." Hamilton reached for the stack. King of clubs. *How did I manage to get saddled with such a group?* They seemed varied as the cards in his hand. Paranoid, outspoken, almost from another planet. He felt the trek taking on the air of a grade school field trip.

A pigtail snaked from under Wellingham's cap. She fiddled with it while she held her cards close to her face. "How much farther?"

Hamilton glanced at his watch. "Half an hour. We'll be in Wildwood by dark." He closed his eyes. *Won't it be wonderful if the town had a place to lock these monkeys up for the night?*

"Hope they have a hotel." Wellingham played a four of hearts. "I'm not sleeping in this van with you guys."

"You'll be lucky if they've even got running water." Cortez unfolded a state road map. "Place is just a hole in the road. One of those 'blink and you'll miss it' kind of towns."

Sleet splattered against the windshield.

Hamilton studied his cards. Block of treys and a spade run. Next card up, king of hearts. *Should have went with the royalty.* He dropped a seven of diamonds on the table. "Hey, Marcel? Did you get all the toys you need to study this thing?"

He lowered the volume on the stereo a decibel. "You ask me, it haf at bes. Dat woman want us to hunt nutria wid a blindfold on."

Cortez pulled the supply list and scanned it. "Infopaks, portable up-link with direct sat-patch to the *Frontier,* cell phones, state-of-the-art real time imagining software. What else do you want?"

"He wants wireless cable." Oxenthall slapped his knee and snorted.

"Dat would be mah secret wish."

Wellingham fidgeted her boots under the table. "Play cards."

The hand appeared promising, but Hamilton decided not to knock. His five of diamonds went to the pile. He looked up at Cortez. "I'm still not sure why you got volunteered for this. What do S-SMC photos of Oklahoma have to do with Archaeoastronomy?"

"Smack pics," corrected Wellingham. She splayed her cards out on the table. "Gin."

"Not my day. Thirty-seven to you."

As she shuffled the cards she nudged Cortez. "Well? Tell him."

"I requested to be volunteered."

Oxenthall wrestled open a fresh pack of Gummi Bears. "Wish I'd said that."

"Life must be very boring for you, Ox." Hamilton worked his new hand into blocks.

The grin on Cortez's face stifled for a moment. "I've been studying the effect of naked eye sunspots on the ancient Anasazi near Chaco Canyon and Chimney Rock."

"What's it got to do with this?"

"Well, back in 1125 the people of ancient America went nuts about naked eye sunspots."

"He's right." Ox chewed the words around a mouthful of candy. "I was trying to sleep in 1126. They made an awful lot of noise."

A pillow sailed out of Wellingham's hand and bounced off the sweaty man's forehead. "Stuff it, Ox!"

"Thanks, Gina." Cortez fished a pen from his pocket. "They tried to tell us in pictographs and petroglyphs like this." He doodled a spiral on the map. "Even in the way they constructed their kivas. Tied in with the fact some of them moved up to Chimney Rock to observe the lunar stand-still, it all ties together."

Hamilton lowered his cards. *What did all this have to do with anything?* "You're losing me."

"Last week started the biggest sunspot flare-up in maybe the last hundred and fifty years. It's playing ping-pong with communications signals, satellite relays and believe it or not, the weather. Right now we're heading into one big winter storm."

Another glance toward the front of the van confirmed the obvious. The sky seemed to descend toward the road. "So?"

"It all coincides with a major lunar standstill. The Moon reaches its maximum northern declination at 28°46′ once every eighteen point six years." Cortez pulled one of the pulse photos up on his Infopak. "It's like a winter solstice, but about 5° farther north. I have a theory this phenomenon scared those people in a big way."

"Why would staring at the Moon cause a bunch of Indians to get their dander up?" Hamilton held back a yawn and returned his attention to his cards.

Cortez tapped the map with his finger. "Look at the evidence. First they witnessed the explosion of the Crab Nebula when it went super nova in 1054. Sunset crater erupted to the west. Halley's Comet cruised by in 1066. Toss in a couple of solar eclipses for good measure and then the equivalent of astronomic fireworks broke loose on the surface of the sun."

"Fascinating." *Not only a school trip, but a lecture to go along.* "So, what's your point?"

"These pulses might have a direct relation to the sunspots. I want to get a look at the source, first hand."

Hamilton ignored his cards. Something in the lecture made sense. "How come I've never heard of naked eye sunspots?"

"Smog. Depletion of the ozone. Greenhouse effect. Mt. St. Helens." Wellingham emphasized each point with a card as she placed them, one by one, on the table before her. "It's a big cover-up. Big brother doesn't want us to know. Gin."

Cortez settled back in his seat. "The southwestern U.S. is full of enigmas. I want to solve one."

"Whowee. Marry Crease-moose, I tink. We jus pass by de Monarch Lake and it startin' to snow."

Hamilton reached for the Infopak and the map. "These pics are of an abandoned oil field located nine miles north of Wildwood. I can see why they bailed." He handed it across to Wellingham. "If they'd been able to see these back in the thirties they'd never have started drilling in the first place."

She stacked her cards in a neat pile, face down in front of her. Instead of zooming in on the photo she pulled a small magnifying glass out her backpack. "I agree. There's a lot of oil around Wildwood, but this field went bust from day one. Everything's behind the fault, south and west of town. Something smells fishy around here and I'm not talking about Monarch Lake."

As if on cue, Oxenthall crawled from his captain chair, squeezed in behind the dinette next to Hamilton and shoved his open pack of Gummi Bears under Wellingham's nose. "Next stop, Wildwood, Oklahoma. The final frontier. Time to boldly go where no one has boldly go'ed before."

"Well, the sign says 'Main Street'. Let's park over there." Hamilton pointed down the snow covered pavement running perpendicular to the state highway. Lined with stores, their windows boarded, the street transformed into a farm road three hundred yards north. A single security light, atop a leaning wooden pole, lit the entrance to a small grocery.

"Coo! Don stand dere lak a gou gut." Gatreux slipped the van into park, left the engine running and opened his door. "Let see if dey got some dat cold brew averyone!"

Oxenthall pulled a coat over his bulk and bounded out the side. "Man, I love these working vacations. Come on, Gina!"

"Can't you close anything behind you? It's cold out there!"

The door of the general store rattled under Gatreux's hand.

"I'm clearly confused," yelled back Oxenthall. "The light's on, the sign says 'OPEN COME ON IN', but nobody's--"

Hamilton closed his eyes and thought of jumping in the driver's seat and leaving the whole bunch behind, but the commotion brought him back to reality.

"Run, Marcel. The old coot's got a gun!"

Hamilton watched the two men scatter like quail and stared at the scrawny, dried up old man who waved the barrel of his shotgun through the slightly cracked door.

"Sorry teenagers!" The old man spit a brown stain into the fresh snow drift. "Go home to your sorry mamas." The door slammed shut and broken icicles dropped from the eave and shattered on the ground.

Hamilton stepped from the van, placed a pair of fingers to his lips and whistled. "Hey, Ox. Get yourself back here." He then rapped a knuckle on the store window. "Excuse me, sir. Are you open or closed?"

A creak and the crack in the door produced the red brim of the old man's ball cap and the barrel of the shotgun once again.

"There's no need for a weapon, sir. We just want to ask you a few questions. Maybe buy some supplies." Visions of moldy cheese and stale bread drifted through his mind. "Cup of coffee would sure be nice."

The barrel dropped and the door opened.

That's more like it.

Inside the store, the old man smoothed his bristled mustache with a wrinkled finger. "Those sorry kids belong to you?"

Hamilton grinned. "I admit, they do act like kids, Mr.--?"

"Shut the door!"

As they shuffled in from the cold, Wellingham and Cortez mocked surprise at the questionable welcome.

"You're letting all the warm air out. What are you trying to do? Heat the whole sorry town?"

"Well, I can certainly sympathize." Wellingham leaned against the door until it clicked shut. "Ox and Miguel can freeze in the van."

"I cut the sorry wood myself." The storekeeper moved behind the counter and ran a thumb under the shoulder strap of his bib overalls, "and I don't want to waste it. Name's Bellaire. Calvin Bellaire. I own this place. Been in the family since statehood." He smoothed the mustache which Hamilton reasoned looked older than his business.

"'Course that's when Wildwood really lived up to its name. Wild, I mean. Folks call me Cal."

"I guess you know just about everybody around these parts...Cal." Hamilton surveyed the store. Dusty shelves, old can goods. A red cooler vibrated in the far corner like a frightened Chihuahua. By the ad on the side, soda pop still cost a nickel.

The grocer eyed Hamilton up and down and winked at Wellingham. "I should. No place else to buy food around here. Not unless you count the big fancy Superette over at the county seat. No, my customers are loyal, at least when the weather gets bad anyhow."

Wellingham scuffed her boots on the floor.

"Miguel, why don't you and Gina get us some sodas?"

"Go ahead and help yourself, Missy." Bellaire slid his gun onto the counter, next to the antique register. "You can settle up before you leave."

"You're very kind." Cortez lifted the lid of the refrigerated box. "Do you always give immediate credit to newcomers?"

"I trust people generally. Especially fishermen, when they're not boasting how good they are." Bellaire cackled and spit into a coffee can on the floor. "You folks up here to fish? Kinda late in the season."

"No, sir." Hamilton accepted the soda from Wellingham and wondered how to open it.

"I don't sell those sorry twist offs." Bellaire tossed him an opener. "Here, you gotta use Adolph's key."

Hamilton wondered about the age of the beverage, but the cap pried loose with a fizz. "We're geologists. We want to do a little scouting."

Bellaire squinted one eye, backed a step and reached for his shotgun. "Put those pops down boys and girls if you're from Stuart-Dupree. I don't give credit to any of that lot."

"Now... Hold on, Cal." The barrel of the gun looked like a cannon. "We're not from Stuart, what did you say, Dupree? Is that an oil company? I don't believe I'm familiar with them."

The old man moved to the area behind the register until the huge machine blocked most of his body. "You're sure?"

"Absolutely." Hamilton turned to his colleagues. "You two ever heard of Stuart-Dupree?"

"Let me see some i-dent-ifi-cation, Sonny!" The barrel of the shotgun rested on the top of the register.

Hamilton reached for his wallet and pulled out his credentials. He placed the plastic cards on the counter.

"ASTRO?" The old man eased the cocked hammer back into a safer position. "You don't drill for oil, you send those boys up in those rocket ships. What're you doing in Wildwood?"

When the gun once again rested on the counter, out of the old man's grip, Hamilton breathed a sigh. "Tell me about Stuart-Dupree, Cal. Why are you so upset with them?"

Bellaire's crooked finger pushed the identification back across the counter. "You folks rather have some coffee?"

"Depends on how long it's been brewing." Wellingham hid the remark behind her hand so Bellaire didn't hear.

"Good." The old man, oblivious to the statement, moved to the store's entrance and locked the door. "Let's go in the back and have some home brewed coffee. I think we have a lot to talk over. I never have any customers anyway. It's time I had someone come by who wants to talk the good ol' days."

Cortez fell in beside Hamilton and tilted his head toward the door. "What about those two?"

"When they stop running, they can wait in the van."

"I think Gina locked the doors."

Wellingham shrugged and followed the old man into a back room. "Ox has enough hot air in him to keep them both warm."

Hamilton laughed and welcomed the coziness of the well lit and amply furnished kitchen. He selected a straight backed chair on the far side of the table and while the old man poured, inhaled the strong acrid aroma of coffee and stale tobacco. "Now, tell us about Stuart-Dupree and we'll tell you why we're here."

"Well, it's like this." Bellaire spit his chaw in the sink and straddled a chair. His gaze seemed to mist into the steam above his mug. "Guess to tell it right, I have to relate a little bit about Wildwood."

An Infopak appeared in Wellingham's hand. "Mind if I take notes?"

"Naw," the old man eyed the little electronic device. "What I got to say ain't worth writin' down... If it's what you're plannin' on doin with that gizmo."

Cortez sugared his coffee from a glass jar in the middle of the table and leaned back. "We'd love to hear your story."

The old man smoothed his mustache. "In its day, this rated the roughest boom town in the state."

"Oil boom?" Hamilton wondered how much of the tale had any truth to it and how much contained historical fiction.

"What other kinda boom is there? Of course it was an oil boom. Wildwood crawled with roughnecks, geologists, company men, you name it. I staked out the ideal spot, right here in the middle of everything goin' on." A thump of his crooked index finger on the table emphasized the point.

"What year was this?" Cortez retrieved the pot from the stove and refilled the old man's mug.

"Oh, I'd say early forties. I can't be too precise. Say forty-one, maybe forty-two. 'Bout the same time they doodle bugged the West Edmond field over Oak City way."

"Near the beginning of World War II?"

Wellingham counted on her fingers. "Why, you must be well over--"

Hamilton kicked her shin under the table. "Go on, Cal. The beginning of World War II."

"Yeah, that's about right. Anyway, the boom was on. People drillin' and speculatin' and wildcattin' all over the place. Why, they were jabbin' holes in the ground faster than I sold 'em beans. Needed oil for them fightin' boys." He removed his ragged ball cap and bowed his head.

"But I thought most of the area north of here resulted in a bust field," said Wellingham with a distrustful eye toward Hamilton.

"Yep." The old man worked the cap onto his white haired head and winked.

"Then why all the activity?" Hamilton waved a hand to draw Bellaire's attention. "I don't recall ever reading anything regarding an oil boom near here."

"Oh, there was a boom, all right. But not north of town." He pointed at the wall. "All to the west."

"Hold on a second." Wellingham dropped her Infopak on the table and leaned forward. "Monarch Lake is west of here."

"Yep. They finished Monarch Dam in late forty-five and flooded the whole sorry field."

"Strange." Hamilton searched his memory for something to tie all the information together. *Is this old man feeding us a line?* "I thought most of the money went to fund the war. How'd they manage to build a dam?"

"Who knows?" Bellaire pulled a plug of tobacco from his bib and trimmed a corner with his pocketknife. He offered it around the table. "The sorry morons built it and then flooded a perfectly good oil field behind it. Why I bet most of the equipment is still down there on the bottom of the lake."

"Maybe later." Wellingham curled her nose at the plug and pushed the old man's hand away. "Who owned the mineral rights?"

"How do I know? Lots of people. Nobody. Who knows... or cares?"

"What has this got to do with Stuart-Dupree?" Hamilton accepted the offered chaw against his better judgment and stuck it in his mouth. The juice made him gag.

"Now them, I know all about. You sure better be ready if you aim to tangle with those rascals. They drilled north of town while everybody else plugged away to the west." The old man placed the tobacco and the knife in the middle of the table next to the sugar jar. "Even I knew there was no oil up in those sorry mountains."

Hamilton worked the tobacco around in his mouth and tried to keep a straight face. The terrain around town more likely qualified as above average hills. "We understand they didn't have the technology we have today, but surely they must've had some indication of a field."

"Nope. They just kept drilling holes in the ground and filling them up again. Spent their sorry money like nobody's business, like it was going out of style. Sorry greedy worms. 'Course we took it and extended credit after they seemed sound enough despite their ignorance."

"Then what happened to them?"

"Who knows?" The old man pulled a second rusty can from under the table and placed it under Hamilton's nose. "Spit it out, Sonny. You're turning green."

Grateful for the reprieve, Hamilton washed the foul taste down with the cold coffee at the bottom of his mug. Sludge came to mind.

"They skipped in the night, owing me and a bunch of others an awful lot of money. It's what killed the town, that and the confounded lake a few years later. I'm the only one left."

"I suppose since no production held the leases, the rights went back to the surface owners." Wellingham scribbled more notes into her electronic notepad. "Any of their families still around?"

"They still hold the leases. Stuart-Dupree."

"Not possible." Wellingham appeared confused.

"Don't tell me, I've had a lien on them ever since the day after they skipped town."

Hamilton held up a hand. "I'm sorry, Cal. The system doesn't work that way."

"Well it does in Monarch County."

Hamilton scratched his ear. "You've seen a lawyer, I assume."

The cackle which rolled from Bellaire's lips held an air of sarcasm. "A peck of lawyers can't find out how Stuart-Dupree is able to hold those leases and still not pay me what's due. You folks work for the government..." The crooked finger jabbed the table again. "You find out why. But stay away from that sorry ghost rig." His chair kicked back from under him and he stomped through the door into the grocery.

"Ghost rig?" Cortez grinned. "If you ask me, I think the old man's crazy. Really had me going for a minute. Almost believed the part about the mysterious oilfield hidden under Monarch Lake."

"Smack pics say it's there." Wellingham stuffed the Infopak back into her pocket.

"Surely you don't--"

"Smack pics don't lie."

"What about the blue pulse?" Cortez leaned toward her and contorted his face into a ghoulish mask. "Hmm? Wonder if the blue hue has something to do with crazy Cal's ghost rig?"

Hamilton took a deep breath to settle his nauseous stomach. The old man's actions spooked him enough without the mention of haunted oil fields. He put a hand out to separate Cortez and Wellingham. "Now is not the time, you two. Anybody notice if he's got a phone?"

A commotion erupted from the grocery.

Hamilton closed his eyes and wished for an antacid. Instead he got Ox, full in the face, as the overheated man stormed into the room and dusted snow from his shoulders onto the floor.

"Good grief. All the old man's got out there is nonalcoholic beer and stale Banana Bites!"

Hamilton reached for the abandoned plug and pocketknife. "Here, Ox. Try some of this."

THIRTEEN_____

Tate Smullins rotated the toothpick in his mouth from one side to the other, then spit it on the floor of the phone booth. A glance at his watch confirmed the call as late. He rapped his knuckles against the metal shelf and banged his head back into the hot glass. The heat of the late, southern California sun warmed his neck. "Cax, this better be--" The phone rang and he snagged the receiver. "This is Smullins. You're late. The message you left on my machine--"

"I'm sorry." Grant's voice sounded odd. Old and raspy.

Odd indeed. The fat man never apologized for a thing in his life. "Okay, so you've got me standing in a graffiti box in the middle of Pasadena. What's with all the cloak and dagger stuff? Where are you?"

"I'm at the Santa Anita racetrack. Can you be here in an hour?"

"Racetrack?" *Something is wrong.* "What are you doing at Santa Anita?"

"Watching the horses and drinking beer."

Smullins eyed the cradle for the receiver and decided to hang up. Grant had lost his mind. "Look, Cax. Enjoy your retirement. I'll have to pass."

"I think Mitch is dead."

The grandstand restaurant opened to track side. Stale cigarette smoke hung in the air like a toxic cloud. Near the rail, Smullins found Grant wedged between the table and his chair.

The former director of ASTRO looked out of place, like a milk bucket under a bull. Accustomed to finding the big man in a tailor-made, three piece suit, Smullins instead viewed a different man; a defeated man. *A man with a serious wardrobe problem.*

Grant sat alone. His face unshaven. His Hawaiian shirt, loud and garish. *And shorts? Incredible.* The total lack of self respect epitomized itself in the fact he drank a beer, not from a glass, but straight from the bottle.

"Cax?" Smullins put his hand on the man's shoulder.

"Sit down, Tate." Grant motioned a drunken wave to the chair on the opposite side of the table.

"You look beyond terrible." Smullins pulled out the chair and sat. "Do you need a doctor?"

"Doctor can't cure thish hurt. Goesh too deep." He tilted back the bottle and drained it. Finished, he sleeved his lips dry and let go a belch heard above the announcer's call for post time.

"What's this about Mitch being dead? Now I see what condition you're in, I find anything you say hard to believe." Smullins flagged a waitress, pointed at Grant's empties. "Take these away and bring us some coffee stout enough to float Secretariat's horseshoes." Then to his former boss, "What about arrangements? A funeral? A memorial or something?"

"Tate, ol' boy, I'm going to tell you a shecret today I've never told anyone elsh b'fore." The words slurred around the alcohol in Grant's breath. "But firsht I've shome bad news. Bad. Bad. Bad."

"Look, I made some calls. Nobody at ASTRO knows anything." The waitress arrived with the hot coffee and distracted Smullins' attention. The voice over the loudspeaker announced the horses had entered the starting gate. It added a sense of circus to the tragic news. *Wake up Tate.* He gulped half the steaming cup. *It's all a bad dream. A nightmare.* The coffee scalded the back of his throat and startled him back into reality. The horses leapt from the gates and headed down the stretch in a fury of hoof and dust.

When the thoroughbreds crossed the finish line, Grant slammed a fist down on the table. "Mitch ish dead an' Kerry ish not!"

The people below the rail jumped to their feet to scream and yell at the top of their collective lungs. The roar muffled the sound of broken glass when his cup hit the floor. Smullins felt like he'd been gut kicked. Numbness overcame him. He tried to mouth some sort of answer to the news, but in the end nothing came.

The crowd went silent.

Grant pulled a ticket from his pocket. "Losh again."

Smullins lunged at Grant and grabbed him by the front of his shirt. "Get a grip, you drunk! What are you telling me?"

The fat man struggled against the hold. "Don't blame you a bit for being angry. Not a bit." He held up an index finger. "Nex time. Won't go with th' long shot. Wouldn't blame you if you throw me over th' rail." He swayed and peered beyond the edge.

"Don't tempt me!"

"I've made a lot of mishtakes. Meshed up. Didn't realize it 'til Foard told me 'bout Mitch."

"What about Mitch?" Smullins released his grip and shoved Grant back into his seat. "Who is Foard and what did he say about Mitch?"

"Kincade crashed a 'copter into hish cabin. There, I shaid it. Shatisfied? Awful, absolutely awful. Awful. Awful. Awful."

"And this Foard guy, he saw a body?"

"Tell you he'sh dead. I couldn't take it. I called you back, got on a plane an' came out here. I'm sick of myshelf. Now... I've shome unfinished business t' attend. I owe it t' Mitch."

Smullins watched the man raise his hand to signal the waitress for more beer but blocked the delivery of the bottle with his arm. "He's had enough."

"Tate's right!" Grant held his hand to his neck. "Had it up t' here."

The startled and confused waitress retreated from the table, slipping slightly in the puddle of coffee on the floor.

I know for a fact, Kerry Jordon did not die in a plane crash in th' Phil... In th' Phil... In th' Philippines."

"Talk sense, will you? First Mitch is dead. Now Kerry is alive. Make up your mind."

"She's shtill alive I tell you. Shomewhere. Out there. Wishh I knew."

"Cax..." A rage of hate boiled inside Smullins. He wanted to smash his fist into the fat man's face. He wanted to physically beat the man, to punish him for all the problems he'd caused. He wanted to avenge his agony. If the place hadn't been so public, he might have followed through. "What have you done?"

"Hold on, Tate ol' boy." Grant put a hand up in mock defense. "I had good reashon for not telling Mitch, or... Or sho I thought. I wash going t' tell him. Once I found her. Now... It may be too late."

"You have got to be the most inhuman, most insensitive bureaucrat I have ever known." Smullins pushed his chair away from the table. He wanted to distance himself, if only a few precious feet. He stood to walk away.

"Come back. Sit down, Tate." Grant's voice sounded soft, mellowed. "Please."

"No, I don't think I will."

"Kerry Jordon ish still alive. I have reason to believe Alan Dover may know where she ish."

The statement sobered Smullins from his grief and anger. "Are you telling me Dover's escaped?"

"I've got a gut feeling he shomehow switched places with whoever it is they found in hish cell. My personal file on Kerry is missing." He lowered his head to the table. "Dover had access."

"So, what are you going to do?"

"We," Grant looked up with a heavy emphasis on the preposition, "are going to find Kerry first. Before Dover can get to her. That's what we're going t' do. You and me."

"Why now?"

"I've made a lot of mishtakes in my life." Grant's bloodshot eyes belonged to a whipped basset hound. "Many of them in th' besht interest of ASTRO. Sho I thought. Now, I've resigned... I at least owe it t' Mitch's memory t' try."

"You owe him a lot more. A whole lot more."

"I know, but it's too late for anything else."

Smullins recovered his chair and sat while the overhead speaker announced a scratch in the next race. "Suppose I go along. I'll call a truce for now. But when all of this is over, you're going to reckon with me."

"Agreed." Grant nodded.

"Fill me in on some details."

Grant waved to the skittish waitress. "I think food ish in order. Hungry?"

Over a plate of fries and a replacement cup of strong, black coffee, Grant told his story of Kerry Jordon's disappearance. The caffeine and grease sobered his speech. "I didn't know Mitch had been dating her. Apparently they'd been able to keep it a secret since college. Seems they didn't want it to interfere with their professional careers. They sure weren't going to tell me they'd been married."

"So, why the problem?" Smullins spit out a burnt fry. What a waste of good potatoes. The thought reminded him of the farm back home. He unsleeved a new toothpick and gazed at the track. The sun set and the flood lights brightened the grandstand like a used car lot.

"At first I saw no problem. Then during her preflight exam for her next lunar mission, the doctors discovered Kerry's pregnancy. Well, of course we couldn't risk..." Grant massaged his temples. "I couldn't risk, sending her to the Moon. From a scientific point of view we'd have made history, but not by jeopardizing her health to satisfy a bunch of curious doctors."

"I understand all that." Smullins felt the impatience grow inside. Here sat the king of cover-up outlining his masterpiece. "What I don't understand is why you waited until the last second to pull her from the mission. Mitch had already gone into orbit. As I recall, Kerry practically stepped into the launch tower elevator, suited and ready to go."

"We had a problem... I had a problem. At the time I still didn't know they'd been married. The press would have had me for lunch. Congress held a saber to my throat. Any more scandal after the Greg Ward catastrophe would certainly shut the program down again. This time for good."

Another race left the gate and Grant appeared to wait for the noise to die down. "Can you image some sensationalized headline like *'Unwed Mother in Space'*? The mission meant too much to be overshadowed by something so stupid."

"So, you covered it up."

"Yes."

"Why am I not surprised?" Smullins conjured up the thought of a cat in a sand box. "And why didn't you tell Mitch?"

Grant took a slow sip of coffee. "Simple. He wouldn't have gone to the Moon. Would you?"

"Not under those circumstances. But I think Mitch might have, if you'd explained it to him."

"I couldn't be certain."

"Okay." Smullins removed his toothpick and stabbed a fry on his plate. *Too bad it's not Grant's cold heart.* "I don't agree with your tactics, but I understand your position. Now, tell me why you sent Kerry out of the country."

"General Antony Stone, USAF, retired. Know him?"

"Sure. Kerry's dad. The last time I heard, he lives in the... Hey, wait a sec." Smullins gave himself a mental kick for not putting the pieces in place earlier. "He's retired air force. And he lives in the..."

Grant nodded his agreement. "...the Philippines. He's got quite a business going over in the duty-free industrial zone at Subic Bay."

"You two planned it together." Smullins placed the toothpick back in his mouth and rolled it around. It tasted salty. "You sent her to be with daddy."

A rowdy lady, below the rail, celebrated her win on the Daily Double and splashed a soft drink onto Smullins' leg. *Great.* He brushed the icy mess away and motioned toward the exit. "Let's take a walk. I get the picture up to where her plane augered in the jungle. What makes you think she's still alive?"

Grant paid the cashier, a wad of assorted bills piled on the counter, but didn't wait for the change. He broke open a pack of aspirin he'd taken from an impulse display and swallowed the little white painkillers dry. "She never got on the connecting flight from Manila International to Subic."

Smullins stopped and put a hand out like a traffic cop. "You have proof?"

"Not yet."

"You're not making sense again."

"No, I guess not."

"What do you have? What's in the missing file?"

"Antony received a call from Kerry before the flight. He thinks she intended to charter a private plane and fly herself. But there's no paper trail. No report of a missing plane."

"So, where did she go?" Smullins leaned against a wall to think. The concourse filled as people ready to bet on the next race flooded the floor with worthless slips of paper. "Didn't she file a flight plan?"

"None I'm aware of."

"This doesn't make sense. What happened to the plane? She had to return it somewhere."

"We think she fell in with smugglers, most likely posing as a legitimate carrier. If it crashed in the same thunderstorm as the passenger plane... Went down in the jungle too... possibly in the opposite direction..."

Smullins spit his toothpick on the cement concourse and put his face in his hands. "Your story smells like a feedlot." He pointed a finger into the big man's belly. "You've gone over the edge and you're trying to take me with you. Well forget it! Two planes, both buy the farm, either of which she might or might not have been on... You've slipped a gear."

Grant shook his head. "If both planes took off from Manila at about the same time, but in different directions into the mountains, it explains a lot. The passenger plane exploded on impact. No survivors. Nothing to identify. But someone found a small plane. A smugglers plane. Kerry may have walked away from it."

"So, if she survived the impact, why didn't she let someone know?"

Grant put both his chubby hands on Smullins' shoulders. "Tate, this is what we must find out. Before Dover can get to her."

FOURTEEN_____

"I'm so g-glad you made it, Miss Turner." Dover pulled out the Chippendale chair and offered the lady a seat next to his. "I hope you like It-talian."

He glanced at Mordel, standing by the lavish table, first on one foot, then the other. "Well, have a s-seat, Meg."

She opened her purse, snapped it shut again and slipped it beneath her chair. "Thank you. Such a gentleman."

He ignored the sarcasm and admired Lana Turner's blush as he showered her with more attention.

"I'm sorry if I appear uncomfortable, Mr. Dover." Turner lowered into her chair and glanced at the violinist nearby. "I'm not accustomed to dining in such elegant surroundings."

He patted the back of her hand. *Smooth.* Her scent pleased him. A whiff of lilac mingled in the air with the remnants of garlic and oregano from the next table. It produced an intoxicating allure, difficult to resist. "A woman of such beauty should be accustomed t-to no less. Relax. Enjoy the evening. And please, I insist you call me Alan."

"I still don't understand why you want to interview me."

Dover compared her profile to the image in his mind. *The surgery has changed her features, but yes, this is Kerry Jordon.* "Why, didn't Meg explain?" He tilted a quick glance across the table at the private eye and backed her into her chair with his stare.

"Yes, she did mention something concerning an article on health care here in Manila." Turner fidgeted with her crystal water glass and turned her attention to Mordel. "But I thought she's writing it."

Dover congratulated himself. *The cover story is working.* To accent the charade, he pulled an electronic note pad from his jacket pocket like he'd seen the reporters do on television. "Oh, she is. I'm here on a related story and offered to help Meg gather some background information."

"Are you with the same magazine?"

Mordel cleared her throat and fielded the question. "Why, yes. As I told you before, we both freelance for *Time*."

"I'm sorry, but I'm not familiar with magazines from the United States." Turner continued to fidget. She studied the restaurant like a paranoid claustrophobic who inventories all the exits every time they enter a room. "If you say it's a major one, well who am I to question?"

Her brain is really shorted out if she hasn't heard of Time. A sudden craving for Swiss cheese came to mind. "I'm sure if Meg uses anything from th-this interview in her article, she'd be more than happy to forward you a co-copy of the issue."

"Oh, will you, Miss Mordel?"

"Of course, my dear." Mordel retrieved her purse from under her chair and searched it again.

Might as well be an expedition to the Arctic. Dover, satisfied he had both ladies under his control, switched the subject of the conversation to dinner. "Anyone for wine?"

A short, dark-skinned *sommelier* appeared and presented a list with no prices. "I am Ramón. May I suggest a wonderful red *Bordeaux?* The *Château Les Ormes-de-Pez* is particularly excellent."

"Any p-preference, Miss Turner?" Dover angled the list to let her read it and leaned until his cheek almost touched hers.

"You choose for me, Mr. Dover. Like I said before, I'm not accustomed to all this."

Dover signaled for Ramón to come closer. He surmised the better vintages to be on the restaurant's reserve list. "Perhaps instead, a *Chardonnay* is in order, but f-feeling a bit maverick for the occasion, I'm thinking a nice *Johannesburg Riesling*." He focused on Mordel. "Don't you ag-gree?"

"Fine. Whatever. I have no idea what you're talking about. Make sure it's not decaf."

"Excellent choice, sir." Ramón departed for the cellar and Dover turned his attention back to his prey. He reached for her hand and caressed the smooth skin. "P-P-Please, Miss Turner. I insist you call me Alan."

"Then I must insist you call me Lana."

"Lana it will b-be."

Mordel looked ready to explode. The crimson in her cheeks matched the red in her hair. She clutched her purse to her chest and pushed her chair back from the table. "If you two will excuse me, I'll return shortly." In an instant she'd made her way across the crowded restaurant toward the exit, an unlit cigarette already wedged between her lips.

At first Dover felt anger toward Mordel for abandoning him so, but he considered the matter further and realized Turner appeared more at ease. He gazed into her eyes and tried to compare her face to the old photo from the newspaper clipping in the file he'd had stolen from Grant's safe. Older now, her features still beautiful even though her soft complexion reflected scars, expertly covered by make-up. Her eyes confessed the sorrow of someone who'd endured a lot of pain and loneliness.

"Forgive me for being so forward." He tempered his voice to portray a false embarrassment. "I c-can't help asking..."

"Asking? About what?" She didn't retreat, but allowed him to inch his chair a little closer to hers.

"It's silly really. Has n-nothing to do with Meg's article." He bit his lip. "I sense from your voice, your appearance... Well I sense you're misplaced in this part of the world."

She suppressed a smile and laughed quietly. "Why, Mr. Dover, it doesn't take the eagle eye of a reporter to notice that."

He laughed with her, but felt stupid for moving too quickly. "The person who answers to 'Mr. Dover' is my d-d-dad and I don't see him in the room. You must c-call me Alan. My feelings depend on it."

"I'm sorry." She dropped her gaze when Ramón arrived with the wine and presented it for inspection. "I'm so used to addressing everyone formally at the hospital with mister or sir or ma'am. It's just a habit."

"To be expected." He accepted the cork and sniffed the sweet aroma. After the *sommelier* had poured the white wine, Dover sipped and washed the rich, full-bodied taste over his tongue. "This is fine, Ramón." He turned Mordel's glass upside down. "Fill these two. I want to make a toast."

"Shouldn't we wait for Miss Mordel?"

"Let's have this one b-between you and I. Shall we?"

"All right." The *sommelier* gone, she raised her glass. "What shall we toast?"

Dover scratched his ear and thought for a moment. "How about to... breaking old habits... achieving our objectives... defeating our enemies."

Turner ballooned her cheeks and blew air through her lips. "Quite a large toast for such a small glass of wine." She laughed and her beautiful smile grew larger.

"F-Forgive me. Must be the reporter in me. I tend to be a little over-dramatic in m-my presentation."

"Let's just toast to breaking old habits." She clinked her glass to his.

He laughed and reached for the bottle. With each glass of wine, Dover watched her confidence grow and gained a foothold on her friendship.

"Before we order, fill me in on a little b-background information." He motioned for Ramón to bring a second bottle to lubricate her memory. "How'd you come to work in the hospital? We've already established you're not from around here."

Her expression changed from happiness to confusion and the smile disappeared from her lips.

"Have I said something wrong?" Dover held up an open palm to halt Ramón's approach.

"Oh, no." Her lashes blinked in rapid succession until she hid her face behind the green linen napkin. "I don't like to discuss my past."

"I'm sorry. Didn't intend to p-pry. I thought it might give me a little insight to what motivates you and your colleagues."

"I don't mean to be private about my past." She lowered the napkin and her voice. "There's so little of it I can remember."

"I don't understand," Dover lied. *Here it comes. This will confirm or deny my suspicions.*

A small tear formed in the corner of her eye, paused for a moment on her lash and ran down the side of her face. She wiped the droplet away with the back of her hand along with a bit of make-up. The smear revealed a slender scar across her left cheek.

It's her! Dover tried to hide his reaction, but the shock on her face confessed a deep embarrassment.

She grabbed the napkin and held the linen to her cheek. "I wonder what's keeping Miss Mordel? If you'll excuse me, I'll check on her." Like a rabbit, she darted her way between the tables and disappeared around the corner.

Dover savored his wine, but the smell of residual smoke told him Mordel had returned. He didn't look up.

She stood alone, arms akimbo. "What did you say to her?"

"Nothing. Why?" Dover crossed his legs and drained his glass.

"She's in the ladies room crying like a baby. You didn't tell her who you think she is, did you?"

Dover drilled his stare into her. "Don't be rid-ridiculous. I may have moved in a little too fast. She's touchy on the subject of her past. It's going to take a little more t-time than I expected to get the information I need."

"Well, ease up on her."

Dover slammed his glass down on the table. "You fail to understand something here, Meg. I don't care what happens to her. She's my pipeline to Jordon. A pawn." He arched his eyebrows and pulled Mordel down into her chair. "As you are, my dear."

She jerked her arm away with disgust. "I don't like you."

"I'm not paying you to like me, Meg. I'm paying you to do a job."

"No amount of money is worth this."

"Pity, I'll phone the I.R.S. and t-tell them you're too dead to pay your taxes." He uncrossed his legs and motioned for the waiter to bring a menu. *Fettuccine with a ricotta and spinach sauce will round out the evening nicely.* "Now, get yourself in gear and check on her!"

76

FIFTEEN_____

The records vault beyond the County Clerk's desk in the Monarch County courthouse looked cramped, like the bunk Cortez occupied in the camper-van the night before. A low watt bulb hung from the ceiling and battled the gray light which filtered through the dusty skylight overhead.

"Okay, Marcel. Hamilton says we're Landmen today. Let's see those township and range coordinates for the blue spot."

Gatreux searched the pockets of his parka. "Ah tink you have dem."

"No, Gina gave them to you this morning." Cortez nodded a greeting to the clerk behind the desk. She imparted the cold, hard stare of a grade school librarian over the top of her paperback book. The pinpoint kind which made you feel guilty in advance.

Cortez reverted his attention to Gatreux. "Maybe you left it back in the van." When Hamilton had sent them on this fact finding excursion, the Cajun made a point of cleaning all of Ox's empty Gummi Bear packages from the floorboard. "Could have fallen out of your pocket."

"A no. Dem all patch numbers still in dat girl's had." He pointed at his scalp. "Wan me coil her at de grocery an ax her?" His cell phone appeared in his hand.

The brusque clerk with the Tower of Pisa bouffant lowered the white cover book, cleared her throat and pointed at the sign over the vault door.

"No cellular phones," read Cortez. "Great. Go try outside. Since we left them afoot in Wildwood, I'm sure she'd love to get a call. What else is there to do? Watch the weird old storekeeper's chin hairs grow?"

Gatreux handed over his Infopak and headed for the door. "Be rat back. Hope ah kin member de number."

A man came out of the vault and shrugged into an overcoat from the rack on the wall.

The clerk looked up from her book again. "Headin' home J.D.?"

"Gonna be a long drive to Tulsa, Darlene. Think I'm all done here.

Probably won't be back for a couple of weeks."

"Well, be careful on those roads." She smiled as he exited and then refocused on her romance.

Cortez tried a pleasant smile as he walked past her desk, but failed to gain any response. *Cold weather must have froze her to the chair.* A step over the threshold and he entered the vault. Thick rows of red backed legal volumes lined the shelves from floor to ceiling. In the center of the cement room a chest high work table waited for researchers to prop against it for the day. The air smelled musty like a used book store.

The temperature inside felt chilly compared to the heat provided by the propane stove in the clerk's office. Cortez decided to keep his coat on for a bit longer.

He ran his fingers along the spines of each volume and acquainted himself to the system. When Gatreux returned with the proper coordinates, he'd be ready to pull the correct books. He scanned the wall for a sign which prohibited the use of computers and rested the Infopak on the metal table and plugged in a small, portable keyboard. A press of a button and the little information center hummed to life. A quick perusal of the files found a preprogrammed poker game and he debated for a moment whether to play.

"Dey no answer." Gatreux shuffled through the door and tossed the yellow piece of paper onto the keyboard. "I foun dis here. De weather is got de phone oil gogo."

"Or the sunspots." Cortez selected a datapad program and typed in the numbers. "They mess with telecommunications."

"Ah know. Mah toys, deh don lak." He wrinkled his nose. "Pooyie! Dis room stanks lak swamp gas!"

Cortez removed his coat. "Getting colder outside?"

"She startin' snow again. Ah worry 'bout mah pet gator back ome. Ah ever show you a picture of her?" He pulled a photo from his wallet. A big ugly beast sat with its toothy snout sticking out of a doghouse, the words 'FIDEAUX' stenciled over its head. "She mah pride an joy."

"Wonderful. Let's get started." Cortez turned to the top row of volumes. "Help me find tract index T6N, R20E." He worked his way along the shelf, his head tilted to read the numbers sideways. "Township two north. Three north." The next volume skipped a number. "Five north?"

"Wha de matter?"

"A book's missing." Cortez scratched his chin. "Not really missing, it's like there's no space for it."

"Don make no sense."

Cortez turned, cleared his throat and crooked a finger at the clerk. "Excuse me? Ma'am? Darlene? Can you come in here a moment?"

"How you know her name?"

She pursed her lips and slammed the romance novel onto the desk blotter so hard it made her bouffant hairdo bounce.

That woman looks about as inconvenienced as an ambulance driver digging for change at a toll booth.

"She don lak mah ponytail." Gatreux moved to where the table blocked a direct attack from the irate county employee. "Ah tink she gon cut it off. Watch out for dem scissors."

"Ease up, Marcel. You'll scare her off."

"An dat bad?"

The sour woman stepped over the threshold, dangled her butterfly glasses on the chain around her neck and tugged a pink sweater over her shoulders. "We do not pull books for you, sir. That is not part of our job."

Cortez held up a palm. "No, ma'am. We'll gladly pull our own record, but I can't locate the index I need."

She tapped the toe of her shoe on the floor and her impatience echoed from the ceiling. "Which is?"

"T6N, R20E."

The clerk bit her lip and went white. "Why do you want T6N, R20E?"

"Just routine research." Cortez glanced at Gatreux and made eye contact. The Cajun's reaction indicated his own puzzlement. *If he had Fideaux with him, he'd probably set the gator after that woman.* "Is there a problem?"

She continued to chew on her lip like a piece of gum. When it seemed she might swallow it, she said, "We keep it up on the top shelf."

"Why?"

She squirmed inside her sweater. "Nobody ever uses it."

Cortez decided not to press her. "Well, if you'll point me in the right direction..."

A wrinkled finger pointed over his head. "Up there." She cut her eyes toward Gatreux. "You won't find what you're hunting for." The revelation proclaimed, she returned to her novel with the picture of the lifeguard on the cover.

"Full a mystery. Ah!" said Gatreux. "Dat ol' byok is a conja. She try an put de gree gree on me."

"She's creepy, like the old storekeeper. Gina tell you what he said? Something about a ghost rig?"

"Why you tink she sleep in de bad wit de light on an a slug ranch in her had oil night?"

Cortez chalked it up to her paranoia, but he had to admit he'd checked the lock more than once. He watched Gatreux reach for the thin volume on the top shelf and blow the dust from its cover. He lowered his voice. "The old bag is right. This thing hasn't been opened in years."

Derek Bullard

After he'd licked his thumb, Gatreux turned the pages one by one. "Let see now..."

A glance at the yellow scrap of paper in his hand gave Cortez further coordinates. "Section seventeen. Northwest quarter of the southeast quarter. Here. Stuart-Dupree. Find the lease."

"Rat cheer." Gatreux's finger traced down the paper. "Annabelle Jacks. It's--" The sound of the vault door interrupted him.

The clerk stood hands on hips at the threshold. "I'm afraid you men will have to leave. Because of the bad weather, we're closing for the day."

Cortez felt cheated. "But you just opened."

"Leave the books on the table. We will file them in the morning."

"A moment longer?" *Something smells. And it's not this vault.*

The woman became more insistent. "Now. I want to get home before the roads ice completely."

"Les go." Gatreux fumbled the book onto the floor. "Why look what I don gone and don," he said loudly as he knelt behind the counter. "Dropped dis here book on mah foot. Caused mah boot to come untied. Made mah toe sore." He slammed the cover as he arose and plunked the book on the table.

"Wait a minute." Cortez struggled against the pull on his jacket. "Marcel, she can't--"

"She don did. I say les go." Gatreux led him out of the vault. "Now, 'fore she bites us."

"I still don't see what this has to do with anything, Marcel." Cortez pulled the hood of his parka tight about his head and stared out onto the frozen lake. "We get stuck in the snow next to a trash can, a picnic table and a rusty roadside marker covered with dead weeds. We need to try and figure out how to get back to Wildwood and you want to see what this thing says."

"Red it again."

Cortez brushed away the white fluff which had mounded on the top of the three foot high sign. "I could read this thing ten times and--" The words leapt from the marker.

OKLAHOMA HISTORICAL MARKER #1229
MONARCH LAKE

Formed by the construction of nearby Monarch Dam and named in honor of United States Senator Ryan Scott Monarch, killed in an automobile accident along with United States Senator Simpson Jacks near this spot on April 13, 1945.

"You see?"

"Simpson Jacks."

"Ah! You mind work lak lightnin' in a bottle. Careful or you melt de snow."

A cold flake landed on his nose and reminded Cortez of the old hag in the courthouse. "That lease had the same name on it."

"It shore do." Gatreux pulled a folded paper from under his coat and spread it out on the marker. "Ah tear it out while she thinks mah toe is smashed."

"You didn't?"

"She no wan us to read dis. You know dat. Ah know dat. Ah figure. Wah not? She no come after us in dis snow. Ah figure, Ah put the gree gree on her."

The cell phone twirped from somewhere in the folds of Gatreux's coat. Cortez accepted it from him and answered.

Hamilton's voice mixed within the static in the tiny speaker. "Miguel, where are you?"

"Stuck in the snow. Out by the lake. Where are you?"

"Getting ready to see if the guy at the garage will lend us his truck. Didn't think about you guys leaving us without anything to drive. Appears we're both stranded. Why aren't you at the courthouse?"

Cortez related the events of the morning and finished with a reading of the historical marker. "And get this." He traced his finger along the lease. Surface rights are still retained by someone named Annabelle Jacks. Must be the dead Senator's land."

"You suppose she's still alive?"

"This is an old lease, but she might be. Or an heir." The phone phased in and out. "I'm losing you again."

"Okay, get the van back on the road. I'll take Gina and Ox with me. Maybe old Cal will know if Annabelle Jacks is still around."

"Or her heirs."

"Right. Be..."

The signal faded out and the phone went dead. "Sunspots." Cortez folded the useless device and handed it over to his friend. "Now I know why they bugged the Anasazi."

"They get lousy service too?"

"They didn't... Oh, funny." He followed Gatreux back to the van and crawled into the passenger seat. Through the window he watched a huge fog bank roll across the lake and engulf the vehicle. Water droplets formed odd patterns on the windshield. "Can you believe this weather?"

Gatreux waved the lease in the air. "Ah tod you dat woman put de gree gree on us."

The van rocked back and forth and Cortez had to grab a handful of seat to keep from banging his head on the windshield. A loud roar filled his ears and then the engine stopped.

The key clicked in Gatreux's hand and he looked up, the puzzlement back in his expression. "She dead."

The van bucked up in the rear like it'd been lifted by a gust of wind, but the fog remained thick and motionless. "What's going--?"

"Coo! An no lak dis. It de abdominal snowman." Gatreux tried his door handle, but he couldn't get out.

Cortez tried his own while the front of the vehicle bucked several feet off the ground. "Hey! What's going on?"

A bright light filled the interior of the van and blinded him. "Marcel? Can you see anything?"

No answer.

Cortez squinted and held his hand to shield his eyes. Gatreux had disappeared.

An ear splitting sound like a thousand soda cans being crushed assaulted his senses and the roof of the van started to collapse.

The door handle remained frozen.

A window cracked.

The light grew more intense.

A carrot smell of burning wires filled the van.

Blood trickled from his ears and ran down his neck. He felt the scream in his throat, but never heard it. Then all went black.

SIXTEEN_____

"**Y**ou're a lucky man." The beam of Dr. John Keene's examination light flicked back and forth in Jordon's right eye. "The cold kept your bleeding to a minimum."

"How are the wounds?" Jordon leaned back into his pillow. "My arm feels numb."

"Considering the circumstances, not bad at all. The bullets went through cleanly. Missed your clavicle by a couple of inches. Good thing your canoe rocked or he'd have hit the subclavian artery."

The doctor lifted the bandage and peered underneath. "Numbness is from the painkillers. I cleaned some cloth out of the wound and irrigated it before I stitched. Don't think you'll need any surgery. Maybe later on to touch up those scars. That'll be up to you."

Jordon glanced over at A.J. Crandell, who still occupied the chair under the television, his forehead covered with several butterfly bandages. "I can live with mine if you can."

Crandell touched the tiny wounds with his finger. "Gals love a man with a scar. Gonna write me a song 'bout it someday."

"Never helped me any, Chief." Foard sat on the bed occupied the previous night by the injured pilot who'd been moved to ICU. He chewed on his unlit cigar and pointed to an ugly pink line on his own neck. "Would you believe a Dolphin gave this to me?"

"As for your ankle, no permanent damage. It'll be a bit sore." The doctor placed his stethoscope in the pocket of his green scrubs and looked up when a commotion erupted at the door.

A second later, Veronda Winston plowed her way into the room with a small black briefcase. A whiff of rosy perfume followed. "How long, doctor? When can this one be on his way?" Her slender finger pointed at Jordon.

"At least she's figured out who I am," he said.

"Now, hold on, Miss Winston." Foard blocked her progress with his bulk. "We moved the pilot out of here because of your behavior last night. Let's not have a repeat--"

"Sit down, Clifford." She pushed him back with the briefcase. "This does not concern you."

The doctor held up a hand and cleared his throat. "Excuse me! It concerns everyone in this hospital. I had you physically removed last night and I won't hesitate to do it again."

"When can he be ready?" Her volume did not lower.

Jordon wondered if it ever did.

"Couple of days, maybe a week. This man has been through a lot, he needs some peace and quiet, not to mention plenty of rest. I've given him a tetanus shot and started antibiotics. Although chances are slim, we'll be watching for gangrene."

Jordon scratched his arm, below the bandage. *I can be on my way tomorrow, but Doc will put me in a body cast, if he knows it will make her mad.*

"A week? I need him now!" Winston barked the command like a drill sergeant in the physician's face. She turned her wrath on Crandell. "And why is this man still in the room? Clifford, have you checked him out? Does he have security clearance? If not, I want him out of here. Immediately!"

Dr. Keene slammed his hand down on the tray table and took Winston by the arm. "I must insist you leave this room. No, let me rephrase that. I'd prefer if you'd leave the state of Colorado altogether."

She pointed the dagger finger at the doctor and backed it with a cold stare. For the first time her voice dropped to a whisper. "Do you get any federal money at this little M.A.S.H. unit you call a hospital?"

"Why, yes. But I don't see--"

"If you want to continue to receive funding, I suggest you do what I say and prepare Jordon for immediate dismissal! If not... Well, I'll promise you'll be scrounging for green fees, because your tax dollars are going to dry up faster than spit on a hot stove."

Jordon witnessed enough. The gall of the woman. Dover had been bad. Grant even worse. But this bureaucratic loudmouth made Lizzie Borden a role model for the Camp Fire Girls.

He pushed the bed control and brought himself to a sitting position. "Foard? Do something."

She squirmed away from the two men. "I'm Veronda Winston. I will not be treated this way."

"Doesn't carry any weight with me," said Jordon. "Why are you so gung ho to get me out of here?"

"Grant's left the nest, I'm acting Executive Director of ASTRO."

"What?"

Foard moved away from her and circled around behind Jordon's bed.

The big man bit through his cigar and bits of tobacco dropped on the pillow. "Where did he go?"

"He's left the country. So? What's the big deal?"

"Why?" asked Foard. "I just talked to him."

Jordon couldn't see his face, but from the sound of his voice, Foard hadn't expected the news.

She pointed at Crandell again. "Remove this man and I'll answer your questions."

"I can take a hint." Crandell stood and shuffled toward the door. "But I ain't leavin' this hospital until somebody pays for my truck. I'll stick to Mr. Jordon like glue if you don't. Come on, Doc. Introduce me to some of those pretty nurses."

The doctor opened his mouth to say something to Winston, but bit his lip and followed Crandell from the room.

That leaves me and an ex-football jock alone with her. Odds still in her favor. "Now, what's this about Grant leaving the country?"

Winston pulled Crandell's vacant chair over to the bed and sat. "He thinks you're dead."

"Well, tell him I'm not!"

"It's not so simple." She shrugged. "Old grump didn't say where he was going, just he needed some time away. I guess he's pretty shook up. I didn't think he cared about anybody."

"Sounds to me like you're not going to try very hard to find him." Foard paced like an expectant father between the window and the bed.

Beyond him, through the glass, Jordon observed a snowplow slog across the parking lot.

Winston stood and maintained her ground. "Look, mister. With Grant gone, I'm in charge. Now my projects will get the priority and the funding they deserve. I'll make policy and you two gentlemen will follow it."

Foard stopped in his tracks. "It's temporary. The President will appoint a new Director."

"And it will be me." A huge cat and canary grin spread across Winston's red lips. "He owes me one." The smile vanished. "So, let's get down to business, Mitchy."

In all his days, Jordon never experienced such a show of blatant, self-indulgent behavior. He didn't know whether to salute her or thumb his nose. The thought made him chuckle. Being called 'Mitchy' though, didn't.

Foard, on the other hand, let loose with a huge belly laugh.

"What's so comical?" Winston clearly missed the joke. "I don't think I like your attitude."

Jordon held himself tight against his bandages. "I have no business with you, Miss Winston." He held back the urge to call her, 'Veronda-poo'. "I don't work for ASTRO. For Cax on occasion, but not for you. Pack your bag and go home."

"I thought you'd say that." She placed the briefcase on top of Jordon's outstretched legs, opened it with a ceremonious flare and produced a folded piece of paper. When she waved it in front of his nose he judged it to be a legal document of some type.

"What's this?" Foard intercepted the paper and read it slowly. "I can't believe you'd stoop this low."

"What is it?" Jordon tried to lift himself, but the IV tube tugged his arm and prevented the movement.

"Big trouble, Chief." Foard shook his head and turned the paper for Jordon to see.

He grabbed the document and recognized it in an instant. His glare shifted to Winston. "How did you get your hands on this?"

"That's your original signature. Is it not? I particularly enjoy the part of the resignation you added in your own hand. Nice touch. No wonder the old man hates your guts."

This lady may well prove to be a formidable adversary. From now on, I'll be careful not to turn my back. "Yes, this is the original. Answer my question. Where'd you get it?"

"From Grant's private file." She tapped the top of the paper with her finger. "Notice he never accepted it."

"I told him to get his own pen."

"Ha. Ha." Winston moved her briefcase to a nearby feeding table and leaned her weight into his mattress with both fist.

"What are you saying?" The tug of the sheets put a strain on his wound.

She stared down with coal black eyes. "It means, Mr. Mitchy Jordon, your arm isn't the only thing in a sling around here. You still officially work for ASTRO. Right now that's me. You're mine and there's not a thing you can do about it."

For the first time in his life, Jordon wanted to land his fist right in the center of a woman's nose. With all the painkillers, the thought of getting away with it seemed feasible. "Clifford?"

"Don't know, Chief. I'll check on it." Foard grabbed the paper and departed from the room.

Jordon fought the tension and relaxed into his pillow. "What do you want, lady?"

"I have a job for you to do."

"And I'm the most healthy candidate you can find? No wonder you feel the need to blackmail me into it."

Winston straightened and returned to her briefcase. The locks snapped into place. "A bit of insurance. I predicted your protest."

"Oh, you haven't heard the first of it, lady." Jordon stared at her. As always, he felt his curiosity grow. Since birth, he'd never been able to suppress it, even in the face of disaster. The curse of the unknown haunted him. Teased him... Beckoned him... "What's your game? What do you want?"

An air of excitement trickled into her voice. "I want you to join a geological survey team I've sent into an Oklahoma oilfield."

The statement flew in from left field and hit him squarely between the eyes. "Excuse me? An oilfield? This is all about oil?"

"That's what I want you to find out," she said. "I've already got the team in place with Caesar Hamilton. Mousy little man. I'm not sure if he can handle it. I want an expert. I want you there."

"Hamilton's a good geologist. He can deal with anything that crops up."

She moved the briefcase back to the bed and released the locks a second time. "He may be over his head with this." She activated an Infopak with her thumbprint, selected a file and tossed the little device onto his chest.

Oh, how I hate these things. He perused the file and immediately recognized what he saw. "S-SMC." He scrolled through the photos. "Some call them smack pics. These are pretty good. ASTRO must have a new bird up there."

"Well?"

Since he had to wait for Foard's return, Jordon decided to humor the lady. The higher he raised her expectations, the farther he could drop her. "What's the story on this blue pulse?"

"Every thirty seconds exactly. No more. No less."

"Interesting. What's in this oilfield, a missile silo?"

The blank expression on her face indicated she didn't catch the jest of his question. "Why do you say that? Is there something here we've missed?"

"No, not really. I've seen this before. Not exactly the same pattern and not sub-surface. It's similar to radar images they used to put out around nuclear missile silos to camouflage the site. Yesterday's technology."

"Radiation? Hamilton didn't think so."

Jordon studied each photo a second time, but independently. "He's half right. Not radiation. Different pattern all together. The radar images I've seen were picked up by the old Lacrosse series of imagery satellites. They can see through clouds and darkness. Surface stuff. This is weird. Smack pics are sub-surface."

She directed him to a second file. "Surface maps made shortly after Hamilton and his team left Houston. The big snow storm has distorted them a bit."

"Are these of the same area?"

"Inch for inch."

Jordon compared two photos, one from each set. "You've stumble on-to something you shouldn't have."

"Now, it becomes more interesting." She moved around the bed and looked over his shoulder.

"More curious than interesting." He maneuvered the two photos side by side, the one on the right a map-like picture of dirt roads and trees and hills, the one on the left the same scene several hundred feet under-ground. "If you believe this, there's nothing there."

"Just a bunch of trees and rocks." She fidgeted with excitement until the bed rails rattled. "The closest thing of interest is this road which ends abruptly three hundred yards from where the first set of photos shows the pulse to be." She pointed a painted fingernail toward the spot.

He settled back into his pillow again and closed the files. "I suppose you've had these enhanced?"

"Yes, but the detail doesn't get any better. Same story with simple magnification. Nothing washes out."

Jordon took a deep breath and sorted his thoughts. "Okay. So, you've got some mysterious underground pulse which flickers on and off every thirty seconds. Why the sudden interest? Surely this region's been mapped. There's an oilfield all around it. Why hasn't anyone noticed this before now?"

"These are the first S-SMC of the area since the new system on the *Frontier* went on line. Yes, you're right on target about the upgrade. Why the oil companies haven't mentioned it? I haven't been able to find out. I've called every agency I know with an initial in its name. Nothing. You'd think we wanted information about the Bermuda Triangle."

Jordon tossed the Infopak into Winston's case. "It's an underground phenomenon. It interests the geologist in me, but I don't understand why you want ASTRO involved. Turn it over to the Department of the Interi-or, or the appropriate state agency or how about the University of Okla-homa? They've got the people to handle it. Their geology department's one of the best."

"Because we found it and we, namely you, are going in there to ex-plain it."

"And if I don't?"

She rounded the bed and pointed the finger at his nose. "Don't threaten me."

As Jordon mustered a response, Foard pushed the door open and entered the room. "I can't find out anything until late this afternoon. Legal department is tearing into it right now."

"Very well." Winston stuffed the briefcase under her arm. "You'll see." She stormed past Foard and disappeared into the hallway, but her scent remained thick in the air.

Jordon shook his head. "I don't like that woman, or the horse she rode in on."

"Makes two of us, Chief." Foard pulled the chair back toward the bed. "It's turned into a nightmare out there. Tell me, which is scarier? A walk on the Moon or an audience with Queen Veronda?"

"You have to ask?" Jordon nodded at the paper in the big man's hand. "What did you really find out about my resignation?"

"I don't believe it, Chief. Do you read minds too?"

"No." Jordon smiled. "I figured you'd let me know first."

Foard returned the grin and lowered his voice. "I'd hoped to buy a little more time for your shoulder."

"I appreciate the effort. Now, what did you find out?"

"Basically, the suit boys agree. Legally, she's got you by the loopholes."

"I figured. I can fight it, but after the satellite photos... She's in way over her head. I'm not going to let her take you and a lot of other good people down with her."

"What's she up to, Chief?"

Jordon scratched his chin. It always helped him to sort things. This time it didn't. "I haven't got a clue. I'm tempted to make her think I've caved in to her demand. I'd like to see how this thing pans out."

"Wha..." Foard sputtered like he'd choked on some petrified hospital food. "You can't be serious!"

"Now, do I give the impression of the kind of guy who goes out hunting adventure?"

"No..." said Foard. "But I do get the impression it finds you and makes friends." He leaned toward the bed. "Speaking of adventure, I've got more information on Grant's trip."

"Way out of character for Cax. Does it make sense to you?"

"No, and neither does the fact your old friend Tate Smullins went with him. Didn't even tell his wife."

Jordon grabbed the rail and pulled himself into a sitting position. "Tater thinks I'm dead too?"

A nurse arrived with a small white paper cup and a hypodermic the size of a basketball needle. "Medication time, Mr. Jordon."

"Oh, and another piece of interesting news from the suit boys." Foard winked at the nurse. "You're gonna love this one, Chief."

Jordon gulped his pills and rolled over to expose his backside. He winced when the shot entered his hip. "Any more excitement and they'll have to sedate me."

Foard nudged up against the rail. "Get this, Chief. Since your resignation wasn't accepted when you gave it to Grant, Ol' Veronda is going to owe you a load of back pay."

SEVENTEEN_____

Caesar Hamilton trudged through the snow with the conviction of a kid who'd been abandoned by his parents at the fair. Stranded without the van he decided to make the best of it and explore the north end of Wildwood.

Ahead, Oxenthall and Wellingham bickered like an old married couple until Ox took a snowball in the face. "Good grief, Gina!" he yelped as he dug slush out of his eyes.

The young woman raced past Hamilton and ducked under a barrage of icy orbs. "You couldn't hit the broad side of a--"

The next shot pegged her in the neck.

"Aaak." She yanked her gloves free and massaged the injured area. "Lucky shot, Gummi boy!"

Hamilton cleared his throat and watched his breath fog into a swirl. "If you two want to play, I'll see if I can find the garage by myself."

Oxenthall packed another snowball tightly with his hands. "Watch me let loose with a linear curve." He wound up like a major league pitcher and let it sail high into the dark sky. It hit the Quonset hut down the street with a thud hard enough to knock the snow from a rusty overhead sign. "Hey, boss? Think I've found the front end of what you're looking for."

The mechanic shop lay hidden behind a drift which had slid down the side of the corrugated half cylinder roof, a collection of multicolored sheet metal, patched many times over the years. The sign read "BUCKSAW GARAGE" and rattled again when Oxenthall's second volley made contact.

"Ease up, Ox," said Hamilton. "If you knock a hole through this old building, the guy will never lend us his pickup."

Wellingham peeked from under the fur lining of her parka. "You believe that old storekeeper? No way anybody's gonna loan us anything."

"Let's find out." Hamilton reached for the handle on the door. It creaked an unoiled protest. When he stepped across the threshold a wave of warmth sucked past him. "It must be a hundred degrees in here."

Oxenthall pushed his way past. "Hello? Anybody in charge of this randomly organized operation?"

At the far end of building, about fifty feet away, Hamilton spotted a station wagon with the hood raised. A short, dark-skinned man with a long black braided ponytail stood on a metal milk crate and worked a ratchet with his hand. A small gas heater on wheels, beyond a beat up tool chest, roared with the intensity of a blast furnace. The shop smelled of gasoline and used oil.

"Excuse me?" Hamilton kicked snow from his wet boots and signaled for his minions to fall back. "Mr. Bucksaw? Excuse me. Sir?" A lanky mongrel appeared from behind the station wagon and barred its teeth. Thoughts of a junk yard massacre sprang to mind.

"What a cute doggy," said Wellingham.

The mutt growled and took another step forward.

"Poor thing's got three legs!"

Hamilton froze in his tracks and eyed the dog, then its owner.

The dog barked.

"Shut up, Limp!" The man under the hood turned and threw an empty oil can into a barrel. He reached a greasy hand to his half moon glasses and slid them up the bridge of his nose. "Don't pay no attention to him, folks. He's full of sass and vinegar. And don't feel sorry for him neither. He's still got one more leg than you do."

Scolded, the dog tucked its tail against its lone hind leg and approached with a kinder attitude.

"One of you yahoos hit my roof with a snowball?" The mechanic reached for a red shop rag and wiped his hands.

Oxenthall leaned toward Hamilton and whispered into his ear. "Get a load of Cherokee Charlie - local outsider."

Ignoring the remark, Hamilton stepped toward the station wagon. "Are you Bucksaw? Cal at the--"

"Well, I'm sure not Cherokee Charlie. I'm the owner, mechanic, bookkeeper and janitor of this little gold mine. Least it says so on the sign out front." Bucksaw switched off his droplight, slammed the hood and stepped toward Oxenthall. He waved a screwdriver in the sweaty man's face. "You ever heard of the last of the Mohicans, boy?"

A lump rose and fell in Oxenthall's throat. "Yes, sir."

"Well, I'm the first of the Poshony." He slapped his knee and snorted like a mule.

Hamilton glared Oxenthall back toward Wellingham. "Mr. Bucksaw, if we could have a word..."

The mechanic tossed the screwdriver into a cleaning vat and headed toward the heater. "Dictionary's full of 'em, son. Take your pick. My favorite one's 'lunch'." He flipped a small side panel open on the portable furnace and extracted a tin can. Steam rolled from the open top. He pulled a dirty spoon from the pocket of his coveralls and dipped it into the soup. "Turtle. Want some?"

Hamilton gulped. "No. No thank you. Maybe later."

"Suit yourself." He shoveled a mouthful and wiped his lips on the tail of his shirt. "Name's Lincoln Bucksaw, son. But Cal done told you that or you wouldn't be out. Folks here 'bouts call me Linc." He pointed the spoon. "You do the same."

"Caesar Hamilton. This is Ox and Gina."

Wellingham waved and received a wink in return from the old Indian.

"What brings you bunch of yehaws out in this kinda weather?"

"We've got a sort of dilemma..."

Bucksaw snorted again. "Life gives you dilemma, you make dilemonade."

"The old geezer is an idiot savant." Oxenthall turned toward the door. "Come on, Gina. I'm gonna go make a snowman."

"Wait a second, there." Bucksaw lowered his can to the top of the stove, his demeanor serious. He wiped his hands on the rag and shuffled across the floor. "Do I know you?"

Oxenthall rolled his eyes. "Certainly doubtful."

"Yeah. You're that movie star. Old what's his name." He cocked his head to study the young man's features. "You know if you'd grow a mustache and shave it back off, you'd look just like Jabba the Hutt." He slapped his knee again and snorted.

If Oxenthall hadn't been so red-faced to start with, Hamilton swore he blushed.

"You, my friend, are clearly confused."

Bucksaw moved toward the car and slid behind the wheel. "Listen to this." A loud crank and a backfire erupted before the starter caught on the second try. Once the engine warmed, it slowed to a quiet purr. Satisfied with his work, he switched off the ignition and crawled out of the car. "Runs smooth, like good Kentucky Bourbon, don't she?"

Hamilton held his breath and waited for the exhaust to clear.

"Like an Indy car," said Oxenthall. "Circa 1926."

A grin spread across Bucksaw's face. "So nice to have someone of my caliber to spar with. He slapped Oxenthall across the back and waved the trio to a dusty set of truck seats propped against a wall near a metal work desk. "Now, what did you say Cal sent you for?"

"We want to rent your spare pickup."

"You folks aren't from around here, are you?"

Hamilton stared back Ox's anticipated retort. "No, we're geologists out on a field expedition. Unfortunately, a couple of our crew took the van and haven't returned."

"I see." Bucksaw moved to his workbench and retrieved a disassembled carburetor. "How long you need the truck?"

"A couple of days, I guess." Hamilton looked at his watch.

"Where you plan on taking it?"

"Does it matter?" He removed the dead timepiece from his wrist, shook it and held it to his ear.

"It might."

"We don't have any specific plans."

The wrench in Bucksaw's hand landed at Hamilton's feet. The sound of metal on cement drew his attention away from the watch.

"Don't be playing games with me, boy. I've been around the sun a whole lotta times. That's why my tan's so even. My guess is, you're heading north." He moved toward a set of sliding doors and parted them wide enough to move the car outside.

The snowstorm had intensified.

"Out of here, Limp." He followed the command with a sharp whistle.

Hamilton, startled by the old man's insight, stuffed the useless watch into his pocket. "It's one direction. Why?"

"Oh, no particular reason," the mechanic said. "I need to deliver this car up to Miss Jacks' place. 'Bout six miles north of here. You can give me a lift back. Otherwise, I'll have to walk."

"Well I don't know if we'll have time." Hamilton glanced at his companions. Both took his cue and consulted their wrist.

"Hey!" Wellingham wiggled her arm in the air. "My watch has stopped."

Bucksaw ignored the remark. "I'll let you use the truck rent free if you'll help me out. Too cold to walk. Nearly froze when I went to get this thing." He slapped the side of the car and reached for the dirty shop rag to wipe his upper lip. "Noses run in my family, son." He nudged Oxenthall in the side. "Bet feet smell in yours."

"Thought you said you're the first of the Poshony. How you got any family?" Oxenthall shuffled his feet on the cement. "Explain that one."

Hamilton shivered when the cold air replaced the warmth of the heater.

"Besides, we're talking Stuart-Dupree country." Bucksaw opened the door of the station wagon. "I'd soon invite OSHA in for an inspection than go up there. But, business is business and it puts groceries down my throat. Believe me, you don't want to venture north without an escort."

"Why?" Hamilton's interest perked at the reference to the unknown oil company.

Bucksaw snorted and turned the key. "Because you won't come back!"

✗   ✗   ✗

The awful jokes ceased at the end of Wildwood's Main Street. Hamilton rode with Linc Bucksaw while Oxenthall followed with Wellingham in a rickety pickup which long ago lost its bed. The team leader glanced over his shoulder, through the rear glass of the station wagon, in time to see the truck bounce as it hit the slushy dirt and gravel farm road that led out of town and into the low hills.

Limp chose to ride with his head out the backseat window on the driver's side and a blast of frigid air chilled the interior. It took a moment for Hamilton to figure out the climate controls on the old car, but soon warm air circulated about his feet. In light of the temperature drop, the effort seemed wasted.

Bucksaw's behavior changed entirely at the city limit. One moment he hardly spoke and acted like he wished Hamilton had not come along. At others, he rambled on about the weather, sports and how good the fishing at nearby Monarch Lake had been the previous year. But the humor disappeared. For some inexplicable reason, the Jekyll and Hyde mood of the trip turned more serious with every fence post passed.

Hamilton tucked his gloved hands under his armpits. "You say this Miss Jacks lives six miles up in the hills?"

Bucksaw nodded and kept his eyes on the slick road. "Give or take. Six miles by road, not so far as the crow flies. Up ahead, there's the most awful mess of lease roads you've ever seen. Go every which direction."

"How do you find your way around up here?" The speed of the car increased and Hamilton tried to count fence posts.

"Just know my way." Bucksaw fishtailed the vehicle around a curve to the east. A mile later the road drifted back to the north again. "If you ever get lost, you can always find your way back."

"How's that?"

"See those rock markers? Ones with the orange paint splotched on them?" He pointed at the shallow ditch. "Follow those at every corner or each time the road forks. Always go to the side of the rocks and soon you'll be back on the main road."

Hamilton watched for the markers and noted a large pile of stones stacked at the next intersection. The bright fluorescent orange stood out against the white snow like a sumo wrestler in a ballet recital.

Bucksaw slowed but did not brake at a crippled stop sign. Instead, he turned the vehicle right onto another section line road and continued west.

Hamilton peeked over at the odometer. "Everything is laid off at even miles."

"Yeah, here, but wait." The mechanic ignored the next turn and continued straight ahead through an open gate and over a cattle guard. "Now, it gets confusing."

The remainder of the trip consisted of no less than ten forks and crossings. Some roads split into five or more new roads. Some doubled back on themselves. An elevation and grade increase at every turn appeared to be the common denominator.

Concerned with the increase in speed, Hamilton continued to glance back for the pickup and he discovered Oxenthall had done an admirable job of keeping up in the slick mess.

A cabin appeared through the trees and Bucksaw toed the brake. "End of the line. This'll be Miss Jack's place."

The pickup arrived shortly thereafter and Hamilton joined his companions in the vehicle while the dog jumped out and hobbled in the snow after Bucksaw, who parked the car in a side garage then headed for the porch with the keys.

A grandmotherly woman answered the door and invited Bucksaw into the cabin. A foot shorter than the old man, she gazed up at him as he pointed toward the pickup. The old woman nodded and disappeared inside. A minute later, she returned with money for the repairs, a treat for the dog and a small wicker handled basket with a red checkered cloth draped over the top. Bucksaw waved good-bye and headed back across the snow covered yard.

"Is that what I think it is?" Hamilton inhaled the steamy aroma of fresh baked bread which wafted from the basket.

"Get on here, Limp." Bucksaw tapped the naked frame where the bed had been removed. He waited for the dog to balance on its tripod stance and handed the basket to Wellingham. "Miss Jacks says she never wants to see strangers go hungry."

"Does she live alone?" Hamilton accepted a tear from the loaf, his stomach grateful since the last offer of turtle soup. He tried to avoid the sad eyes from Limp through the back glass, but the dog's pitiful stare enticed Wellingham to share her portion.

Oxenthall slid out from behind the wheel and yielded his seat to Bucksaw. "Kinda crowded in here." He hefted himself onto the frame and propped against the cab. "I'll ride out with the dog."

Wellingham pulled a muffler from under her parka and handed it over. "You'll freeze out there, Ox."

"I'll be all right, long as Linc heads straight for the Bahamas." He accepted a coil of lariat rope from Bucksaw. "Oh, boy. A genuine imitation Jethro Bodine seat belt. My lucky day."

Hamilton watched Oxenthall secure himself to the frame. "Miss Jacks live up here alone?"

Bucksaw gobbled a mouthful of bread and turned the ignition. "You asked me already." The engine clattered to life with a belch of smoke.

"Does she?"

"Practically owns the whole mountain. Part of four different counties I've heard tell."

"Guess she must know everything that goes on in the area." Hamilton pulled in his shoulders and yanked the rusty door shut. Wellingham squirmed next to him.

"Not much does," Bucksaw said. "She don't allow anyone up here."

Wellingham fished a second loaf of bread from the basket. "Linc, has she ever mentioned anything strange going on north of here recently?"

"What do you mean by 'strange'?" Bucksaw slipped his hand between her knees, grabbed the stick shift and ground the transmission into reverse.

"Oh, I don't know." She squirmed again and Hamilton felt her lean into his side. "Sounds, tremors, things like that."

"No." The engine gunned and Bucksaw reached for the stick again.

"Thought I'd ask. Allow me." She pried the old man's hand from the shifter and worked it into first herself.

The pickup rolled back into its original tracks. Over the clatter of the engine, Hamilton heard Oxenthall's head bang on the back of the cab. *Shouldn't have volunteered,* he thought. The next statement from Bucksaw surprised him.

"You aren't talking about the phantom rig, are you, girl?"

Hamilton caught his breath. *The other old man at the grocery rattled on concerning the same thing.* "Rig? What about it?"

"You've never heard tell of old lease number seventy-six?"

A pile of orange emblazoned rocks passed by in a blur.

"No."

"Too bad."

Wellingham turned to look out the back glass and screamed.

"What the..." Bucksaw lost control of the pickup and slid into a fence. "Calm down, woman."

Hamilton held out his hand and tried to keep his face from making contact with the windshield. The vehicle rocked to a stop and he kicked his door open.

Wellingham crawled across his lap, tossed the empty basket into the ditch and belly flopped into the snow drift. When she regained her footing, she slogged back up the road.

A quick survey of the back of the vehicle indicated Oxenthall had been thrown free. "Hey, Ox! Where are you!" The dog appeared behind the rear wheels and whimpered.

"He's back this way!" Wellingham waved for assistance.

Bucksaw reached behind the seat and extracted a shotgun. "I don't like the looks of this," he said and set after the girl.

"What is going on?" Hamilton followed in the old man's tracks. "Did Ox fall off?"

"No." Wellingham stopped and waited. "Something grabbed him when we came under those trees." She bent over to recover a piece of rope. "This has been chewed through."

"Did you see what did it?" Hamilton held a hand to his forehead and scanned the road ahead. A group of oaks guarded the next quarter mile on both sides.

"Yeah, I saw." Wellingham started to cry. "Some kind of ghost, I think."

EIGHTEEN_____

The jeepney rolled to a halt. Dover steadied his knees and crawled from the backseat. The Filipino driver grinned at him with a huge white smile, proud of his ornamental vehicle with its crocheted curtains, multitude of radio antennas and over abundance of headlights. Nickel plated horses stood guard on the roof, bookends for a sign with plastic wings.

"Chinatown. We here."

"MASTER OF THE ROAD, huh?" Dover read the sign aloud. "Ought to r-read MASTER OF THE HIGHWAY ROBBERY." His wallet still felt the sting of having to pay extra Pesos for all the empty seats. Finally more Pesos convinced the toothy driver to leave. "D-Don't wait for me. I'll find another r-ride back."

The driver nodded and raced the sideshow taxi away to search for more tourist fare.

The Roman Catholic hospital, shy of a fresh coat of paint since the second World War, loomed in the distance. Dover walked into the lobby and caught his breath. Greeted by an assortment of medicinal smells, his assaulted senses forced him to pull a handkerchief from his jacket pocket to cover his face.

A dark-skinned, teenage girl studied a schoolbook behind a flimsy reception desk.

Dover cleared his throat and flashed a bogus press card in her face.

"*Ha unsa kinahanglanon?*" she asked

"I speak English. *¿Habla inglés?*"

The girl arched her brows.

"I'm here to see M-Miss Turner. She's expecting me."

Dark brown eyes lit at the mention of the name. "*Pagtangdo. Pagtangdo! Lana!*" She held up an index finger. "*Babayeng hamtong Lana.*" Excited, she dropped her book on the desk and dashed down the hallway. A moment later, she returned with a breathless Lana Turner in tow.

Dover nodded. "Thank you, young l-lady."

Turner stroked the girl's hair and whispered something in her ear.

"Ikaw maayong pag-abut."

"She speaks *Cebuano*, it's the second most common language around here. She says 'You're welcome'."

Dover fished in his pocket and presented the young receptionist with a crisp American dollar. The reaction he received told him he'd offered quite a prize.

The girl grinned and returned to her book. "Thanks for the dollar, mister."

Nice. Trick the gullible American. "So, Lana? How are you this beautiful morning?"

"I'm sorry for your wait, Mr. Dover." Even dressed in a simple white smock, Turner maintained her loveliness from the night before.

"Alan, please. We ag-greed."

"I'm sorry. Alan."

"That's more like it." He allowed her to escort him to a small sunlit courtyard and inventoried the garden's exits as they walked. Palm trees and crumbled, odd sized benches dotted the grounds and he chose one of the larger white ones, near a dry fountain.

She accepted his offer to sit and perched herself on the edge, like a tiny bird anticipating a quick escape. "I'm really surprised you came." She held her head low and avoided direct eye contact. "After last night and my stupid little scene in the restaurant, I thought you'd make some excuse to stay away."

The ruse continued to work. Here sat Mitch Jordon's bride and she didn't have a clue. He savored the anticipated sweet taste of revenge. "Think nothing of it." He comforted her with a touch on the back of her hand. "I c-can understand your f-feelings. I'm s-s-sorry I upset you so."

She scooted a little farther back on the warm bench. "Oh, it's not what you said, Alan. It's..." Her chest rose with a deep breath. "I get too emotional when I think about it."

A small, blue and orange butterfly lit softly on the leaf of a tree across the path. Its wings pulsed in rhythm with the slow motion sway of the brown egg-shaped fruit beneath. She stood and took a step to admire it. "I feel sort of like this little guy. Faced with what to do with the Chico, he's a bit overwhelmed."

"Why?"

"It's hard to explain." She sighed. "It's like I've been born all new again. Free, independent, capable of going wherever and whenever I please."

"What's wrong with that?" He watched her coax the fragile creature from the fruit into her cupped hands.

"I have no past." She turned to show him the butterfly perched on her finger. "I don't remember being a caterpillar. I've got an unlimited future, but it's blocked by an intense desire to know where I came from. Like I can go anywhere I want, long as that place is home." She laughed. "I know it sounds contradictory, but it's truly how I feel."

Dover noted her beauty. He wanted her to be totally in his control - then tell her the truth. Maybe a moment before he killed Jordon. The thought made him tingle.

She lifted her hand, set the butterfly free and watched it catch a small breeze as it circled the fruit tree. It gained lift and soon disappeared into the open sky of the courtyard. "You see, it can go home, wherever home is. I can't. I don't know where home is. I don't know how to find out. I'm hopelessly trapped."

"No, you're not." Dover watched her reaction. It bordered on surprise.

"What do you mean?"

"If you'll t-tell me all you know about how you got here, for Miss Mordel's article of course, I-I'll try to help you figure out your p-past."

"You can do that for me?" She returned to her seat on the bench and put her hand on back of his.

"Let's say I know people.

"But how?" She pulled back.

Maybe one of these connections will be able to help us out."

A strange look crossed her face.

"Wh-What's w-wrong?" *What have I said?* "Aren't you excited?"

"I think so, but I'm a little scared. A little apprehensive."

"Understandable. But, there's no need to be." He tightened his grip on her soft hand and pulled her close.

"What if you do find out who I am and I don't like what I hear?"

Dover smiled. *If you knew how close I am to checkmate.* He pressed his lips to her ear and whispered. "Lana, we all have a past. Good or b-bad. From talking to you I'm sure yours is fine. But if I find out anything to the c-contrary, I'll keep it to myself."

"Don't you dare!" She said. "I want to know everything. Good or bad."

"Agreed." He loosened his tie and pulled a small electronic organizer from his jacket pocket. "Now, let's start from the beg-g-ginning. What do you remember and how did you get here?"

She sat back, closed her eyes tight and took a deep breath. "Every once in awhile I get these flashes of memory. Like pieces of a puzzle, but they never fit in the right order. I do remember a terrible storm and an accident, somewhere up in the Zambales Mountains."

"Do you know when?"

"Months ago. Years ago. I'm not sure."

"I see." He tapped useless information onto the small screen with the stylus. "Did someone b-bring you to this hospital?"

"Not at first, but this is where I ended up. The sisters tell me I slept for a long time, like in a coma."

"Explains your memory loss."

"The doctors think so. Anyway, after the crash, some *Infugao* hill people took care of me until they brought me out of the mountains to the city. I have a vague memory of some houses built on piles with a sacrificed pig fixed on the outside. Creepy. I'm told they're headhunters."

"How did you s-survive?"

"You'd be surprised at the medical knowledge the *Infugao* have. They've been doing it for centuries on Luzon. They don't need doctors or medicine because they rely on the *hilot*, a healer who uses herbs and prayers. All natural. All from the Earth." She reached down the neck of her smock and pulled out a thin chain with a small amulet. "They gave me this. It's called an *anting-anting*. Supposed to protect me from evil."

Dover felt uneasy. *Superstition is not getting in my way.* "So, you d-don't know how long you stayed with these people? What brought you to the m-mountains in the first place?" *Be careful*, he decided. *Don't let her figure out for herself what will be revealed later.*

"I don't know. Guess I might have been on a trip of some kind."

He paused to loosen his tie farther and consulted his bogus notes. "You mentioned m-memory flashes, like the pieces of a puzzle. Can you d-describe them?"

She thought long and hard, stood a moment and sat down again. "I keep remembering a baby being born."

Dover stared into her eyes. *Now, we're getting somewhere. Jordon has a child. Excellent! The game progresses. From chess to high stakes poker.*

"Don't look so startled, Alan." She stuffed the amulet back down the neck of her smock. "That's all I remember. No details."

"Was there anyone else w-with you in the accident?"

"I don't remember." Her shoulders slumped, the energy drained from her body. "I'm sorry. I'm getting one of those stupid headaches." She stood and extended her arms to both sides. "This is where I ended up. My whole world begins and ends here. Simple. Nowhere else to go. The sisters have taken good care of me. I've made a few friends, nobody I really talk to though." She glanced down at him, then turned her gaze upward. "The people who brought me to this hospital left no money, so I offered to volunteer to pay back my bills. They give me room and board, so I can't complain."

"Any chance of finding the p-people who brought you here? These *Infugao?" Perhaps they know what happened to the baby.*

"No." Turner cradled her forehead in the palm of her hand and shifted her attention to a Royal Palm a few feet down the path. Two steps and she leaned against its trunk. "People like that don't leave names and even if they did, they don't have addresses. I'm grateful to them, but I doubt if I'll ever see them again."

Dover pocketed his organizer, stood and offered her a hand. "Are you all r-right? I've d-done it again, haven't I?"

"No." She wrapped her arms around his neck and let him support her weight with a tight hug. "It's the headache. I get them from time to time when I try too hard to remember."

"I underst-stand."

She pulled away. "I'm being selfish. In the excitement I've completely forgotten Miss Mordel's article. Let's discuss it instead."

He shook his head. "Not today. I think you've had enough. I've been taking helpful notes. B-Besides, there's a nun coming this way. Must be time for you to get back to work."

She grabbed him by the arm and headed for the entrance, away from the stern looking nun. "Alan, thank you for caring."

He patted the jacket pocket with the organizer. "Least I c-can do."

"I'm very excited about this," she said when they approached the reception area.

"So am I." *A truthful statement.* "You'll soon know where home is."

The amnesic Kerry Jordon leaned and kissed him lightly on the cheek. The nun cleared her throat. "I've got to go," said her Lana Turner personality. In a moment she disappeared down the opposite hallway.

Dover glanced at the sister and stepped out onto the sidewalk. He waited a moment for her to move on and reentered the hospital. The teenage fraud sat behind her desk and grinned. He pointed at the rotary phone. "I'm going to use this."

"Sure, for another George Washington."

He pulled a bill from his pocket and dropped it in her lap. "There's got to be a law." He lifted the receiver and dialed 555-09-16. After the tenth ring, he slammed the receiver down hard and plucked the dollar from the girl's hand.

"Hey!"

As he stomped his way back to the street, he wadded the bill into a ball and threw it in the bushes. "Why is it, Mordel, you're never around when I need you?"

103

NINETEEN_____

"Tate Smullins, I'd like to introduce you to General Antony Stone." Grant moved back on the portico of the large manor house and allowed the retired military leader to step around his manservant and offer a handshake. "This is Kerry's father."

"It's a pleasure, sir." From Grant's description, Smullins had prepared for first sight of the famous 'Stony' Stone. The legend of the skies stood straight and tall, despite the spiraled cherry wood cane supporting his weight. "Under better circumstances..."

"Times like those are rare, I'm afraid." Stone's voice sounded rough, like a dog's growl. Below the left embroidered cuff of the General's short sleeve shirt, Smullins noted the scar Grant had mentioned. It originated at the elbow, reappeared up his neck, and snaked across his face. The ugly graft ended at the hairline of his fuzzy burr with the most grizzly damage hidden by a black eye patch. He considered it a miracle the man survived the heart stopping ejection through the malfunctioning canopy of his crippled jet.

General Stone turned to the servant who waited by his side with patience. "Thank you, Efrem. I'll take it from here."

The short, dark-skinned man with crinkled hair gave a courteous bow, closed the large glass doors at the end of the hall and departed.

"Efrem is very loyal." The General gestured them into a study and selected a large red leather reading chair for himself. "Excuse me if I sit. This is the end of the southwest monsoon season, dry today, but I can feel a change in my bones. It'll be sultry and wet again by morning, mark my words."

He settled in and dropped his cane to the floor. "Sometimes Efrem will sit and listen to me ramble for hours. A childhood accident hampered the development of his vocal chords. The conversations tend to be a bit one sided. It's a nice change to have someone who can talk back."

"It must be quite lonely for you, Stony." Grant moved toward the sofa, the largest seat in the room. "Why don't you move back to the states?"

Smullins wandered about the study and admired the decor. For the home of an Air Force man, it occurred odd the room be decorated with artifacts and reminders of the American Revolution. Sabers adorned the walls, while muskets and tricornered hats showcased the entire south end of the room. Behind the desk, the preamble of the U.S. Constitution hung next to a painting of Washington with his arm around another soldier.

"That's Chappel's rendering of old George's emotional farewell to his comrades." Stone beamed with pride at his collection. "New York, near the end of 1783. Of course the document needs no explanation. Have you seen the original in the National Archives?"

Smullins shook his head. "Not much of a history buff in school."

"Too bad. Take a gander at the medallion on the desk. Inside the glass box."

Smullins leaned for a closer inspection. The clear box contained a small silver medal, its polished surface reflected the light. "What is it?"

"Congress gave it to one of the three captors of the spy, Major John André, after they hung him. It's priceless."

"Very interesting, sir." Smullins pulled the chair from behind the desk and moved it to halfway between the two older men.

"There's no need to be formal, Tate. Call me Stony."

"If you don't mind, I'd be more comfortable with 'sir'... sir."

"As you wish. Can't fault a man for his training." The General grunted and leaned to his side. From a refrigerator hidden in a small cabinet, he retrieved three dark bottles and an opener. "San Miguels anyone?"

Grant licked his lips and accepted the offer.

"So, tell me about your first visit to what the Spanish called *El Insigne y Siempre Leal Ciudad* - the Noble and Ever Loyal City."

"Manila's one interesting place to shop." Smullins eyed Grant's new wardrobe, a remarkable improvement over the Hawaiian tourist getup he'd worn over on the plane. "But we didn't come for the bargains."

Grant, obviously uncomfortable in his new suit, shifted his bulk. "I don't understand, Stony. A man of your experience and education has endless opportunities in the states." He gestured about the study. "I can't think of a more patriotic man. You'd be a natural for a seat in the Senate."

"Now, Cax. You're the last man I'd expect to ask someone to run for Congress."

"They need someone who can be trusted."

The General lowered his head. "My life is here."

"Wasting away in the past. You're not that kind of man." Grant took a swig of his beer and swallowed hard.

"No, old friend, I'm looking toward the future. He held his dark bottle in salute. "With my investments in the duty-free and industrial zone over at *Olangapo*, near the old Subic Naval Base, I'm financially set. But the root of why I stay is for precisely the same reasons you're here today."

"In hopes of locating your daughter."

"Exactly. She's alive and still in this country. I can feel it deep down. Especially now."

"I don't understand." Smullins gulped his beer. He discovered why Grant grimaced. The brew tasted oily and thick. Combined with the jet lag he felt, the pit of his usually billy goat like stomach rebelled the intrusion.

"Cax told me about Mitch's death. A sad affair. To lose a special friend. I regret never having met the man."

Smullins placed his half-empty bottle on the desk. "Your daughter's husband? It's hard for me to believe your paths never crossed."

The older man shook his head and appeared suddenly tired. Sad. "Pity really, having to get to know one's son-in-law through sensational headlines. Not every man can say a member of his family walked on the Moon." He held up his hand, palm out. "Now, don't misunderstand me. I've no doubt he did every gallant and heroic thing the papers reported, but I regret not getting to know the man my Kerry fell in love with. I feel she wasn't drawn to his courage, fine quality that it is. No, I'm certain he must have been a very warm and caring man. A man with an understanding of life."

"All - and more." Grant held his beer in the air.

"I'm certain of it." The General leaned to clink his bottle.

Smullins completed the trilogy with a tap of his own. He compared the two men before him. Both much alike. One, on his way down a lonely spiral because of his past. The other on a similar course, but in a more dignified manner. "Why do you think Kerry is still alive? After all this time?"

Grant reached for a framed photo, of Kerry and her father, on the table next to the sofa. He tilted it and Smullins decided she hadn't changed a bit since he'd met her.

"I feel it deep down. Surely as I can predict tomorrow's weather. I'm never wrong. Efrem will back me up."

Smullins cleared his throat of the oily taste. He wanted to formulate his next statement, politely if possible. "I'm sorry, sir. But a feeling's not much to go on. Is there any hard evidence?"

The General grunted again. "Don't doubt the human spirit, young man. Sometimes a father's gut feelings are more truthful than you think." He held his head high again. "But yes, I do have a little to go on besides. Never hurts to confirm your instincts, no matter how strong they are."

Grant drained his bottle and sat it to the side of the photo. He rubbed his hands together. "Please, enlighten us with details."

The General reached for his cane, steadied himself and moved to the desk. He pulled a key from his pocket and unlocked the top drawer. "I've had a private investigator on it for some time now." He rummaged through several folders and selected one. "Someone brought this to me shortly after Kerry disappeared." He extracted a sealed plastic bag from the folds of the report and held it out for inspection.

Smullins stood and crossed the distance to the desk in a few steps. "It's a ring." He examined it for a moment and passed it over to Grant. "It's been in an accident. The gem's chipped."

Grant stuck his fat fingers into the bag and pulled the contents free. He laid it in the palm of his hand and studied it from several angles. Despite the damage, the oval ruby glinted in the light. "College class ring. Date's right. So's the school. I can make out the carving of a telescope with the word 'ASTRONOMY' across a banner."

"Look inside." The General moved closer and pointed with his cane.

The ring rotated between Grant's fingers and he examined the shank. "Fourteen karat."

"No, no." The General shook his head. Impatience betrayed itself in the shuffle of his feet. "There's something else."

Grant held the ring closer to his eye. "I see initials. KRS."

"Doesn't mean she was alive when it was removed." Smullins felt foolish the moment he spoke, too late to pull the statement back. The glance from Grant burned like a hot poker and confirmed the slip. "Uh, I'm sorry, General Stone. A thoughtless comment."

"You don't have to tread lightly with me, Tate. If you have any ideas, speak your mind."

Smullins nodded, relieved the General would be able to face the unpleasant truth, should it become the final logical alternative.

"Too bad the ring can't tell us a story." Grant moved to the refrigerator and helped himself to more San Miguel.

"Kerry gave it to a family in payment for help or food or something. I think that information alone erodes your theory, Tate."

"It does indeed." Smullins waved off the offer for another bottle. He'd spit out motor oil which tasted better.

Grant leaned back on the sofa and crossed his ankles. "Is there anything else?"

"Yes, an interesting new development. My investigator called shortly before you arrived."

"Any hints?" The second beer drained from Grant's bottle and rippled down the inside of his jowls.

"No. I'm told it's important."

"Well," Grant said with a heavy sigh. "I guess we wait."

The General leaned on his cane. "Perhaps you'd like to take a stroll in my garden. Efrem has such a talent with flowers."

Grant prodded the pillows on the sofa. "Why don't you go along, Tate? I'm quite comfortable where I am."

The General motioned toward the French doors. "Come, Tate. I think you'll find this most relaxing." Suddenly, he turned to Grant. "Oh, by the way, Cax. I've invited Ambassador Goe for lunch. He'll be beneficial in cutting through some of the red tape."

"I look forward to it." Grant's expression didn't agree with the statement. He held out the ring. "You better put this in a safe place."

"No," said the General. "Keep it and put it on Kerry's finger when you find her."

Smullins felt sorry for the former director. He'd seen the man sink lower and lower since his first encounter at the race track. Depression and fatigue pulled him into a pit from which no escape appeared likely.

Through the gardens Smullins strolled, deep in thought. Hopeless situations did not set well with him. Alternatives always presented themselves when least expected. Why not now?

"Tell me about my son-in-law." The General's attitude changed the moment they'd left the study.

"You already appear to know a lot."

"Yes, but I want to know the true Mitchell Jordon, not his media image."

"Well for one thing, he's a--" A tight lump formed in his throat. "I'm sorry. Was... A private man." Smullins struggled with the thick words on his tongue.

"You haven't come to grips with his death, have you?"

"No, I guess I haven't."

"With time..."

"Maybe. It's tough. Mitch did so much for me. Like a brother."

The walk continued in silence. When they neared the end of the path, the General shifted his weight on the cane and took Smullins by the elbow. "What's your rank?"

The question seemed out of context. "Lt. Colonel. Why?"

"Can I speak to you truthfully? One military man to another? In strict confidence?"

Smullins sensed the serious tone of the gruff voice foreshadowed unpleasant news. "Of course, sir. I have every respect for you..."

The man's face muscles twitched and he ran a finger over his patch. "Since my accident, Tate, I've become a deeply religious man. My concept of what is morally right and wrong has evolved into something of a higher understanding."

Smullins bit his lip and listened.

"I think Cax did the wrong thing. I think what I did measures equally wrong. We felt ourselves arrogant, above God's will. Clearly mistaken." He tapped his cane on the cobblestone walk and took a deep breath. "As a result, my daughter's missing and her husband is dead." He moved to the edge of a small, flowing fountain. "Everyone sees God in a different way, but in the end the truth is always the same. Believe in him, Tate. Your faith will make you stronger. Grow with him every day."

Smullins hadn't expected a lecture on religious beliefs. The moment felt awkward.

The General leaned toward a rose, careful to avoid the thorns, and inhaled its deep aroma. "Can I confide something in you, Tate?"

"Sure."

"After Kerry disappeared, I wanted to tear Cax's heart out. It's difficult to be in the same room with him. He knows something, but he's always held his cards close to the vest. I find it hard to trust him."

Smullins laughed. "I think you're standing in a long line."

The General lowered his head and stared at the ground. "I'm sure you're right. I blamed him for everything. But over time, I've absorbed a lot of the guilt. Now I have to find my daughter. Not for my sake, but for his. Cax doesn't deserve to carry the entire burden by himself."

"I think Mitch would have disagreed."

"Yes. And it's precisely such thinking which got him killed." The old military man paused, eye closed. "Did you know Mitch to be a religious man?"

"In his own way. I suppose." Smullins ground his toothpick between his teeth and studied the petals of the rose. He felt the General's grip tighten on his elbow.

"Thank you, Tate."

"We'll find your daughter, sir. If you believe she's alive, so do I."

"As is Mitch."

The statement startled Smullins.

The older man tapped him gently on the chest with the top of his cane. "Tate, in your heart, he'll always be alive."

The General rose from his seat and steadied himself on his cane. "Ambassador Goe! We're honored to have you as a guest."

Efrem led a tall, thin, middle-aged man with an overabundance of gold jewelry into the study.

"I'm sorry to hear your lovely wife is not well."

Smullins recognized the politician immediately. A former Senator from Hawaii, he'd headed the appropriations committee which caused Grant so many ulcers over the years. Too bad he'd changed out of his tourist outfit.

The Ambassador bowed at the waist. "Ahlani regrets it as do I, Anthony. She misses the conversation with fellow Americans." He eyed Grant with a neutral expression. "Caxton. How are you?"

Smullins wondered if Grant wanted to go on the defensive, but the reply surprised him.

"Nice to see you again, Ambassador. You appear well."

With a swipe of the cane, Smullins allowed himself to be herded into the dining room with the two bitter foes. A long table, lavishly set with enough food for twice the present guests, greeted them with a pleasant aroma of fresh cut flowers and steaming dishes. Four chairs, grouped at the end, waited their arrival. Two on one side for Grant and himself with the Ambassador seated opposite and the General at the head. Hidden speakers piped classic Baroque into the elegant setting.

"I miss our friendly confrontations." Goe unfolded his napkin with meticulous care.

Grant pursed his lips. "I recall many confrontations. But, friendly? I think not."

The Ambassador laughed until he held his side. "We'll allow history to be the judge."

Smullins fished a fresh toothpick from his pocket. *Let the games begin.* He perused the feast while the General explained each dish. Kidney beans, sweet potatoes, charcoaled ribs, mangoes, pineapples, bananas and rice. Lots and lots of rice. After a description of the pitch black stew and the mention of intestines, he decided to avoid that end of the buffet.

"As you can see, Efrem has prepared a wide variety of native cuisine."

"Well, Caxton..." Goe spooned a large heap of swamp cabbage onto his plate. "Anthony's filled me in on a few sketchy details concerning your visit, but I'm hazy on one particular point."

"I'm sorry, Ambassador. What?"

"Why now?"

Grant touched his lower lip with his napkin and took a sip of wine. "It's time to repay an old debt. Overdue, to be sure, but it's something I feel I must do. I'm not content to... What did you say? 'Allow history to be the judge'?"

Smullins sensed the Ambassador's eyes move to him.

"And you, Tate? What's your part in all this?"

"I'm the guy who keeps score."

The Ambassador laughed again and fiddled with a gold link bracelet which dangled from his wrist. "I suppose someone must always keep track of the winners and losers, eh? How do you classify yourself?"

Smullins worked the toothpick from one side of his mouth to the other. He surmised a trick to the question. Either answer right - either answer wrong. "A winner."

With a clap of his hands, the Ambassador leaned back in his chair. "Excellent! There's no room in this world for second place!" He returned his attention to Grant. "Do you agree, Caxton?"

The big man's expression remained neutral. "Having never lost an election as you did the last time out, I wouldn't know."

General Stone cleared his throat. "Gentlemen, might we save the political discussion for later? Perhaps over brandy and cigars?"

Smullins tipped his glass to Grant and thought he discerned a slight smile near the corner of his lip. He took a slow sip of wine. *Round one to the fat man.*

The Ambassador fidgeted with his bracelet again until a sound near the door drew everyone's attention away from the table.

"Ah, Efrem!" said the General. "Your timing is perfect."

The small man made a series of hand gestures and the General stood to excuse himself from the table. "It seems the person I'd been expecting has arrived. Please, continue. I won't be long." He reached for his cane and pushed himself free from the chair.

Smullins stood in tandem. "Can I bother you to point me toward the bathroom, sir?"

"This way."

With a wink at Grant, Smullins left the room, accepted the directions and when the General cleared the hall doubled back and peeked through the crack in the French doors. He didn't want to miss a second of the battle between the old adversaries in the dining room.

The next several minutes would have made the Romans proud. Without leaving their chairs, Grant and Goe went at it like two gladiators. Instead of sword and mace, they substituted accusations and innuendo. Denial served for shields. Threats hit home with the force of a heavy bludgeon.

"You, sir, are the most pompous man I've ever had the unfortunate displeasure of meeting." Grant backed the politician away from the table. Sweat poured from his brow like blood. "The gall of you to think I deliberately caused the death of any of my people. How dare you!"

The Ambassador retreated, hesitated and with fresh found venom advanced with a new barrage. "You lie to me. You lie to the General. You lie--"

"I do not!"

"Show me this 'file'. The one with proof of her survival."

"I don't have it."

"Exactly my point."

Smullins hadn't seen the former director so upset since his glory days at ASTRO. *Why did Kerry's father invite Goe, when he knew...*

"Haven't you lambasted enough? You never saw fit to approve my budgets, but if I recall, you also never turned down a pay raise!"

"Of course," Smullins whispered to himself. "Good plan, General. Grant's most effective when he's mad. Mad like a bull in a blender."

The tap of a cane on the tile floor indicated the General impending return. Smullins toed the door open with his foot and grinned when he saw Grant nose to nose with his enemy.

"And don't you forget it, you gold-plated leech!"

The Ambassador sputtered like he needed a lawyer.

Smullins returned to his chair and scanned the table for desert. "Did I miss anything?"

Grant turned and faced the door as it opened again. He appeared refreshed after the heated confrontation. "The honorable gentleman from Hawaii has pledged his utmost cooperation."

Smullins fought to retain his composure.

Goe nodded.

If Grant has his way, the little jewelry covered man will personally eat every yard of red tape we encounter.

The double doors parted and General Stone escorted a woman toward the table. "Gentlemen, I'd like to introduce you to my private investigator. This is Meg Mordel. I believe she has the most interesting information to tell us."

TWENTY_____

"**W**e've got a really bad problem, Jordon." Veronda Winston stormed into the hospital room with the intensity of an arctic cold front.

"You sure are excitable, lady." Jordon kept his attention on his bowl of mashed potatoes. He'd found amusement in infuriating the woman. It helped to ease some of the pain which lingered in his shoulder. Sort of his own version of irresistible force vs. unstoppable object. But for some inexplicable reason the laws of physics didn't apply when Winston hovered about.

She planted a foot and crossed her arms. "We've lost three men. I need you in Oklahoma now."

Jordon held the spoon halfway to his lips. She appeared concerned, preoccupied with something other than herself. "Back up." He searched under his sheet for the napkin, gave up and wiped his chin on his sleeve. "What do you mean 'lost three men'? That's kinda like the pilot telling the controller he's lost an engine. Makes a difference whether it stopped running or fell off the plane. Which is it? Lost or dead?"

She fidgeted back and forth, her high heels clicking frustration on the polished floor. "We don't know. They've disappeared."

The bland food lost what little appeal it held and he pushed his tray table away. "Tell me what happened. Let's start with the short version."

She dropped into the nearest chair like a rag doll charged full of electricity. Her hair a rat nest, with a botched attempt at make-up to accent the fact. "I don't have the whole story. The phone lines went dead while I was talking to Hamilton." She scooted her chair closer and lowered her voice. "He wanted to have some information rechecked at the county seat, so he sent two men, Cortez and Gatreux. They went to the courthouse while he and the rest of his crew headed up into the pulse area. I guess they rented a Jeep or truck or something."

Jordon saw fear in her dark, bloodshot eyes - as if all her calculations failed to add up. As if she'd rather panic than regroup.

"The two who went to the courthouse never came back." Winston's hands trembled, but she continued to tell a bizarre story about an ox, a dog with three legs and an old Native American with an attitude.

The final bit of the tale perked Jordon's interest to the next level. "Ghost? Sounds a bit farfetched, don't you think?"

She held her palms out in mock defense. "Hey, I'm telling you what he told me. He's pretty shaken over the whole thing. Frankly, I found him a kind of weak man to start with."

Leave it to Winston to refer to the head of her crack survey team as 'weak'. Jordon worked his shoulder and tested its limitations in the sling. "Did Hamilton contact the police?"

"No."

"No? Why not?"

"I asked him to wait."

"Asked or told?"

She hugged herself and shook her head. The room temperature felt cozy to Jordon. *Cold isn't making her shiver. It's fear.*

"Told," she said. "But what's the difference? Hamilton wanted to, but I vetoed the idea."

"Why? What are you trying to hide?"

She stood and raked a hand through her hair. A second stretched to two before she aimed an index finger in his face. "I--"

"Lady, didn't anyone ever tell you it's not polite to point?"

She ignored the remark. "This is an internal matter, Jordon. I don't want outsiders involved."

So, at least her mother won't be putting in an appearance. The day can only get better. "You're not above the law, lady. Neither is ASTRO. Things like this have a nasty tendency to fall down around your ears. Your predecessor can attest to that."

She pushed the chair out of the way and paced the space between the beds. "Something funny is going on. I don't know who is involved. It's imperative I keep a lid on this until you find out more information."

He gazed out the window and watched the snowplow make another swath across the parking lot. A losing battle against a growing pile. "I think ASTRO needs to adopt 'KEEP A LID ON IT!' for its official motto. Maybe print some bumper stickers. But, you know what, lady? Sometimes when you keep it on too long, the contents explode in your face. I've heard this song for years, different verse, but the same old tune. ASTRO's covered up more stuff in the name of secrecy than most bury in two lifetimes."

"That's not the point." She nibbled at the tip of her nail.

"That, Miss Winston, is precisely the point. I tell you what. Put today's date on my resignation and read it again. Nothing's changed."

"Be reasonable, Jordon." She continued to gnaw at the nail. "See it from my perspective."

He laughed and returned his stare out the window. "You don't even listen to yourself. Why should I?"

She circled the bed and blocked his view. "Do this one last assignment. I promise I'll have your resignation approved."

"I submitted it to Grant."

"I'm in charge now." It appeared any moment steam clouds might blow from her ears. A moment passed - she cooled, then started in on a second nail. "The offer stands, take it or leave it."

She's desperate beyond belief. "You know this is blackmail, don't you? Pure and simple."

"Call it what you like." She tried to clear a fleck of nail polish from her lip and turned her back. "What's it going to be? I don't have all day."

He maintained his silence for a great while. The click of her heel on the tile floor increased in tempo until his brain ached. He waited a second and watched the plow exit the lot. "Three conditions."

She spun on her toes, the tip of her finger still in her mouth. "Within reason. Let's hear them."

He struggled against his IV to get out of bed. After a little effort, he stood and tested the weight on his ankle. *Better.*

Winston not so much raised an eyebrow to help.

"Number one." He clutched at the gap in the back of his gown. "I want Clifford Foard to go with me to hold me up until I can walk by myself."

She crossed her arms. "Done."

"Second." He steadied himself and moved around the bed, the metal rail cold under his grip. "I want you to give Crandell a job. He goes with me."

She shook her head, jaw set like a vise. "No way. I don't like that man."

"Well, I'll not spare your feelings to tell you his opinion of you is mutual."

"And give me one good reason why I want to put the grimy old man on my payroll. I'd like to give him a good hosing down instead."

"For one thing, we wrecked his truck when Foard used it for a landing pad. Or have you forgotten? Besides, I happen to like the guy and you don't. I'm not asking you to go out on a date with him."

"Okay." She started to chew on her next nail. "ASTRO just gained a truck driver."

"Third," he said before she changed her mind. "I want complete control of the field operations in Oklahoma. If your reports are accurate, Hamilton's fouled things up. I've got to call the shots. Also, I want access to any equipment I'll need, plus I want you to keep your nose out of it."

She moved forward and stared at him with contempt. A little girl who had to share her tea set with the neighborhood boys. "That's five conditions."

"Take it before I add a sixth."

"Very well." She studied her mangled manicure, took a deep breath and turned to leave. When she reached the door, she spun on her toes again and pointed toward the closet. "Oh, by the way, you'll find a change of clothes in there. I've already convinced the doctor to dismiss you. Transportation to Oklahoma is waiting at the local airport. You've got one hour to get yourself, Foard and that stinky truck driver on board."

"Someone talking about me?" Foard's voice preceded him at the door. He sucked in his gut and nudged past the boss. "Did I hear mention of an airport?"

Winston ran mutilated fingernails through her hair and disheveled it even more. "One hour, Jordon. Don't be late."

"And where are we supposed to land when we get there?"

"It's all taken care of."

"Is it now? I don't know how this is going to pan out, lady. And I hope you don't plan on coming along. But, if you do, I'm sure A.J. will save you a seat next to his."

"No." A hateful smirk accompanied the reply. "I received a call back to Houston on important business."

"Thank you Houston!" Foard mouthed the words and watched the door close with the irritating woman on the other side. He reached to help Jordon back onto the bed. "Maybe the suit boys have come to their senses and appointed a real director."

"I think the only appointment in her future is at the hair dresser," Jordon looked at Foard. "Cliff, my curiosity will be the death of me yet, if my bad luck doesn't run out first."

The security man unwrapped a fresh cigar and clamped it between his teeth. "Mind if I'm late for the party and take the bus, Chief? After our last little aerial circus, I'd rather go Greyhound."

Jordon cocked his head toward the window. "In this blizzard?"

"Exactly. I'm not going up in another flying machine until somebody figures out how to keep them from falling out of the sky."

"My new boss lady will be crushed."

Foard smiled a wide grin. "Okay by me, Chief." He pulled a match from his pocket, studied its tip and flicked it, unlit, into the sink. "Hey, and good news regarding our pilot. He'll need a little dental work, but he's going to be okay."

"Good to hear." *One less thing to worry about.* "You know, Winston never even inquired to the young man's condition. She's nervous." He eyed his unfinished potatoes and decided to start a new diet. "I've just met her and watched her go from arrogant to downright shell-shocked."

"You're telling me, Chief. I've seen Superbowl rookies with more composure than her."

"Any ideas?"

"Not one, Chief. I've been on the phone, but nobody's whispered a word. But, if you want my opinion? I'm glad she's got things so fouled up. It'll get her bounced out of ASTRO a whole lot faster."

"And us with her."

Foard removed his cigar and studied it. "I thought you wanted--"

A muffled scream came from somewhere down the hospital's hall-way. A moment later, Crandell shuffled through the door, red-faced.

"What's going on out there, A.J.?" asked Foard.

"Not sure." Crandell ran the back of his hand across his beard stub-bled cheek. "I winked at that Winston woman and she slapped me."

TWENTY-ONE_____

"**D**over is here?" The large man who'd been introduced as Grant, threw down his napkin and forced his chair away from the table with the fury of a CPA ambushed at a tax audit. "Now, how is that possible?"

The sudden outburst made Mordel drop her cigarette into the china cup on the table. *The boss warned me to steer clear of this guy. Easy to see why.* "Yes, but I don't think he knows where she is yet."

"This is preposterous." While Grant moved about the dining room, his face grew a deeper shade of red with each step. "When I left, Clifford Foard informed me Dover died in his cell. Now, you're telling me you've see him alive. I'm sorry, my dear, but I don't... I can't believe you."

"You're not implying Miss Mordel is a liar, are you?" asked Ambassador Goe.

The General's cane clicked on the floor. He circled behind her and placed a firm hand on her shoulder. "Miss Mordel's credentials are impeccable."

"No." Grant shook his head and leaned to stare her square in the eye. "I prefer to believe you've been fed some bad information."

Mordel gained little comfort from the General's supportive squeeze. Without a word, the manservant appeared on her blind side and replaced the ash filled cup with a new one. The rattle made her jump and she forced herself to inhale the strong, acrid coffee to settle her nerves. Grant continued to stare down his nose until the lump in her throat made it difficult to speak. A quick glance over at the man introduced as Smullins offered no help. *Why is such a handsome guy mixed up with this bunch?* "Do you believe me?"

He rolled a toothpick from one side of his mouth to the other, then removed it to inspect the damage. His manners appeared smooth and deliberate. His smile mischievous, almost playful. "I don't know. Some proof would be nice."

She forced a hand out toward Grant and retrieved her bulky purse from the floor. "Give me some space. I'll show you proof." She dug past a spiral note pad and a bottle of aspirin. "I have a photograph of him outside a local hospital on my digital camera. Told the nuns he was looking for the General's daughter. Now where is it? Like I told you before, he hasn't found her, but he may be very close." The tiny camera appeared under her last pack of cigarettes. A quick flip through the contents produced the image on the viewscreen. "Here."

Grant snatched the camera from her hand. His expression conveyed an instant recognition. "It's him all right. Still alive!"

He passed it across to the handsome one, who bit his lip and nodded a confirmation. "America's ten most wanted, all rolled into one greasy package."

Ambassador Goe interrupted his attack on a second bowl of lemon custard and pointed at the camera. "This photo, I gather, complicates things."

"Dramatically." Grant moved toward Smullins and took a second look. His whole body trembled. "I can't believe it. Has the world turned upside down?"

"When did you take this?" Smullins asked.

"This morning." Mordel continued to watch Grant's hand make a fist. *The boss has gotten me into a real mess here.* The danger expected. The pay reflected the risk. But she'd as soon try to rake leaves in a hurricane as get between the big man and the stuttering psychopath.

"How'd you know about this traitor?" Grant started to move around the table again, the camera concealed in his hand.

Mordel considered options. *Certain things I can reveal. Others... Perhaps now is not a good time. Not yet anyway.* She cleared her throat and gulped a mouthful of hot coffee. "Dover's been checking a lot of the same places I have. You know, people will say a man has been there before me. I found out he's posing as a reporter for *Time*. A few more questions got a name. Doesn't even bother to use an alias. I figured it's important, so I took his picture."

"What do we do now?" The General appeared satisfied with her response and moved back into his chair at the head of the table.

"We move faster than he does." Mordel checked out the dessert options, but the knot in her stomach convinced her to stick to the caffeine. "Instead of days, we have hours. If Dover gets to your daughter first, General Stone, there's no telling what he'll do."

"But why is he so interested in her?" The Ambassador pushed his bowl away and studied the gold chain on his wrist, his interest seemingly split between personal decoration and the conversation at hand.

"And why will Dover risk being found out?" Smullins waved off the

119

manservant's offer of fresh coffee and propped his boots on the adjacent chair. "He's taking a huge chance."

"He's after Mitch." Grant continued to squeeze the camera in his big paw. Something cracked. "He's doesn't know we're here."

Mordel snatched the device from his hand. "For Pete's sake..."

Grant returned to the table and planted his mass on the relatively small chair. "He intends to use Kerry as a pipeline. We must also consider something else; he doesn't know Mitch is dead."

Mordel felt the lump swell in her throat again. *The boss didn't tell me Jordon's dead. The helicopter crash - fatal?* She ceremoniously veiled her surprise by dropping the camera into her bag. "Uh, nobody said anything to me about Mr. Jordon."

The General held up a hand. "I'm sorry, Meg. I didn't have a chance to tell you. Killed by one of Dover's accomplices."

"Well, isn't that the end of it? Dover won't have any reason to continue searching for your daughter." Mordel's mind raced. She'd talked to the boss a few minutes before her arrival. She didn't know exactly what position he held at ASTRO, but knew he had excellent inside information. *Why didn't he tell me? Something doesn't add up. How can I play Dover against Grant if the center of the controversy is dead? But Jordon survived the attack. Can it be they don't know? Has Grant, in his zeal to track down Dover and settle a personal vendetta, cut himself off from his network? Nothing else makes sense.*

"You may be right, Miss Mordel." Grant's voice brought her back into focus. "However, I think it is safe to assume when Dover discovers the truth about Mitch, he'll come after me. He's a sick and demented man. Revenge will be foremost on his mind. If he finds Kerry before we do, he'll maximize his threat to the fullest. We must either find Kerry or stop Dover. Either way, it's not going to be easy."

The Ambassador admired his watch.

Has to be a Rolex, thought Mordel.

"Anthony," said the Ambassador, "I'm afraid I have another meeting in a few hours. My man will be here with the limo. I'll make a few calls on the way to the office. The authorities will begin an immediate and discreet search for this Dover. The sooner we get him off the street, the better for all concerned, eh?"

"Thank you, Ambassador." The General cut his eyes toward Grant. If the big man felt any concern, he didn't show it. "Efrem will show you out."

The politician nodded toward Mordel. "A pleasure, Miss." His cologne surrounded him like an invisible shield. "Perhaps we'll meet again." He bowed at the waist and kissed her knuckle.

She waited for him to clear the door before she wiped the back of her hand on her blouse and checked to see if the ring had disappeared from her finger. Grant's stare intimidated her once again.

"What else do you know concerning the whereabouts of Kerry Jordon?" The big man, despite his girth, managed to appear in the chair next to hers.

Wonderful. A blimp with stealth capabilities. She fished a cigarette from her purse and lit it with a shaky hand. *Now the lies get a bit more creative.* "I haven't found her either, but I think I'm closer than Dover."

"What makes you so sure?"

"Experience."

"And you have a lot of it - I suppose?"

She glanced at the General, moved her gaze to Smullins, held it there for a moment and then turned her head to blow smoke in Grant's face. "You don't care for me very much, do you?"

He waved a hand through the gray cloud. "This is a delicate situation. I expect you to be the best."

She took another drag and reached for her cup and saucer. "I'm the best."

"It doesn't really matter if I like you or not." He coughed and leaned forward until she smelled the beer on his breath. "Now does it?"

The big man's presence eclipsed everything else in the dining room. Dishes rattled. Efrem cleared the table, but she didn't take her eyes off Grant. His stare pinned her back until she forced him away with a more powerful puff of smoke. "Do you want me to escort you to the hospital where I took the photograph?"

Smullins continued to play with his toothpick. "Seems to me, if Dover didn't find her there, we'd be wasting time following in his tracks."

"I agree." Grant leaned back into his chair until it creaked. He crooked his finger at Efrem and pantomimed his desire for another bottle of beer.

"Where do you want to start?" Mordel watched him drain the one he had in one swallow.

Grant dried his lips on a linen napkin. "You say you are the best. You tell me."

Smullins rapped his fist on the table. "Ease up on her. She may be our last hope."

"I suppose you're right." Grant sighed and nodded at Efrem. "I'm sorry, Miss Mordel. It's been a long and most unrewarding day. I'm afraid this is more than I'm used to."

She drained her coffee while the big man guzzled his umpteenth beer. *The man's a human sponge. If he belches, we may all die.*

Lit by a single street light, the shabby rooming house entrance attract-ed the homeless Filipinos like flies to a road kill. Mordel held her breath against the reek of boiled *Kang Kang* and hopped over one decrepit soul after another until she reached the top of the steps. *Grant doesn't have a clue who's alive or dead*, she thought. *He should see this place.* The stench from the clothes of a skinny man on the landing overwhelmed the aroma of cooking as her key slipped into the lock. The click sounded like a mes-sage from heaven. She gave it a forceful twist, skitted through and slammed the door behind her.

A quick knock, with the proper pauses, on her second floor door brought a curious Lana Turner to answer. She grabbed Mordel by the purse strap and pulled her into the dim apartment. "Where have you been, Meg? You told me to wait. You'd be back soon. Well, 'soon' came and went hours ago."

"Change in plan." Mordel pushed the thin, wooden door closed with her back and turned to slide the chain in its slot. A cigarette slipped be-tween her lips and the purse, minus the disposable lighter in her hand, sailed through the air and landed on the green vinyl couch. "These guys the boss set us on, have got things royally confused. You wouldn't believe it."

"Try me."

Mordel watched the smoke halo over her head and circle the weak bulb on the ceiling. "Grant thought Dover was dead."

"What?"

"It gets better." Mordel took the two steps to her battered recliner and dropped into it like a boxer who'd survived fifteen rounds. "Dover thought you were dead. They all think Jordon is dead." She kicked off her high heels and massaged her feet. "The only thing I'm sure of, is my dogs are dead. The boss has sure backed us into a mess."

"Jordon's dead!" Lana backpedaled and landed on top of the purse.

"No, silly." The foot rub felt good and began to ease the tension. "The boss says he's okay. At least the last I heard. He's due to get out of the hospital and on his way to Oklahoma. I'll tell you one thing. It's getting where a girl can't tell the good guys from the bad." Mordel pulled anoth-er drag and let her thoughts drift back to her childhood through the haze she exhaled. The simple days when she watched *Gilligan's Island, Mayber-ry,* and *The Brady Bunch.* Andy and Barney - always true and good. Rob and Laura always kissed and made up. No need for anybody to be bad, or if they strayed, it all worked out after the last commercial. Barnaby Jones would have a stroke trying to figure this mess out.

"He's hurt?" Lana squirmed to a better position on the split cushion.

Mordel missed her black and white television. She missed Hawkeye and Trapper. "Calm down. He's all right. If I can get our plan back on track, you'll be in his arms in no time." She inhaled more smoke and closed her eyes, but the daydream didn't come back. "Play both ends against the middle, things always get out of kilter." When she opened them again, Lana had moved to the window and parted the shades.

"You didn't tell them about me. Did you?"

"You mean, who you really are?"

Lana nodded and surveyed the street below.

"No." Mordel inhaled again. "I take risks, but I'm not an idiot. Told them I picked up your trail. Trust me, Lana. Everybody else does."

"But they know about Dover. They'll search for me twice as hard. Which means they'll find me twice as fast." She released the blind with a snap and kicked the recliner. "Doesn't your stupid boss know that? I wish you'd tell me who he is."

Mordel craved a cup of coffee, some of Pa Cartwright's advice and a slice of Aunt Bea's apple pie. "Believe me, the less you know regarding the boss, the better." She left the chair and headed for the kitchen. "And get this. Old Ambassador what's his name, the Hawaiian guy with all the jewelry, even offered to kick in his two cents worth. Book em' Danno." She searched the cabinets for a clean mug. "You, my dear, are a hot ticket."

Lana reached over Mordel's shoulder and slammed the cabinet door. "What have you done, Meg?"

"I've made sure they don't find you. At least not right away; not until we're ready." She flicked her ash into the sink and looked back toward the recliner. Her favorite ashtray sat on a folding table next to the couch. "I showed them a picture of Dover outside the hospital. Took it when he came to see you." She laughed. "Boy, they got upset!"

Lana's expression indicated she didn't appreciate the humor. "What if Dover is smarter than you think. What if..."

Mordel debated whether to go for the tray or continue to use the sink. "...if he searches for you here? No way. Why will he think you live with me?" She thumped Lana on the forehead with her finger. "Get your head straight, girl."

Lana ran a hand through her hair. "I suppose you're right."

Mordel located her favorite mug, the one with a picture of Dr. Johnny Fever, *WKRP's* ultimate coffee drinker. She pointed at the percolator. "This fresh?"

"No, I made it a couple of hours ago. We're getting low."

She emptied the pot and watched her ashes swirl down the drain. "When this is over, I'll be rich enough to have a servant like old man Stone. And he better be able to make some good--"

The phone rang and caused the cigarette to drop from her lips. "I gave Grant my number. Can't believe he's already calling." She reached toward the wall and lifted the receiver. Heavy breathing assaulted her ear. She cupped her hand over the mouthpiece and pointed at the percolator. "Make some fresh, will ya?" Her attention back to the phone, she said. "At the tone,--"

The voice boomed in her ear. "I KNOW SHE'S THERE, MEG!"

Dover! She dropped the receiver and watched it bounce across the counter.

Lana froze, but her eyes asked 'What?'

"Dover." She pulled the receiver back to her ear by the cord.

"I know she's l-living with you, M-Meg. I'm very dis-disap-pointed in you."

Mordel gripped the receiver until her fingers numbed. "Now, hold on. You don't know what you're--"

"Oh, I kn-know all right. I know when I've been t-two t-timed by someone who thinks she's smarter than me."

The cord twisted around Mordel's fingers like a poison snake. "Let's discuss this." She smelled smoke. "Where are you?" She felt an uncomfortable, warm sensation in her chest and stumbled back into the refrigerator.

Lana slapped at her blouse. "You've caught yourself on fire!"

Mordel screamed into the receiver. "I want to know where you are, Dover!"

"RIGHT OUTSIDE YOUR DOOR, MEG!"

Something with the force of a wild animal slammed into the thin door and the wall across the room rattled in protest.

Mordel threw the receiver to the floor and grabbed Lana by the sleeve. "He's here! Get out. Now!"

The molding near the lock split.

"No!" *Where's my purse? Need to find...* "Lana! Don't stand there. Go through the window."

The frame broke free from the wall. The door crashed across the room and landed against the recliner. Dover stood at the threshold with rage in his eyes. A cell phone slipped from his left hand and hit the floor with a pronounced thud. In his right, he held a small automatic pistol and silencer. "Hello, ladies. Sorry for th-the intrusion. I happened to be in th-the area and thought a certain amnesia victim might like to g-go on a trip."

Lana took a step toward the evil man. "Alan! Why do you have a gun?"

Mordel bit her lip. *Be careful. One mistake and Dover will kill us both.*

124

"I k-know who you are." Dover grinned like a boy who'd found the Cracker Jack prize. "I've con-confirmed your true identity."

"What?"

"Ever heard of M-M-Mitch J-J-Jordon?"

"No." Lana edged toward the couch. "Should I?"

The grin crawled even wider across Dover's face. "Surprise! He's your l-long l-lost hubby. He wants to see you real b-bad."

"Alan, if you think this is funny." Lana took a second step toward the couch. She turned to Mordel and her eyes cut to the right as if to signal something. "Meg?"

My purse. It's on the couch. She raised her hands to speak, timed her next move and bounded over the back of the divan. Even before she crashed through the folding table, the sting in her chest and the hole in the mug told her she'd been shot.

"Meg!" Lana screamed and grabbed the purse.

The sound of the second shot didn't register in Mordel's mind for a moment, but the sensation of a red hot poker ran the length of her spine. *Dover moving in the room...in slow motion. Lana. The purse. Floor. Ceiling. Pain in my back. Light. Dark. Dover's voice in a tin can.*

"A matter of payment for a job well done, M-Meg."

The hot tip of the gun pressed against her temple.

"I found out an interest-ting fact from my source inside ASTRO. G-G-Grant is here in Manila."

Mordel fought for breath. "Your plans are... Grant says Jordon dead... Kincade kill him..."

Dover's laugh echoed like the wail of a freak show between her ears. "Kincade! What an idiot. He's the body G-G-Grant thinks is J-J-Jordon."

A stickiness touched Mordel's cheek. Her sight diminished. "How you... Who source..."

"You know, for a woman with th-three slugs in her." He fired into her shoulder. "Excuse me, four slugs in her, you ask a b-bunch of stupid questions."

A scream. Lana's?

"Okay, Kerry J-J-Jordon. Get used to your former name. We're g-going to Oklahoma."

A kaleidoscope of color raced through Mordel's mind. Sounds. Images. Life. Death. *I Dream of Jeannie.* Dover's cell. A childhood memory. *'Call the man. Aunt Bea.'* She inched her fingers toward the phone. The lid flipped open. First number. Second...

"General Stone here."

Mordel formed the words in her mouth but didn't know if her tongue passed them on. "Yoooor daughteeeer."

125

"What. Who is this?"

"Doooovvver haaas Kerr…"

"Dover has my daughter? Is this Meg Mordel? Where are you."

"Shhhot."

A convulsion racked her body and she sensed the phone no longer on her palm. The room felt cold. Empty. A powerful message repeated over and over in her mind. *You got us into this Clifford Foard. You better not let that lowlife hurt Lana. She's the only sister I've got!*

TWENTY-TWO_____

"Queen Veronda will throw a shoe." Wellingham bit into the final remnants of stale Moon Pie and pushed the marshmallow and chocolate goo around the inside of her mouth with her tongue. The image of a glass slipper bouncing off a Prince's forehead skipped through her mind. "She told us to wait for Jordon."

Hamilton continued to ignore her. He'd been pretty tight-lipped ever since he stuck his head outside Calvin Bellaire's general store and declared, "Hey, sky's clearing. Let's go have another look round."

Nerves, she thought and jammed the sticky wrapper in her pocket.

'Another look' constituted their third venture north of town since Ox disappeared along the lane of oak trees. Vanished seemed a more appropriate description. Bucksaw refused to accompany them, fear evident in his manner. Instead, he offered unlimited use of the antique truck. Now Hamilton had driven her all the way up to Miss Jacks' cabin again.

The wispy clouds overhead played shadows on the surrounding timber. Like fluffy, powdered Christmas trees, they resembled an army of smothered infantry. The air carried a fresh aroma of pine, cedar, damp snow and chimney smoke. Her tired imagination took the creepy movement a step beyond, until she felt like Dorothy in the haunted forest. Winged monkeys lurked on every bent branch.

The remains of a second stale pie in her mouth, she put a foot on the bottom porch step. "Caesar! What's up with you?"

Hamilton turned, his stare colder than the icicles beneath the eaves. "Since when do you take Veronda Winston's side?"

"Now, wait." Wellingham pushed her ball cap up into her parka hood. "I'm with you one hundred percent on this, but she calls the shots. And besides, with Miguel, Marcel, and Ox gone missing, I'm not real keen on this idea of yours."

Hamilton looked back at the borrowed truck, then the cabin. He kicked his heels together to dislodge the packed snow from his boots. "The Jacks' name keeps cropping up. Maybe the woman who lives here can give us some answers."

"Let's wait for Jordon. I've heard stories about him. He'll get to the bottom of this."

"What's eating at you, Gina?" Hamilton ran the finger of his glove along the chinks between the logs. "You're not afraid of a little old lady, are you?"

She shook her head. "I don't know. Linc told me--"

Hamilton continued to rub the palm of his glove along the smooth log. "Is that what has you worried? Bucksaw's tall tales? He's one strange old man and his stories are stranger still. I think he's smokin' too much locoweed or drinking antifreeze or something. Phantom rig? Please." He turned to face the carved wooden door. "Wise up, Gina. We work for ASTRO. We put men on the Moon. We don't believe in ghost."

Wellingham tested the next slick step. "Sorry. It's just... Well, with Ox missing, I..."

Hamilton retraced his tracks to the rail. He extended his hand and pulled her into his arms. The bear hug offered comfort and security. "It's going to be okay. I promise. I understand how you feel. Feel the same way myself. We'll talk to Miss Jacks and try to figure this thing out. Okay?"

Wellingham broke the hug and shuffled toward the door. Carved into its surface, a huge bald eagle snagged a trout from a lake. The polish looked dull and weathered; the knob tarnished and unused. "Maybe you're right. Shall I knock?"

He ran his glove over the intricate work as if the eagle spoke to him in Braille. "Go ahead."

The door felt solid under her cold, bare knuckles, so she made a fist and pounded for a few moments longer. "Miss Jacks? It's Gina and Caesar. We rode up with Lincoln Bucksaw when he brought back your car. Miss Jacks? Are you home?"

No answer.

Hamilton added his fist to the summons. He stopped and pulled his glove free. The edge of his hand along the little finger grew red and puffy. "This place is built like a fort. Door must be pretty thick. Doesn't even rattle the frame." He stepped to the far edge of the porch and swung a leg over the rail. "Let's have a look see round back."

Wellingham followed and scanned the droopy evergreens. "She's gotta be home, there's not any tracks." Her voice echoed across the white patch of snow and perked the ears of a jackrabbit. A second later, Limp bounded from nowhere and chased the bunny across the road. "Hey? Isn't that Linc's three-legged dog?"

"Had to be."

"You suppose Linc followed us up here?"

"No way," said Hamilton. "He couldn't walk faster than we drove. Dog probably followed the truck."

"Suppose you're right." She crawled over the rail. "Is the car still in the garage?"

He nodded his head. "Still there. No tracks to it either. You notice this place doesn't have any windows? Now, who builds up here in the woods and forgets to leave a way to see out? It's not natural."

A bulge in the snow behind the cabin caught Wellingham's attention. No back door, she thought. Must be a cellar entrance. She dug into the drift with the heel of her boot until she struck a handle.

Padlocked.

"What is this place? A bank?" Hamilton continued to circle around the cabin with her close behind him until they returned to the porch. He backed away and pointed at the chimney. "She's got a cozy little fire going in there, but it appears we're not invited."

"Why is this place built so solid?"

"Maybe she's afraid of tornadoes."

Wellingham shivered beneath her heavy coat. "Hurricane Veronda and the Big Bad Wolf couldn't blow this place down."

Hamilton laughed. "They're not one in the same?" He signaled toward the road. "Come on, let's walk a ways on up. See what we can see."

She pointed at the truck. "We've got wheels. How 'bout we use 'em."

"Can't risk getting stuck. We won't go far."

"Sure would like to see the inside of this place." Wellingham turned away from the cabin and considered her options. Nice warm truck. Cold forced march. Hamilton grew smaller in the distance, then disappeared around the bend. She made up her mind, zipped her parka tighter under her chin and stepped into his tracks. "When this is all over," she yelled, "I'm going to open a snowmobile rental shop right next to Bucksaw's garage."

The clouds darkened above and the wind-whipped drifts left a path down the middle of the road, so the going progressed easier than Wellingham anticipated. After what felt like an endless mile, she worked her way across a narrow frozen creek. On the other side, she passed a rickety, wooden shack. A busted mattress leaned where a door once opened and offered a modicum of privacy for the occasional forest bum who might drop in for a stay. Spits of sleet peppered the rusty tin roof. "Hey, Caesar! I'm freezing back here."

"Tough it out a bit further." He slowed his pace, but didn't stop.

A second creek came into view, or maybe the same one as the first. *In these hills*, she thought, *who can tell?* "Okay, Caesar. Enough fun for today.

Let's head back and get our merit badges." Her lungs ached from the frozen air. Overhead, the clouds thickened even more to paint the road pale gray. "This is getting ridiculous. We're not going to find Ox. Let's go back and wait for Jordon."

Hamilton stopped and raised a hand, yanked his parka hood down and cocked an ear to the wind. "You hear something?"

"Besides the sleet?"

"Besides the sleet. Hear it?"

"Yeah, my heart beating out of my chest."

He held a finger to his lips and shushed her.

"I'm getting hungry," she said. "You can march all the way to the North Pole if you want to." Then she heard it too. *A horn. The truck horn!* "Hey!"

"You hear it now?"

"Yeah, sounds like SOS or something."

He licked his finger and stuck it in the air. "Winds coming from back the way we came. Gotta be Bucksaw's truck. Maybe Miss Jacks woke up from her nap and saw our footprints." He trotted along the backtrack of their original route.

Wellingham followed him. Around the next curve she spotted the truck parked in front of the dilapidated shack. Smoke puffed from the tail pipe, but no one sat behind the wheel. "How did that get there?" She stopped in the middle of the road and looked both ways into the trees. "Surely the old lady didn't... I don't like this, Caesar."

Hamilton led her toward the ditch, away from the shack. "I've got the same feeling in the pit of my stomach. Let's keep to the trees until we get a bit closer."

She ducked for cover behind a stubby cedar and bent to whisper in Hamilton's ear. "Horn stopped."

"I noticed. See anybody?"

"No."

"What next?" He parted the branches.

"You're the troop leader on this one." She struggled to clean her glasses with the inside of her coat sleeve.

"I'm going to go check out the truck."

"Bad idea."

"Why?"

"Sounds like a bad idea." She crouched. "A really bad idea."

Hamilton inched forward and knocked snow onto her head.

"Hey!"

"Shhhh. I'll go and have a peek. You circle round behind the shack and come at it from the creek."

"I don't think so!"

He hunched his shoulders. "If everything is all right, I'll signal you. If not, beat it back to Miss Jacks' cabin. See if the old lady has a phone."

"I didn't see any wires. I don't think she even has electricity. Besides, she pulled the welcome mat and put it in storage."

"She's home. Lie down in the snow and scream bloody murder if you have to. She'll come out."

"Then what?"

"Call the state police."

"Yeah, right. And tell them a ghost put the kibosh on you. They'll come and lock me up."

Hamilton grabbed the brim of her ball cap and pulled her nose-to-nose. "You got any better ideas, Gina?"

"No, Caesar. I don't."

"Thought so." Hamilton took a deep breath and sidestepped the cedar branch. "Wish me luck."

"I wish you carried a gun."

She watched him crawl through the ditch. Once he'd crossed it, he hunkered toward the truck. The motor continued to putter as he raised himself and peered into the cab. The signal came back 'thumbs down'. His next move put him at the door, alongside the battered mattress.

Don't go in there. The trip around the back of the shack didn't look promising, but she stepped deeper into the woods and started her trek. She stumbled on small stones under the snow until, faced by a small outcrop of granite, she decided to climb over.

A slight wind shift peppered her face with tiny ice pellets as she scrambled her way up the ten or so feet of jumbled and overturned rocks. The clouds grew darker still and the frosty downpour increased. "Lovely. Frozen rain. What we need right now is cold water in yet another form." Her footing continued to deteriorate until she reached the top. A new sound came from the front of the shack, which like the cabin, possessed no extra doors or windows on any outside wall.

The truck motor revved louder.

She jumped into the air and raised her fist in victory. "Way to go, Caesar!" A few steps later she trod around the corner of the structure and stepped into the center of the road.

Exhaust still puffed from the tail pipe, but no Caesar. "Now, where did you go?" The mattress no longer rested in the doorway. "If I've told him once, I've told him twice. Nap time is after recess."

She cupped her hands over her mouth and yelled at the shack. "Are you in there?" Sleet peppered her glasses as she inched forward. "This is not very funny."

A peek into the interior prompted more questions than answers. Shafts of light streaked through nail holes overhead. Empty, save for the nasty mattress which lay flat on the dirt floor. "What gives, Caesar? You've got to be in here somewhere." *Simple architecture. Maybe eight by twelve feet. No place to hide.* Her glasses fogged. *Great.* "I'm giving you to the count of three."

No answer. ·

She removed her spectacles and looked over her shoulder at blurry snow and ethereal trees. She held her watch up to her nose and tried to focus. *Still stopped.* "This is ridiculous. I'm going to take the truck. You'll have to walk back."

Silence.

"Caesar?"

Nothing.

"Ox?"

The sleet pelted the tin roof. "This is too crazy. I'm getting--" Something covered her head and she dropped her glasses to the ground. A chemical smell mixed with the musty odor of the shack - a sensation of a hammer on anvil rocketed through her brain - then blissful blackness.

TWENTY-THREE_____

Tate Smullins flexed his upper arms and repeated a second set of isometric exercises. The limo's back seat offered little else to occupy his time on the way to the Aquino International Airport. It appeared the speed of their Philippine exit threatened to exceed the pace of the evacuation following Mt. Pinatubo's eruption.

He craved a fresh toothpick and prayed the commuter jet the Ambassador promised had an ample supply.

On his left, Caxton Grant stared at the back of the driver's head. His troubled thoughts no doubt a few thousand miles away.

"What a totally fouled up mess." Smullins' muscles tensed, ready for action.

If Grant heard, he didn't respond.

Smullins considered the events of the past hour.

They'd found the crumpled body of Meg Mordel in her cluttered apartment. Somehow, she'd survived Dover's vicious attack and managed to punch the letters O-L-K-H-M-A into the memo minder of a blood covered cell phone. The unfortunate sleuth lived, but according to the General, who'd accompanied her to the hospital, she'd never walk again.

Dover's sick reputation made the senseless assault appear deliberate and methodical.

Grant's call from the backseat of the limo to ASTRO headquarters in the states revealed an even more bizarre scenario. Upset, and unable to speak to Clifford Foard, he handed the phone to Smullins. "I refuse to talk to this bombastic woman. See if you can make any sense of her ramble."

Veronda Winston's voice whined through the static to relay the one good news item of the day. "Jordon is alive. No, I can't reach him. Yes, Foard has gone along. No, I can't say more because I'm not sure of a secure channel."

"Where are they?" Relief washed over Smullins like a cool April shower.

"Wildwood," she reported and the connection broke.

I once went fishing on a lake near a town called Wildwood," Smullins told Grant. "Long time ago. I remember this old man who sold me live bait."

The big man perked at the news of Jordon's return to the living side of the obituary column. "You think this is where everyone is going?"

"Has to be. It all points to a place halfway around the world. In Oklahoma."

Lana Turner's wrist bled. She struggled against her bindings. Her elbows, held tight against the arm rest, throbbed in hot agony. The first time in a Lear and she felt like a galley slave.

Dover, the plane's other passenger, sat across from her and sipped Champagne with the attitude of someone on a simple vacation to a remote Caribbean resort.

A recent issue of *USA TODAY* rested on the carpet near his feet. The headline, two days old, repeated over and over in her head. *IS MOTHER NATURE GETTING EVEN???* Two photos, side-by-side, told the story without words. The first, a close-up of the sun, showed massive eruptions of orange and yellow from the corona. The second, depicted a map of the states with the graphic of a dump truck unloading snow across the Great Plains.

She didn't care about the sun or the snow or even Dover at this point. Her concern drifted to the twisted body of her sister. *Meg? Are you alive or dead?* Anger mixed with apprehension. *Who is this 'Boss' you kept referring to? Will he be waiting in Oklahoma?*

"Hey, Chief? What's all this stuff for?" Clifford Foard stumbled under the weight of the pile while Jordon stacked another white snow suit on top. "Tents, emergency rations, thermal underwear. Are you going to buy the whole store out?"

Jordon moved down the next aisle and caught his sling on an ammo box. "No, Veronda Winston is." The high schooler with the nose ring, sat behind the counter and ignored his wave. "'Scuse me? Hey kid? You got any snowshoes?"

The teenager glanced up from his comic book, but didn't turn down the volume on his 80's era boombox. "Two rows over, man. Next to the gas masks. Can't..." The deep bass thump from a cracked speaker drowned the rest.

A.J. Crandell appeared from the rear of the shop. "Found me an old cassette player and some good country-western tunes. Those army boys sure got taste. Better than the junk squawkin' outta that punk's radio." He held a yellowed plastic case to his face. "I ain't heard 'TRUCK STOP LOVIN' since before I snagged my old lady."

Jordon pointed him toward the counter. "Put it on our tab. See anything else you want?"

"I'll keep lookin'." Crandell turned and moved down the next aisle.

Foard couldn't see him, but by the sound of metal on metal, the old driver found treasure.

"Well, I'll be. Whole box of Spam. Those boys sure knowed how to live."

The so-called 'music' on the boom box faded and a young DJ's voice crackled, "This is the top of the hour news from WMTN. Colorado and surrounding states can expect more problems from the recent sunspot activity. Scientists report a third superflare will reach Earth late this evening. As reported yesterday, previous flares have caused havoc in China and Central Europe. The space station *Frontier* reports minor damage and several communication satellites have been crippled. Speculation is the next twenty-four hours may rival the massive Quebec blackout of '89. Unfortunately due to cloud cover in the mountain region, the magnetic storms will not be visible. The auroras, however, will be seen far south. The *Yucatán* Peninsula will get quite a show. In sports..."

"Hey, Chief? You hear that?"

Jordon continued to pile on the supplies. "Will make for an interesting flight."

Foard considered more argument, but bit his lip. A flashlight rolled onto the top of the pile and the burden grew heavier. He dropped the assorted field camp to the floor and brushed the grime from his hands. Everything in the place smelled damp, oily, or musty. "You trust all this secondhand stuff, Chief?"

"I went to the Moon on the back of a rocket built by the lowest bidder." Jordon studied the interior of a crate. "Answer your question?" From deep in the box he pulled three stuffed parcels.

Their use became immediately apparent and a lump the size of a small kitchen appliance formed in Foard's gut. "Now why do we need parachutes, Chief?"

"How else are we going to sneak up on that thing?" They'd referred to the blue pulse as 'that thing' ever since leaving the hospital. "You don't think we're going to land at the airport, do you? I don't care if Winston does manage to pull enough strings to get the nearest runway clear. We don't want to announce our arrival."

"But, Chief. I don't know the first thing about jumping out of an airplane."

135

"You learned how to get a helicopter from point A to point B."

"Yeah, point A being the sky and point B the back end of A.J.'s truck. You didn't tell me point B would be the back of A.J.'s truck."

Jordon smiled. "Didn't know A.J. at the time." He moved to a shelf and reached with his good arm for a book. He opened it, tore out the final third of the thin pages and tossed it on the pile. "That will do. Hope you got your Visa."

Foard focused on the title of the book at the top of one of the torn pages. *"How to Parachute in Ten Easy Lessons."* He tapped Jordon on the back. "Why'd you rip out just this part, Chief?"

"All you need is the last lesson. You can bone up on the way." He tilted his head toward Crandell. "You may have to show A.J. the pictures, though. Not sure if he can read."

The mangled manual looked promising - like a case of poison ivy. Foard forced a laugh. "You're kidding me, aren't you, Chief?"

Jordon headed for the register and the pierced teenager. "Consider it another crash course. Now, let's go to Oklahoma."

Lincoln Bucksaw studied the deep snow from the door of his garage. Trouble came and trouble went over the years, but this time it aimed to stay for a while.

He stared into the swirls of his coffee and conjured up memories of the past. The forties brought World War II and the Stuart-Dupree Oil Company to his peaceful little town.

Soon after Annabelle's grandfather had been killed in a car wreck, the ghost rig appeared. Then, some stupid idiot decided to build a lake over the best oilfield in the state and name it and the whole county after the uppity Senator Monarch instead of the local boy, Simpson Jacks.

The coffee felt thick in his throat and tasted bitter like the memories.

In nineteen forty-five, a week before he died, his friend Franklin asked him to do a favor. Young, fresh out of college, Bucksaw considered it an honor to follow through on the President's request.

In forty-eight everyone moved out of Wildwood except Cal, the storekeeper.

In forty-nine the clocks stopped.

In sixty-one, the headaches began.

Now, this morning, all those young geologists disappeared, he'd lost his truck, and his dog ran off.

Bucksaw poured the dregs from his cup into a barrel and reached for his coat on the nail. Time to finish paying off the favor. After all these years. "Man, I hate Oklahoma!"

- PART III: FRANKLIN'S FOLLY -

"A secret is like a rattlesnake
in a box."

Theodore Shay

TWENTY-FOUR_____

The ground came at Jordon like a blanket of pure white illusion. No depth. No width. A total indiscernible landscape. To judge the instant of impact required a miracle.

The landing approached too fast. He'd have to rely on instinct at the moment his boots touched the snow. *Feet together. Be ready.*

A gust of arctic wind pulled the parachute tighter against his harness and he tugged the steering toggles in response. *Any second now.*

The open field appeared to be his best bet, but how far away from the blue pulse, he couldn't be sure. The pilot had told him of erratic instrumentation readings, even advised against the suicidal action. To complicate matters, the jump sight landed them squarely in the middle of an area marked "Prohibited Air Space" on the aeronautical charts.

Impact came in an instant and Jordon's mind told his body to bend at the knees, tuck, and roll. But the snow around his waist refused to allow the maneuver. Instead he stuck in the deep fluff like a lawn dart at a backyard picnic.

He pushed his goggles onto his forehead, yanked the rigging lines free from his harness, and scanned the afternoon sky for Foard. No doubt the big man added a month's worth of foul language to his vocabulary on the way down. The white military chute and matching commando suit proved hard to spot against the background of clouds and haze.

His canopy gathered toward him, Jordon used the silky material to make a pad on top of the snow. He tested the pain in his shoulder before he crawled from the white crater he'd made on impact. The wound felt numb, thanks to the subfreezing weather.

Out of the corner of his eye, he caught sight of Foard's thick-soled boot coming at him a second before the hefty ex-jock collided. A full acre of fresh snow and he'd zeroed in on exactly the same spot.

"Touchdown!" Foard grunted as he flipped forward and landed on his face. "Wow! What a ride. I'm never gonna climb higher than my bed

139

again. If my feet can't touch the ground, I don't want no part of it."

Jordon worked his stiff shoulder. "Another textbook Clifford Foard landing."

The big man rolled onto his back and gasp for air. "Hey, Chief. Made Pro Bowl six times with tackles like that." He clawed at his goggles and pulled them down around his neck. "You see A.J. land?"

"No." Jordon dug into his backpack and located the compass and a walkie-talkie. "I'll see if I can raise him."

Foard rubbed a glove over his nose. "You believe that old truck driver used to jump out of planes in the service? He grabbed my belt and pulled me out after him!"

The thought brought a smile to Jordon's face, but a glance at the compass changed his outlook. The needle spun wildly from north to south like the very poles of the Earth had lost their way. A quick radio check proved disheartening. "Equipment is useless," he said. "Get your snowshoes on. It'll be dark soon and if we don't find A.J., he'll have to find us."

The tune echoed through the snow covered pines with the cadence of a first year cub scout troop. The craggy voice sounded unmistakable and belted out a anthem irritating enough to wake the dead and any immediate ancestors. Another crooner joined the recital until a crow protested from overhead.

Jordon held out a hand and crouched on his haunches.

"What is it, Chief?" Foard stooped low and cocked his head. "Somebody gutting a live moose?"

"A.J.'s got somebody with him."

Through the trees, two bodies emerged from the haze. "Hey, boys! Look here. I found me a friend out in the middle of this desolate place."

The two men stood side by side - like salt and pepper shakers with Crandell in his snow parka and the other in a fur covered jacket.

Jordon leaned to Foard and whispered in his ear. "Keep an eye on the edge of the woods. A.J.'s new buddy might not be alone."

Foard backed away.

Jordon approached the stranger.

"This here's Linc Bucksaw." Crandell put his arm around the man's shoulders. "Man after my own heart. Knows all the words to *Jailbreak Honeymoon*."

With his left arm extended, Jordon offered to shake hands. If the wrinkled old man carried a gun, he concealed it well under his coat. "Glad to meet you, Linc. I'm Mitch Jordon. Big guy over there is Clifford Foard. I guess A.J. told you we're out on a hiking expedition."

Bucksaw eyed the gloved greeting.

"Don't mind it none, Linc," said A.J. "He took a bullet a couple a days ago. He'll be fine. Won't you, Mitch?"

For the first time since he'd met the likable driver, Jordon wanted to strangle him. "A.J.'s a kidder. Aren't you, A.J.?"

A large grin crawled across Bucksaw's weathered face and Jordon realized him to be a Native American. "For a moment I pegged you for bank robbers on the run. I seen your mug on the news." He pointed at Foard. "His too. You fellers come across a three-legged dog? Tracks are easy to spot."

Foard approached and stuck a cigar between his teeth. "Sorry, Chief. Ain't seen your dog." Jordon felt a poke in his back. "We better be moving on. Gotta make camp before dark."

Bucksaw eyed the cigar. "Name's not 'Chief'. Got any more of those?"

Confusion raced across Foard's face. "Uh, yeah, Ch... I mean, Linc." He pulled two from inside his parka. "Help yourself."

"Much obliged." Bucksaw bit the end from one of the cigars and spit the tip in the snow. After he'd accepted a light, he leaned against a tree and savored the smoke. "When I happened across A.J. here, thought I'd run into another one of those haints."

"Haints?" asked Foard.

"Ghost. Apparitions. Bogeymen. Spirits. Spooks." A smoke ring disappeared into the haze. "Woods is full of 'em."

Jordon stared into the ancient man's wise eyes. Not easily fooled. Without a compass or means of communication, he'd have to ask for the old man's help. "Perhaps you'll give us some information."

"Fresh out of information." Bucksaw continued to puff away as if the day contained a hundred hours. "But this is a fine cigar. Worth a couple a hints."

Jordon pulled a folded topographic map from his pocket and wrapped it around the trunk of the tree at eye level. "I'm interested in this area." He tapped the center of a red circle he'd drawn.

Bucksaw rolled the cigar between his fingers and leaned in for a better inspection. "You don't want to go there."

"Why not."

"Just don't."

"Why? What's there?"

"You're not from around these parts."

"Obviously."

Bucksaw nodded at Foard. "Thanks for the cigar, Admiral. I'll be on my way. Got to find my dog."

"See you later, friend." A.J. waved a glove in the air. "Glad to know you. Let's me and you go fishin' someday."

Bucksaw stopped in the deeper snow at the edge of the trees and turned. "Stay away from up there."

Jordon stepped forward. "Afraid our minds are made."

His head hung low, the old man retraced his steps. "Listen to me young man. Don't go up to the ghost rig." He took a long drag from his cigar and didn't exhale for several seconds. "Nobody ever comes back."

"Tell me about it."

"Not much to tell."

Jordon fought impatience. He needed the old man to save them time. Every moment counted with the geologic survey team missing. "Tell me what you know."

"It's the old Liberty Lease. Number seventy-six."

"Who owns the mineral rights?"

"Stuart-Dupree, they own all the leases up on Miss Jacks' land."

Jordon tapped the map in his hand. "And it's here?"

Bucksaw's finger landed on the exact coordinates of the blue pulse. "Rig sits on location, right where you got this circle."

"Pulling unit or drilling rig?"

"Oh, it's a drilling rig, no doubt about it. All clean and shiny. They sure do keep it nice and polished."

"They?"

Bucksaw leaned against the tree again and continued to puff. The smell of the foul smoke hung in the air and mingled among the low branches. "Miss Jacks lets me hunt up there. Far as I know, no one else does. She says I can hunt anywhere I want, long as I stay away from the old Liberty Lease. It's her way of paying me for doing odd jobs."

"How long have they been rigged up on this location?"

"Oh, sometime in the late thirties, early forties."

"Nineteen forties?" asked Foard.

"Yep"

"Doesn't pan out." Jordon's sixth sense of curiosity moved to a higher level. What didn't make sense before, made even less now. "All those years on the same location. You say they keep it clean? Why do they want to maintain an abandoned rig?"

"Who said it's abandoned?"

Foard cleared his throat. "How long since you saw it last?"

Bucksaw studied his stogie. "Maybe a month. Maybe two."

"Is it stacked out?" asked Jordon.

Foard raised his hands and formed a T-shape. "Time out. I'm not making any sense out of this at all."

"Neither am I." Jordon leaned toward Bucksaw. "Are you telling me somebody's put a location up there and the rig's been in operation since the early forties?"

Bucksaw took a deep breath and ground the stub of his smoke out on the trunk of the tree. It sizzled and melted the ice. "Not the same rig. Keeps up with the times. Every few years it changes. It stays modern. So I call it a ghost rig, because we never see anybody going up there or coming down. Strange."

Foard pulled Jordon to the side. "If a drilling rigs up there, why doesn't it show up on the aerial maps?"

"I think that's what we're here to investigate. Most spy sats can spot the pimple on the fuzzy tail of a rabbit. We'll have to go up there and find out." He turned his head back to Bucksaw and raised his voice again. "Will you show us the way?"

"You're looking for those young people from the space agency, aren't you?"

Foard stepped in front of Jordon and grabbed the old man by the collar. "You know about them? Where are they?"

"Clifford!" With his good arm Jordon pulled the security man away.

"Hey!" said Crandell. "Go easy on our new friend."

Bucksaw adjusted his coat and headed off in a new direction. "Yeah, I seen them," he said over his shoulder. "Ghost got 'em all."

Crandell appeared confused. "Where's he goin'?" He tightened the laces on his snowshoes and trotted after the old man. "Hey, Linc? Wait up. These are good fellers. We really need your help."

Bucksaw stopped and shook his head. "All right." He waved for them to follow. "It'll cost you though."

Jordon folded the map and put it in a pocket on his parka. "Name your price."

The old man walked up the hill. His voice echoed softly through the trees. "I want a box of those fine cigars and fifty pounds of dry dog food."

TWENTY-FIVE_____

"**I** think he's leading us with his eyes closed, Chief." Foard pulled the goggles from his face and wiped snow from the bridge of his nose. He waddled nearer Jordon and signaled for a break. "If I have to crawl through one more barb wire fence..."

Crandell joined the pair. "Cliff's right, Mitch. Done gone and ripped my pants clean down to my long johns. Got me a draft what won't quit."

"I can see how you'd think the old guy's lost, but so far he's avoided some pretty questionable terrain." Jordon watched Bucksaw trudge ahead. "What I can't pan out is why he changed his mind so fast on leading us in."

Foard held his gloves under his armpits and turned away from the wind. "You think we're heading for a trap?"

"Can't be sure. Keep your eyes open. A.J., you want to take the point?"

"Suits me." Crandell cinched the rip in his pants and aimed in the direction where Bucksaw had disappeared into the pines. "Wind's already blowed away the tracks."

Jordon grabbed Foard by the elbow and pulled him closer. "Checked your watch lately?"

"No. Don't want snow getting up my sleeve." He glanced into the ominous sky. "Sun's going down. Be dark soon."

Jordon held his timepiece in front of Foard's face. "Ever see one do this?"

Foard's expression contorted behind the goggle lenses and his eyes grew wide. "Thing's running backwards!"

The slope proved too steep to attack head on, so Jordon zigzagged his way to near the top of the ridge where Bucksaw and Crandell waited. Huddled together under an evergreen, they pointed into the night sky.

The clouds cleared and for the first time since his rescue from the train tunnel, Jordon viewed the Moon, now low on the horizon. Breathless from the climb, he dropped to his knees and marveled at the eerie light show which dominated the rest of the heavens. Like a ghostly veil, the atmosphere quivered streaks of red, yellow and blue.

Foard straggled by and turned to see. "What in the world?"

"Magnetic storm. Worst I've ever seen."

"Is that what's fouled up your watch and compass?"

Jordon studied the auroras with childlike fascination. "Doubtful." He forced his gaze toward Bucksaw. "How much farther to this so-called 'ghost rig'?"

The old man stuck a thumb over his shoulder. "Other side of the ridge. Lot more interesting than the fireworks show."

Crandell rummaged through his backpack. "If the wind dies down, I'm startin' me a fire for some coffee."

From his own pack, Jordon withdrew a small pair of high powered binoculars. "Can't risk it. We'll run a cold camp tonight." He located a hex tent and pulled it from a protective sleeve. "Know how to pitch one of these?"

"Old lady made me sleep in the yard a time or two."

"Good. Try to stay out from under the taller trees. With this wind, the broken limbs will bust your skull."

Crandell took the small shelter and searched cautiously for a level spot in the snow. He gathered an arm full of pine branches and fashioned a tidy lean-to for a windbreak. "Cold don't begin to describe this camp." He pointed at Bucksaw and grinned. "We can't have a fire, 'cause Mitch's 'fraid you'll send off some smoke signals."

At the moment, Jordon didn't know what to be fearful of. "Good job, A.J. Why don't you get inside and have a bite to eat? Be careful of your light." He motioned to Foard. "Want to come take a look over the ridge?"

"You don't think I came all this way to miss the last two minutes of the game, do you?" He dropped to all fours and crawled alongside to the rocky top.

Jordon raised a gloved finger to his lips. "Stay quiet." Over the top of the ridge a bright light reflected off the snow. In contrast to the rainbow of colors from the magnetic storm above, it made the bowl shaped location look like a Christmas globe, shaken to let the sparkles drift quietly to the bottom. In the middle of the blustery white setting, a modern drilling rig stood tall and ready for use. "Man, it's a big thing. Must be a good two hundred feet, floor to crown."

The wind died down and the silence became so intense, Jordon heard his own heart beat in rhythm with his breath.

"So, it is there!" Foard said, his tone amazed. "Thing's lit like a tourist attraction. Why didn't it show up on the recon photos?"

"Looks brand new don't it?" Bucksaw worked the dormant stub of his cigar around in his mouth.

Jordon handed the binoculars to Foard. "Be careful of the lights. Don't let it reflect off the lens."

Foard nodded and pulled his parka hood further over his forehead to shield the field glasses. "This stuff's foreign to me. Explain what I'm seeing." He worked the focus. "All I know about oil is it keeps the motor from falling out of my SUV."

Jordon wondered if he'd have the same reaction at a football training camp, with the roles reversed and Foard pointing out the details. "Well, don't use this as an example. Things aren't what they seem." He turned to Bucksaw. "It always lit up like this?"

"No, and those three trailer houses parked over to the edge of the location are new."

"Appears normal to me," said Foard. "Except for the motorcycle leaned next to the first one."

"It's not what's there, but what's missing." Jordon reached for the binoculars and took a second look. "This place is constructed like a movie set. No substance. If they're drilling for oil here, I'm J. Paul Getty."

Foard shook his head. "I don't get you, Chief."

Bucksaw grunted, but Jordon ignored him and handed back the binoculars. "Okay, first let's catalog what we do see. Rig's an average size derrick, built on a steel structure that keeps it above the ground. Up on the floor is the doghouse, the long white room at the top of the steps. It's a place the crew can rest and get in out of the weather."

After more adjustments, Foard nodded. "I see it, but everything else is covered by big, blue tarps."

"Right. To block out the wind and cold or to keep us from seeing the stack underneath. My bet is there's nothing between the floor and the ground. No B.O.P.'s or anything."

"Too much jargon. You're losing me, Chief."

"Sorry. Blowout Preventers. See the long platform that descends from the floor at a slope and levels off to the left?"

"Yeah, I got it."

"Called a catwalk. Should be some pipe or equipment on it, but there's not. Not any in the derrick or on the racks either, just snow. And I don't see any mud pits or flow lines. Cable coming down from the crown appears to be brand new."

"Is that a pond over there?" Foard pointed to the far side of the location. "Wind's blown most of the snow off of it."

Jordon took the binoculars and studied the cleared area. Reserve pit. It's full of fresh water."

146

"From the sound of your voice, I get the feeling it shouldn't be."

Jordon nodded. "You're catching on fast. It should be full of waste or used drilling fluids."

"How can you tell it's fresh water?"

"Easy. Its surface is frozen solid. You called it a pond and that's all it is. It's smooth and clear in the lights. No discoloration or junk in the ice."

Foard continued to scan the area before him. "Lots of footprints, so the snow's not very deep. Cleared recently. I can see gravel patches everywhere. I think the old man's three-legged dog has been near the far trailer. Odd pattern of tracks beside the tires."

Bucksaw grunted. "Who you callin' old?"

Without a reply, Foard adjusted the stance on his elbows. "Barb wire fence completely encloses the perimeter except where it crosses the center of the pit. There's a cattle guard over to the right where the road leads in. I see a man, or at least I think it's a man, inside a booth next to the gate across from the cattle guard. He's wearing orange coveralls and a hard hat. Some printing on his back, but I can't quite make it out."

"Stuart-Dupree Oil Company logo," said Bucksaw.

"How do you know?" asked Foard.

"Easy. I got eyesight like a hawk. Besides, it's their rig."

Foard continued to stare through the binoculars. "Guy's hard hat sure is clean. What's he doing?"

"For some reason they want this to look like a tight hole."

"Say what?"

"Some of the bigger oil companies use a guard at the gate to keep pesky salesmen and other oil company representatives off the locations."

"So, you think this place is a phony?"

"As a three dollar bill," said Jordon. He inched a bit closer. "It's a front for something, and they're putting on a show tonight. My bet is, they know we're here and all this is for our benefit." He held a hand to his ear. "Notice there are no engine sounds. This thing must be pulling a whole lot of electricity from somewhere. Linc, you ever notice any high line wires heading up this way?"

"Now you mention it. No."

Jordon rubbed his chin. "Cables must be buried underground. Makes sense if the rig's been here a long time."

Foard handed the binoculars back to Jordon. "Be back in a minute." He backed down from the observation point and walked away into the dark woods.

Bucksaw moved closer. "You're a pretty sharp observer."

The praise seemed out of place, thought Jordon. "What makes you think so?"

"I've been watching this location for years," said Bucksaw. "Took me a long time to figure out what you just did in a minute or two."

Jordon rolled to peer into the old man's eyes. The illumination from below made it easy to see the fear. "You've been stonewalling us the whole time, haven't you?"

"Needed to be sure I can trust you."

"Trust me for what?"

"To help me get on the floor of that rig."

Jordon studied the expression, tried to pull a meaning from the voice inflection, willed himself to read the man's mind. Nothing. He sensed the truth depended on his answer. "Are we talking sabotage?"

"I'm not sure."

"You're not making any sense."

Bucksaw reached for the field glasses and studied the perimeter of the location. "Don't suppose I am. Problem is, I don't know the whole story."

"Well, tell me the part you do know."

The heavy sigh indicated a certain degree of defeat. "Years ago a man gave me a message to relay to someone on that rig. He didn't say why, but did tell me, I'd know when."

"And you think now is the time?"

Bucksaw bobbed his head. "Thing's been real quiet up here for years. Now, all the sudden, people disappear. A lot of activity down there. Has to be the time, cause I feel it in my gut."

"What's the message?"

"Can't tell you. Franklin made me promise to deliver it to whoever is in charge of that rig."

Jordon worked the pieces of the puzzle around in his mind. The rig. The abductions. The old man. "Who's Franklin?"

Bucksaw opened his mouth, closed it quickly and pointed down the ridge. "Jeep just came up the road. Stopped at the guard booth."

Even without the binoculars Jordon identified the man who stepped from the vehicle and followed the orange clad worker to the middle trailer house. A lump formed in his throat and choked back a flood of memories. *It can't be.* "What's Tate doing here?"

148

FORTY-SEVEN_____

Grant continued to pace the floor of Bellaire's general store. He said nothing to the old man, whom he and Smullins had awakened from sleep an hour earlier. Back and forth, the plank floor creaked under his weight. Counter to door. Door to counter.

Bellaire stroked his matted gray mustache and moved about behind the cash register. A gob of tobacco juice sailed through the air and pinged a rusty coffee can in front of a wood burning stove. "So, you're the boss of that sorry bunch of crazy geologists?" He propped an elbow on the antique till. "You sure that friend of yours can find that sorry rig in the dark?"

"Former boss," said Grant. He turned on his heels and closed his eyes. The old building held its heat well and he felt a wetness under his arms. A smoky smell combined with other easily identifiable odors dated the store like the rings of a tree. Rancid coffee, rotted fruit, musty shelves. *The local health department will probably enshrine the place - a museum to uncleanliness.*

He opened his eyes, approached the counter again and stared at Bellaire's weathered face. "And yes, if your directions are correct, he'll be fine."

"You can bet your bottom dollar on it. That's where they all went all right. Did I mention none of 'em ever came back?"

"Several times." Reminded of the old geezer who tagged along behind Roy Rogers, Grant felt uneasy.

The storekeeper fidgeted again.

What does he have hidden under there? An empty money box perhaps? He thought of Smullins, who'd driven north and wondered if he should've gone along. *What if Tate doesn't come back either? What if...?* He shook the contradictions from his mind and concentrated on another awful truth. "I don't suppose anyone came in before us?" he asked Bellaire.

"Nope." The artesian flow of juice rattled the can again. "You're the first to wake me up tonight."

Grant held his hand shoulder high above the creaky floor. "Short man. Has a stutter?"

"Sorry bunch of..." Bellaire shook his head and continued to fidget. "Now, what did I just say? You deaf?"

"I didn't mean to imply--"

"Know what I think? Those young 'uns got gobbled up. Sorry town's some sort of gateway into some type of devil's triangle. Ain't natural what goes on up there, if you ask me."

The door rattled under a fist and Grant jumped in his skin. He cut his eyes from the storekeeper to the entrance.

"Well, you gonna answer the sorry thing?"

The summons pounded again. This time more insistent.

"Tate?" Grant stepped forward, gripped the knob and yanked the door open. Immediately an intense gale of cold wind slapped him across the face.

In the drift, a shadowy form stood and kicked snow from a boot against the frame. The parka hood lowered and Grant felt his breath pulled from his throat. His stare locked on her face. *Not possible.* "Kerry? Is it you?"

Without an answer, she rushed forward and drove him back a step.

He wrapped his arms around her and felt the binding about her wrist. "What in blazes?"

"Caxton! Watch out!" She continued to bulldoze him into a shelf loaded with canned goods. "He's got a gun!"

"What?" Grant stammered and tried to regain his wind. "Who has...?" Over her shoulder he watched another hooded fur coat step across the threshold. Beyond the mysterious figure, the night sky shimmered over Wildwood like a Van Gogh painting come alive.

The coat raised an automatic pistol to arm's length and pointed it in his direction. "It's b-been a long t-time, fat man!"

Out of the corner of his eye, Grant caught a glimpse of Bellaire as he pulled a double barrel shotgun from beneath the counter.

"You folks are crazy!" The grocer brandished the weapon over the till. "Get out of my store! The whole sorry lot of you!"

The hood flipped back to reveal a familiar face.

It can't be!

Dover took a quick sidestep, grabbed the gun by the barrel and yanked it from the old man's hands. He spun it like a baton and planted the stock of the weapon firmly into the storekeeper's forehead.

Bellaire, unconscious, slumped back into his shelves, then fell face forward onto the cash register. It cha-chinged a 'No Sale' in protest.

"G-Guess I rang gramp's bell." Dover kept the pistol trained on Grant and wedged the shotgun between his knees. He cracked the breech and inspected the chamber. "Old fool." The gun disappeared behind the counter. "Not even l-loaded."

Grant held the woman tight in his arms. She shivered uncontrollably. *Not Kerry Jordon,* he felt quite confident. *But who?* He leaned to whisper in her ear. "It's okay, my dear."

"She's changed a b-bit, don't you think? Airplane crashes tend to muss a g-girl's hair."

She whimpered like a lost puppy and buried her face in his chest. Her skin felt icy cold. "Caxton. Help me."

"Save me all this reunion garbage." Dover stepped forward and stuck the muzzle of his pistol to Grant's temple. "Should've p-put one through your head the last time I did this," He stroked his earlobe with the cold metal. "But this t-time you don't have J-J-Jordon here to save you."

Grant swallowed his fear. He had no doubt Dover preferred to pull the trigger. "What do you want? To kill me?"

"In good time." Dover stepped back and kicked the door shut. "First I want to let J-J-Jordon see his dear wife one last time."

"Mitch is dead." *If Dover has just come from the Philippines, he can't know the truth.* "Your flunky, Kincade, killed him." He squeezed the woman in his arm's tighter and caressed the back of her head. *What else doesn't he know?* "I'm sorry you heard it this way... Kerry."

One corner of Dover's mouth turned up in a smile. "Boy, is your intel out of d-date. I've got an inside man with him right now."

Grant caught his breath.

"Surprise!" Dover laughed and held his side. "I'd like to p-put the expression on your face in a b-bottle and keep it forever. Priceless. Absolutely p-p-priceless. If I didn't want to kill J-J-Jordon so bad myself, I'd have had Foard do it for me months ago."

Grant felt his jaw drop. *How can it be? Not Clifford Foard. Working for Dover? Preposterous.* His chest tightened and constricted his next breath - nausea swept through him like a freight train.

Dover stepped toward the counter and checked Bellaire's pulse. "Foard's been feeding me information since d-day one." He grabbed a candy bar from a wire rack and bit the wrapper open. "You never kept a very tight ship." He made a face and spit the chocolate out. "ASTRO has more leaks than the Ti-Titanic. The real laugher is how you hire a Security Chief who's already on my p-payroll. A gooey white substance barely oozed from the candy bar. "The stale marshmallow in this thing could have plugged more of your leaks than he did."

Grant bit his lip and held his silence. He felt betrayed... Defeated.

"Hey!" Dover tensed and surveyed the store. "Where is S-S-Smullins?

Get him front and center. Now!"

"He's not here." Grant continued to hold the woman close. He didn't want to see her eyes. To sort the truth, he needed time.

"Where is he?" Dover charged forward and stomped his boot on the floor. "Tell me, or I'll put one b-bullet through both of you."

"He left," said Grant. "To get the state police."

Dover rabbit punched the grocer in the side. "Wake up, storekeeper."

Bellaire groaned and scuffed his feet.

"S-S-Smullins. Where is he, g-gramps?" He grabbed a handful of gray hair and lifted his head off the register.

Grant prayed the old man to stay unconscious. He heard him speak, but in muffled words. *Not good. Not good at all.*

"G-Guess I'm going on a little hunt," said Dover after he'd listened to the whispers. He released the old man's hair and waved at a door near the back of the store with his gun. "What's in there?"

"How do I know?" replied Grant and pushed the woman away from him to arm's length. *It's definitely not her.* But one fact gnawed at the back of his mind. The stuttering egomaniac across the room never knew Kerry.

Dover grabbed her by the elbow and pushed her toward the back of the store. "Find some rope, fat man. Now!" He tested the knob on the door and glanced around. "Why doesn't this place have any clocks?"

With one eye on the gun, Grant rummaged the shelves until he located a long, thin extension cord. Careful not to appear anxious, he searched for something to use as a weapon amongst the bags of hot dog buns, potato chips and coffee. *Nothing.*

"Out where I c-can see you."

Grant carried the cord into the kitchen and watched Dover open a pantry door and kick around the contents.

"This will d-do." He held the girl tight and pointed at the floor. "Get all this out of here and pile it behind the table."

Within a few minutes Grant managed to stir up enough dust to make himself sneeze.

"T-Turn around." Dover pushed the girl forward.

Grant did so. He felt the electrical cord cut into the flesh of his wrist and the weight of the woman against him.

Dover coiled the cord around their bodies and cinched the knot tight enough to pull his belly where it overlapped his belt.

Tied like a hog ready for the slaughter house, Grant stumbled into the pantry and bumped his head on a low shelf. The trickle which ran down the bridge of his nose felt like a combination of sweat and sticky blood. His stomach turned when he inhaled a whiff of air which reeked of stale tobacco, body odor and moth balls.

152

"I would g-gag you, but I know you two have a lot of catching up to do. Don't yell for gramps, because I'm taking him along." He pushed them down, slammed the door shut and clicked the lock. "Enjoy your chat." The sound of his boots clattered away until the kitchen door rattled against its frame.

Grant fought against his rage - the cord dug deeper into his wrist. The wooden floor, wet from the melted snow on the woman's parka, soaked the leg of his pants. He concentrated on the light coming under the door and tried to focus. "All right, my dear. Suppose you start by telling me who you are."

For the first time since she'd careened into his arms, she spoke. Her voice, much higher than Kerry Jordon's, quivered with fright. "How did you know so quickly?"

"Kerry never called me Caxton. Always 'Mr. C.'."

She wriggled against the restraint. "Dover is so arrogant. Easy to fool. I knew it would be harder with you."

The pain in his wrist burned and numbness set in. "Not even close. I suppose you favor her a bit. Why the charade?"

"My name is Lana Mordel." For the next several minutes she related an incredible story of lies and deceit, of a sister shot and of someone called 'the Boss'. "I think I've figured out who he is," she concluded.

"Let me guess." Grant sorted through the hodgepodge of information and twitched his forehead to coax the sweat from his brow. "Is it Clifford Foard?"

"Yeah. I put it together when Dover pegged him as his inside man. I took a phone message for Meg once from a guy with the same name. Can't be a coincidence. Can it?"

"Doubtful." Grant sneezed again and winced when the cord cut into his stomach. *What's Foard's game? Working for Dover? Trying to trap him? What about his connection with Jordon? Assassin or body guard? Whatever the case, Dover will soon be in the thick of it.* "Please be careful, Mitch," he whispered into the darkness.

TWENTY-SEVEN_____

"**W**ho's Tate?" Bucksaw lay flat on his belly in the snow and looked toward the location.

Jordon ran a thousand scenarios through his mind, each one unable to explain why his old friend suddenly appeared at a nonexistent, snow covered, Oklahoma oilfield in the middle of the night. "He works for ASTRO. I've known him since college and we went to the Moon together. Haven't seen him in a couple of months."

"He hunting for you?"

"Not unless that idiot Winston woman sent him." He adjusted his binoculars and investigated the middle trailer which Smullins had entered with a rig hand. He studied the motorbike leaned against the side of the steps. "What do they need a cycle for in this weather?"

"Rigged with skis," said Bucksaw. "Seen it before."

The snow crunched under a heavy boot somewhere to Jordon's rear. He rolled over onto his back and motioned with his hand. "Hey, Clifford," he whispered in the still air, "come take a look at this."

A sudden realization struck him like a red hot iron. He worked his gaze up and down the white camouflage suit, the goggles and the parka. Right size, but this guy's got hair, he thought.

Bucksaw, who'd not looked back, elbowed him in the side. "Big truck on the road. Almost to the guardhouse. Think they're gonna pull one of those trailers out of there."

Jordon continued to evaluate the situation. The camouflaged man stood well back in the trees, the shimmering auroras high above his head.

Bucksaw jabbed again, rolled over and caught sight of the intruder. "A haint! And this one's got a machine gun!"

TWENTY-EIGHT_____

The light from the rising sun reflected off the snow with the intensity of an arc welder. Jordon squinted and tried to define the outline of the handrails which extended upward on both sides.

Bucksaw led up the steps to the rig floor, silent, save for the clank of his boot soles against the slick expanded metal.

"Hey, fella! Easy on the shoulder." The barrel of the assault rifle prodded Jordon again and he winced. "You better have good reason to make me go up here. If not, I'm gonna make you eat that."

The heavy door at the top of the landing matched the color of the snow except for the round Stuart-Dupree emblem at eye level. The orange insignia depicted an eagle atop a barrel of oil, but the sight swung away when the latch released and the portal opened inward.

A scrawny man with a massive handlebar mustache and an even larger black cowboy hat came into focus. He held out his hand. "Welcome, Pardner. I've been expectin' you. Why don't you git yourself in outta the cold?"

Jordon felt a shove from the guard and followed Bucksaw across the threshold into a bath of warm air.

The lanky greeter lowered his big hand and opened his other fist to reveal a good sized apple. He fished a pen knife from the front pocket of his jeans, opened the blade with his teeth and sliced into the fruit. "Both of you. Come in here and thaw. How ya doin' Linc?"

Bucksaw dropped back a step. "Don't know you. How you know me?"

After the apple quarter disappeared behind the mustache, the out of place cowboy wiped the knife on the back of his checkered sleeve and offered his paw again. "Name's P.T. Shay. Friends call me Theo."

"What's your game, Shay?" Jordon didn't feel real friendly. A quick scan of the small enclosure revealed lockers, a bench and lots of fresh paint. *All show and no substance. Maybe there's something more interesting hid behind the next door.*

155

"No game, ol' buddy. Unless you count those young 'uns who tried to play hide and seek." He shivered. "Now git your carcasses on in here so I kin shut the door."

"Who do you work for, Shay?" Jordon stood his ground and continued to inventory the room.

"Suit yourself. If you want to freeze your backsides..."

Jordon signaled for Bucksaw to step forward. Behind him, he heard the guard close the door from the outside.

Shay stepped around Bucksaw, spun the spoke wheel on the door and locked it like the watertight compartment of a submarine. "Anybody fer coffee?"

"Answer my question, Shay."

The mustache bristled. "Shoot, I'm the company man fer Stuart-Dupree. Ain't you figured that one out yet?"

"And I'm the Lone Ranger!"

"Hey spaceman," muttered Bucksaw, "don't think I like where this analogy is going."

Shay's cheeks rose with the smile hid behind the brush. "Yes, Mr. Jordon, I can see why you feel like that 'bout now." He pointed at the row of sterile white lockers. "Why don't you and Linc crawl outta those hot bunny suits. I'll rustle you up some proper coveralls."

After a change of clothes and two mugs of thick coffee, Shay cocked his head toward the inner door. "Seems my rig's listed one of the top tourist attractions fer ASTRO employees this winter. Don't see why. Ski season ain't much."

"Cut the good 'ol boy, Shay." Jordon forced down another thick gulp of coffee. "What happened to the geologic team?"

"'Fraid their accommodations are a tad cramped at the moment. Put 'em up in my No-Tell Mo-Tel. Got 'em packed in the middle trailer out there like feeders headin' fer auction."

"Hamilton?"

Shay sliced into his apple. "Yep. Got that crazy Ox, a smart mouth Cajun, one spunky little filly and couple of others hole up in there. Your buddy Smullins checked in last night."

"I want to see them."

"Hold your horses. We gotta talk 'bout some things first. You space boys call it a debriefin'. Or is it the military?" He gobbled the juicy slice. "No matter, we'll cull it all out."

Jordon rose from the bench and took a step toward Shay. The pen knife didn't appear to be much of a weapon, but the big fist told a different story. "After I see everyone." He wondered why the gangly man hadn't mentioned Foard or Crandell. *Are they still on the ridge?*

Shay didn't flinch. "Believe me, Pardner, they're all in fit shape. Sleepin' off a hangover. Give 'em a little elixir to erase their short term memory. They'll have one bad headache fer a spell and nightmares 'bout ghost and such fer 'bout a year."

Jordon looked at Bucksaw and with a nod both pinned Shay to the wall. "You've drugged them?"

The cowboy offered no resistance, but his eyes nervously studied his black hat which had landed and now teetered on the edge of the bench. "Stuff's harmless as a Sunday picnic."

The throb in his arm caused Jordon to release his grip. "And I suppose you intend to do the same to us?"

Bucksaw leaned into Shay's chest. "He ain't gonna poke me with no needle."

"Relax. Ain't nobody gonna poke nobody." Shay stared with dark eyes over Bucksaw's shoulder. "I checked you out, Mr. Jordon. You got level eight clearance at ASTRO."

Jordon wondered how the lanky man had access to such information. He tapped Bucksaw on the back. "Ease off, Linc. Let's hear him out."

Despite the antiseptic cleanliness of the room, Shay dusted his jeans and tossed his apple core into an empty locker. "How 'bout a tour of my rig? Think you'll git a kick outta it. Ain't another one like it in the world. Fully automated." He planted his hat on a hook and headed for the inner door. "An' this darlin ain't ever gonna drill fer one drop of oil."

Entry to the next room required a thumbprint scan and a four digit code punched into a grid pad next to a retinal read. Jordon caught his breath and followed Shay through. For twenty feet across both walls, rows of cold war era computers blinked and calculated.

"Trouble started when your team went pokin' their noses into the courthouse records. My men grabbed 'em on the way back to Wildwood. Would've sent 'em back with ghost stories in their heads, but the rest of the bunch kept trippin' my perimeter sensors. What with the solar flares foulin' up communications and everythin'. Nabbed the whole lot. Gonna ship 'em out this afternoon. Ain't decided where, but they'll be scratchin' their noggins wonderin' how they got there."

Jordon marveled at the bank of instruments. It rivaled the best at Mission Control, circa Neal Armstrong. "How'd you know I'd be searching for them?"

Shay parked his backside in a chair which rode a rail the length of the console. "I knowed 'bout you when you jumped outta that dern airplane. Gutsy, real gutsy." He typed something onto a keyboard and pointed at a monitor. "What I want to know, is why all the sudden ASTRO gets curious 'bout my little operation?"

Jordon watched his entire life history scroll across the black screen in blocky white letters. Information on birth records, academic achievements, marriage. He choked back a bitter memory and concentrated on the conversation. "This rig doesn't show up on any aerial recon photos."

"Not s'posed to. I've got complete stealth capabilities. Some nifty technology we pulled outta the Roswell crash. Came in real handy in the early sixties, what with every commie and his dog launchin' spysats. My predecessor told me he got a big laugh first time they tested the *KH-4.*"

Jordon scratched his chin. "If I remember right the *KH-4 Corona* is one of ours."

"We're tryin' to hide from everybody. The French *Lacrosse* scared us fer a bit, but we got our hands on some salvage from a fresh crash site in Bosnia and that solved that. Some engineerin' way ahead of its time. Really made us invisible."

So, these aren't the real computers, these dinosaurs are window dressing too. "Not quite. You show up as a blue pulse on the *Frontier's* S-SMC."

Shay slammed a big fist against the console. "I knew it! Solar flares. Just a matter of someone pointin' the wrong thing at us at the right time. The pulse comes from a generated image diffractor buried under the middle of this location. It ripples the atmosphere. How's that fer tomorrow's technology today?"

"Why a drilling rig?"

"Now, a military compound is kinda obvious, isn't it? Nobody pays attention to us. Besides at the start they worried more 'bout planes than spysats." He rubbed the edge of the keyboard like the back of a pretty girl's hand. "Yep, this baby eats a lot of power. They built the lake so we can pull all we need from the dam. Monarch's idea, so they named it after him. Big buddies with Jacks who owned all the land 'round here."

"So, you're telling me this is a government operation?"

"You wouldn't believe the half of it."

"Take a stab anyway." Jordon gazed about and tried to locate the source of the light, which came from some hidden panels in the ceiling.

"I'll say one thing. You sure don't use up all your kindlin' to make a fire. I like that. No wonder you got a security level eight clearance at ASTRO."

"So does Tate. Why don't you bring him up here too?"

Shay swung a cowboy boot onto his knee and leaned back into the console. "Because, Pardner, this operation's security level twelve. You willin' to take the responsibility of such knowledge?"

"So, this is a government operation."

Shay nodded. "Yep. One hundred percent U.S.D.A. certified Uncle Sam all the way. Security level twelve."

"That's restricted Presidential access."

"Exactly. The alternative is I drug you." He shook his head and looked at Bucksaw. "Have bad dreams of haints and such fer years. What 'bout you, old man? Keep a secret?"

"Been keeping one since before you sprouted teeth."

Shay's cheeks rose again, but the smile remained hidden. "I know. I've been waitin' fer you to come forward fer a long time. Didn't know if it was you or the storekeeper. Not too hard to figure out. Everybody else went off to other pastures, 'cept fer the old lady."

Jordon moved to the end of the computerized room and spotted an observation port which revealed a look at the actual rig floor. A cable ran from the enclosed ceiling into a hole below.

"Like I told you, ain't no oil down there. It's all under the lake."

"Start at the beginning," said Jordon. "Bucksaw told me this isn't the first rig here, that somehow you keep modernizing it every few years."

"Yep, this is the sixth. First one erected in nineteen forty-three soon after the project began. I'm the third, fer lack of a better description, foreman of this ranch. Came aboard in ninety-six. I work fer a small organization created by an Executive Order which designated this place *Project Liberty Hole*. It also created Stuart-Dupree, a bogus company named after a couple of Roosevelt's aides."

"So, what are you protecting here?"

Shay raised his hands into the air like a bank teller at a holdup. "Believe it or not, Pardner, nobody knows. Roosevelt and the two big hat boys, Monarch and Jacks, cashed in their chips before they let anybody in on the joke. I do know one thing. If ASTRO enjoyed my fundin', your buddies Neil and Buzz would've walked on Mars in sixty-nine."

Jordon continued to stare at the thick shiny cable which ran from floor to ceiling. *It couldn't have been installed that far back.* "Doesn't pan out."

"Consider the times." Shay appeared behind him and put a large hand on Jordon's sore shoulder. "We're talkin' WW II. Ol' man Roosevelt felt he needed to hide somethin' from the world, and he decided to do it at the bottom of this well. Probably thought things might git outta hand over in Europe. Guess he didn't trust anybody, 'cept fer Linc."

Bucksaw shuffled at the far end of the room.

"That true, Linc?" asked Jordon. *He must be way older than he looks.* "F.D.R. tell you what's down there?"

"No."

"Then what?"

The old man approached and peered through the observation port. "My father found a good friend in the President when I was a small boy. Franklin gave me a message to pass on. Told me I'd know the right time."

Shay kicked up his heels and did a jig across to the door and back. "I knew it! We're fixing' to find out what's what." He slapped Bucksaw on the back. "Why'd you wait so long ol' timer?"

"People just now started to disappear in the woods."

Jordon held up a hand. "That war's been over for a long time. Why don't you go ahead and bring it up?"

"Cain't"

"Why not?"

"Fool thing's booby trapped to explode."

"So? Disarm it."

Shay shook his head. "I've gone over this a million times and so did my predecessors. What we got here is a powder keg and we're sittin' right on top of it. No tellin' what's down there. Shoot, they messed with nuclear bombs. Experimented with prototypes and such. This mother gave birth to more secrets than the *Manhattan Project*."

Jordon rubbed his chin and considered everything he'd been told. "You've got an ultra secret operation so hush-hush even you don't know what you're sitting on?"

"Now, your herds movin' in the right direction. But not to worry. My systems are fail-safe." He dropped into his chair on rails. "It's all controlled from this here panel. The junk at the bottom of the well may be antique, but we're monitorin' it with the most modern, state-of-the-art equipment available. You guys at ASTRO will probably be gettin' some of the spin offs in the next ten to twenty years."

Jordon surveyed the controls. "I'm not buying it. This is obsolete junk. I don't care how much fresh paint you put on it."

Shay raised the hinged keyboard to reveal a small box in a recess underneath. It had ten buttons of various colors and shapes and a slightly larger flat monitor with an assortment of grids and graphs. "You got me, Pardner. Here's my hole card. All you need to control a whole fleet of shuttles remotely is this gizmo."

"So, if an invasion did take place, how's it designed to keep the enemy from getting the mystery item out of the well?"

"Several ways." Shay bragged on his equipment like a proud papa. "Titanium cable in the draw works goes into the hole and is connected to a cylindrical tube at the bottom of the well."

He pulled out his pen knife and used it for a visual aide. "That's what contains Roosevelt's mysterious stash. Attached to the bottom side of the canister is the detonator. If it drops and contacts the explosive device at the bottom of the well, kiss your saddle horn, and everythin' within a three mile radius, *adios*. Most of the explosion will be directed upward, destroyin' the bad guys along with all this equipment. Gotta be nuclear.

Nothin' else can pack such a wallop."

"So, how's it fail-safe? Don't you monitor for radiation?"

Shay scratched the back of his head. "Now, why didn't somebody think of that?"

Jordon held his breath for a moment, then released it slowly. "Why do I get the feeling this place's been designed by committee?"

"Now, don't git your lasso in a tangle. Once we start pullin' the cylinder up, it'll take 'bout ten minutes fer it to reach the surface. On the outside of the canister is a security lock sportin' ten digits. If I'm right, Linc knows the password which'll allow the computer to release the code numbers. Whoever opens it has three minutes to git inside the tube and disengage the detonator release. If not, an acid vial breaks and the whole mess drops to the bottom of the well takin' the whole kit 'n caboodle down with it. Which, dependin' on the friction, will take anywhere from two to seven minutes."

"What if they just take the canister?" The story became more unbelievable and Jordon's intense curiosity grew.

"Oh, if they can get it loose before the three minutes runs out, the detonator will drop by itself. There's no way to git it outta the well, it's got a lip on it what catches before it clears the hole. Either way, this place is history."

Jordon moved to the computer console and stared at the monitor which still contained his life story. "So, you're telling me if Linc has the right information you can pull this thing out of the hole?"

"Yep, that's what I've been sittin' on my tail fer day after day. Just waitin' to git the thumbs up. This job's borin', but the pay's good." Shay cocked his head to the side and crooked his index finger. "So, 'ol timer, why don't you tell me what you've been keepin' a secret all these years?"

TWENTY-NINE_____

Jordon watched Theo Shay's big hands dance across the odd keyboard like a concert pianist. *A secret is hidden in the well below. Its time of revelation is now. But, why now? Why here?* He weaved the facts together in his mind, but for some reason square pegs jammed in round holes. The ex-astronaut hated one thing more than anything else in the world. Bureaucracy. This whole operation reeked of a bureaucratic scheme run amuck. A classic example of the left hand not knowing the right hand held a finger on the button.

Shay winked like a man on the verge of a first date instead of his last day on Earth. "All righty, Ol' timer. I got this here thing ready fer your message. I enter it. It'll start computin' out the ten digit code to deactivate the detonator."

Bucksaw grunted.

"Right. Anyhow, I've already primed it to start pullin' that thing outta the hole. Just gotta hit 'Enter' on the console over there." He pointed across the sterile room to a second keypad under the observation window. "But first, I gotta go tell my men to clear the area. Just in case."

Jordon leaned forward and stared at the flat monitor in the recess. "How can this code be in this computer if Roosevelt gave it to Linc back in the forties?"

"Wondered that myself," said Bucksaw.

"Oh, it used to be in a bunch of books. Would've took twenty men 'bout a week to sort it out. Pentagon would kill fer this encryption code. Now, it's all programmed in here." Shay tapped one of the ten keys and brought up a line on the screen. "Ready fer the first password." He looked at Bucksaw.

Jordon studied the ancient face. Serious, behind closed eyes, as if he'd forced himself into a trance to search the depths of his memories. A grin spread across his lips. "James and Sara loved Hyde Park in the Spring."

Shay punched a combination of keys.

On the monitor a prompt for a second password flashed in red letters.

162

Bucksaw closed his eyes again. "Delaware and Hudson."

More keystrokes and the demand for yet a third set of instructions.

"There is no more." Bucksaw shook his head and rubbed his temples.

A warning flashed on the screen:

```
Thirty seconds to enter the third code or the sys-
tem will lock out any more attempts for ninety days
```

"Well, don't that beat all?" said Shay. "I ain't waitin' fer three more months. Think!"

```
Twenty seconds...
```

Bucksaw lowered his head.

```
Ten seconds...
```

"Well, I guess that's that - ain't it?"

```
Five seconds...
```

Bucksaw pushed Shay's hands away from the keyboard and typed. X's zipped across the display, then it went blank.

A buzzer sounded from somewhere behind the console and a blue screen appeared. Jordon read the message.

```
Thank you.
Decoding will commence
in one minute.
Please stand by...
```

"How'd you do that on this crazy keyboard, Linc?"

Bucksaw wiped sweat from his brow. "I'm a fast learner."

"So, what's the password, ol' man?" asked Shay as he lit up a second larger monitor on the wall with the same information as the recessed one.

Jordon studied the new monitor and wondered if Bucksaw had guessed.

The weary old man shuffled backward and landed in the chair across the room. "Does it really matter?"

"No," said Shay. "But what's it gonna hurt?"

The big blue screen filled with thousands of numbers, all of which changed instantly. *A random group which will filter down to ten*, thought Jordon. "What did you type, Linc?"

"Take a guess."

Jordon searched his memories of his old college history books. *Would F.D.R. select something totally out of left field, or a more obvious choice?* A name popped to mind. "Eleanor?"

"Nope." Bucksaw leaned back in the chair. "Warm Springs. My father also suffered Polio, but could not afford treatment. The President helped him go to Georgia, so I offered to return the favor."

With his fingers interlaced above his head, Shay cracked his knuckles. "What a day. While we're waitin' on the code, I'll go tell my hands to clear the area and git that trailer house outta here."

Jordon put a hand on Shay's shoulder. "So, how many men do you have?"

"'Bout two dozen. They got bunkers all over this country. That's how we grabbed your people so easy. Popped right outta the ground. Quick and painless. 'Cept fer those two in the RV. My bunch did a first rate job. The Cajun thought a U.F.O. abducted him." He stood and moved toward the door. "Radio communication's still fouled up, so I'll go out and pass the word. When they're all clear and we got the code, we'll bring the canister to the surface."

"You okay, Linc?" Jordon stepped across the computer room and looked down at Bucksaw. "This will all be over soon."

The old man sighed as if a great weight lifted from his shoulders. "Good. Maybe you and I go fishin' when the snow melts."

"I'd like--"

The sound of bullets pinged off the outside of the doghouse.

Jordon grabbed Bucksaw and pulled him to the floor.

Shay's voice echoed through the door. "Hey! Who do you think you are? Git your stinkin' gun outta my face." The scrawny man backed into the room, bullied by his attacker.

From the floor, Jordon stared up into the eyes of the devil himself. "Dover!"

The corner of the short man's lip curled into a wicked smirk. "So nice of you to r-remember me." He kicked slush from his boots. "But I don't recall an invitation t-to this p-party."

"What are you doing here?"

Shay turned his head. "You know this hombre?"

"Why, we're like b-brothers." Dover laughed and unbuttoned his coat. "Aren't we, J-J-Jordon?"

Pure hatred surged through Jordon's veins. How the madman ever escaped from prison would be a matter best discussed later. For the moment he needed to buy some time. A quick glance at the large monitor told him eight of the ten numbers had fallen into place.

Dover shifted his attention slightly from Shay's face to the scrolling screen. "Is this data imp-important?"

Shay offered a blank stare.

"Th-thought so." The barrel of the rifle swung toward the computer bank and a burst of bullets ended in a shower of glass and metal. "Hope you didn't need that information." An acrid smell of burnt wire drifted across the room toward the ventilation grids.

Jordon held his breath and locked the first eight digits into his memory. The last two would be a matter of trial and error.

The end of the rifle moved back to Shay's forehead. The sweat above the bridge of his nose sizzled from the heat of the hot metal.

"What is th-this place?"

"Your tax dollars at work." Jordon exhaled and tried to maintain his composure. He hoped to draw Dover's attention away from Shay.

"Continued re-remarks like that and Mr. Mustache gets a b-bad case of lead poisoning."

Shay's knees buckled. "We're sittin' on top of a big bomb and you just wiped out the code to shut it down."

Wonderful, thought Jordon. *Our list of options drops to two. Maybe Foard hasn't been captured or maybe Dover keels over dead of a heart attack.*

"Thank you so much for th-the update."

The barrel of the rifle lowered from Shay's forehead. At point blank range the cowboy didn't have a chance as the burst struck him square in the chest.

Jordon held his hands over his ears, but the thunderous echo pierced to the core of his brain.

Eyes wide in surprise, Shay stumbled backward, twisted from the force of the impact, tripped on the railed chair, and landed face first on the console.

"I do believe Hopalong is wearing a vest. Pity."

A second later the rig shuddered.

Dover pivoted and aimed the weapon at Jordon. "What's th-that?"

The floor bucked and a groan of steel against steel reverberated through the walls like a giant come alive from a long, deep sleep.

"Thanks to you, Shay landed on something that has initiated the sequence to bring the canister to the surface." Jordon's mind raced. *How long? Seven minutes. Three to deactivate the detonator.* He'd memorized only the first eight digits. *Not enough time.*

Bucksaw stood on wobbly legs. "Bomb's on the way to the surface. We gotta get out."

Through the door, beyond Dover, Jordon sensed movement. *One of the guards? Or...*

"What's going on in here, Chief?" Foard came into the room like a locomotive under full steam. He pulled up short at the sight of Shay.

Dover turned, but didn't swing the rifle to fire. "Everything's under c-control. You get the guards all locked in the trailer with the others?"

Foard removed his coat. "Thumped a few heads, but the rest went peaceful enough."

"Excellent!"

"What are you doing, Foard?" Jordon tried to pan out the barrage of new facts. *ASTRO's head of security? Dover?* "What are you waiting for? Grab the little traitor!"

Foard rocked on his heels and spun the strap of his snow goggles around his finger. "Now, why do I want to do that?" He nudged Dover on the shoulder. "The spaceman thinks I'm on his side."

"How did he get th-that impression? He must think you're as stupid as you look."

The goggles clattered to the floor and a frown crept across Foard's face. Dover's quip struck a nerve.

Jordon tried to think of a way to fray it.

"Go b-back in the other room. I saw some storage. See if you can find any locks and chain." Dover inched forward and peered through the observation portal. He pointed the rifle at Bucksaw. "Open the door to out there," he said. "I think you two should be right on t-top of things."

Foard returned, a handful of locks and several feet of small chain in his hands. He grabbed Jordon by the sore arm and manhandled him out of the room and onto the floor of the rig. The thick cable quivered as it emerged from the hole in the floor and snaked its way through another one in the ceiling.

Dover clubbed Bucksaw across the back of the head with the barrel of his rifle.

The old man grunted and collapsed next to the hole.

"D-Drag him over there, Foard." Dover pointed at the floor. "Chain his legs to Jordon's on both sides of the cable."

Jordon stared into the security man's eyes. "Why, Clifford? For money?"

Foard pushed him down and wrapped the chain around his ankles. "Ain't it always about money, Chief?"

"The h-hands. Make sure he can't use his h-hands."

Jordon felt the man twice his size pin him to the floor with a knee. More locks snapped through the chain links. "We've got six minutes, Clifford." The astronaut's mental clock ticked in his head. "You've still got time to reconsider."

Foard tested his work. "Not a chance, Chief. I've got everything under

166

control." His expression conveyed the exact opposite. His eyes darted back and forth between panic and fear.

A slight movement in Bucksaw's chest indicated life. Jordon looked at Foard and hoped the nerve he'd sensed earlier frayed close to the surface. "I guess you realize, Dover always bumps off his accomplices when he's through using them."

Foard's cheek twitched.

"Always."

"G-Good work." Dover stepped forward and pointed his weapon at Jordon. "Clifford tells me you suffered a b-bit of an accident. Somebody sh-shoot you in the shoulder?" He glanced at Foard. "Which d-did you say?"

"Right one."

"Bet it hurt." Dover pulled the trigger.

The pain ripped through Jordon's arm like a dull saw. The first two wounds, numbed by the cold water of the lake, felt different. Here, on the warm floor of the rig, every cell in his body screamed in agony.

Through the haze of pain he heard Dover laugh. "Oops. Can't tell my right from my left. Guess you'll have matching scars."

Nausea swept into Jordon's throat. *Must fight back.* He rolled to one side and felt the cable slice into his thigh.

Foard headed for the door. "Let's get out of here!"

"N-Not yet."

"What?"

The blood pooled on the white metal floor under Jordon's cheek. He tried to focus on Foard and Dover.

The short man leveled the assault rifle at Foard's legs and backed toward the far wall. "You know the b-bad th-thing about pro football players?"

Foard's face contorted. "No. What?"

Dover leaned close to Jordon and whispered. "The knees are always the f-first to go."

Jordon lashed out against the chains with his less injured arm and dug the tips of his fingers into his nemeses' throat. "Why don't we ride this one out together?"

Dover spit and writhed. His eyes grew wide. "Let go of me!" He pulled the trigger and a bullet ripped into Foard's thigh.

The rig shuddered again.

Foard clutched his leg and stumbled toward the door.

"The canister will be at the surface in a matter of minutes," said Jordon to Dover. "Stay and watch."

A noise rattled at the doorway.

Jordon pinched his fingers tighter into Dover's throat.

"Hey, fella! Get off my friend." A.J. Crandell pulled at Dover's collar and Jordon lost his grip. "Where's Foard runnin' off to?"

Dover struck the innocent truck driver with the rifle stock and Crandell dropped to the floor with a thud.

All hope lost, thought Jordon. He closed his eyes and concentrated on better times. Over the clatter of the cable, he heard Dover cough.

"So long, J-J-Jordon." The madman slammed the door behind him, but reopened it a moment later. "Oh, I almost forgot to t-tell you the good news. Your wife's alive. I found her after all this t-time. So, while you lie here and wallow, waiting for the b-bomb to blow you up, I'm going to pay her a visit."

Jordon arched his back and felt every ounce of strength surge into his voice. "Kerry!"

THIRTY_____

The rig shuddered and groaned beneath him. A giant, wakened from troubled sleep. Jordon felt a low intensity vibration in the floor. He focused on the cable which zipped between his outstretched legs and disappeared into the hole in the ceiling.

Near the door, Dover stumbled to catch his balance. Bucksaw, his feet chained to Jordon's, jerked in awkward spasms. Crandell's motionless body, curled like a child during nap time, lay nearby. Shay's limp form on the other side of the open door slowly slid from the console and thumped on the floor. The impact awoke him and he clutched his chest and inhaled deeply.

An ache clawed up the base of Jordon's neck and exploded behind his eyes like a sledge hammer on granite. He fought the nausea and from deep down searched for the strength to grasp the last straw available. "Dover! You coward!"

The evil man halted, his foot on the threshold of escape. "Am-Am-Am not!"

"Finish the job! Don't wait for the bomb to do it! Step up to the plate and show me what you're made of."

The floor creaked like the deck of a ship in a hurricane. Dover's face twitched as he raised his weapon. He stepped closer to Crandell. "I've had enough of you, J-J-Jordon."

With a quick shift of his body weight, Jordon planted the flat of his boot into the truck driver's back and pushed hard. The chain caught, but the effort proved enough to roll Crandell's body into Dover's legs.

Off guard, Dover lurched and reached for the closest thing to steady himself. His right hand grabbed the cable. It yanked him toward the ceiling and tossed him in a corner. Something snapped and his weapon clanked on the metal floor. Dover tried to crawl toward the door, but his arm appeared broken. Tight-lipped and in obvious pain, he stood and disappeared into the room beyond.

Anticipating the canister's rise to the surface, Jordon tilted his body and forced the chain around his ankles into the cable. Sparks flew and metal sawed against metal. When the link grew red hot, he yanked hard and broke free. In another few seconds he'd done the same with the bindings on his wrist.

Crandell moaned and sat upright. Blood ran down the left cheek. He reached his fingers to the side of his face. "He smashed my ear!"

"A.J.!" Jordon tried to focus. "You're alive!"

"What? Cain't hear you. Got a smashed ear."

"You're alive!"

"Bee hive?" Crandell stumbled to his feet and swatted at his legs. "Where?"

The cable's velocity slowed.

Jordon worked himself onto his knees and pulled the driver down by the tail of his coat. "Get these wounded men to the trailer. Start the truck. Everybody else is inside. Pull them to safety."

"Why?"

The cable crept and stopped when a large two foot tall black canister emerged from the hole. Oily goo dripped from its side.

"Because this is part of a bomb. You don't have much time to get everyone out of the blast range."

Crandell shook cobwebs from his head. "Cain't. That little idget what decked me, done gone and broke the key off in the ignition. Got real suspicious like when I saw him tie up that old man and dump him in the cab."

"Hot wire it!"

"Yeah! Why didn't I think of it?" He moved toward the door. "What do I do with these guys? Best I can tell, they're all still breathin'. Some better than others."

Jordon crawled toward Bucksaw and slapped his cheeks. The old man groaned and reached to rub his forehead. "He'll have to help me diffuse the bomb," he told Crandell. "Get Shay out of here and save those people. Don't wait!"

"This cowboy lookin' feller?"

Bucksaw lifted his head. "Guess I missed something, huh?"

Crandell blew out a breath, hefted Shay under the arms, and headed for the door. "Gonna write me a song 'bout you fellers someday."

The mental clock in Jordon's mind set at three minutes. He knew the first eight digits of the code, but the last two he'd have to guess. He tried to move his wounded arm, but it dangled useless at his side. "Linc. Help me pry the cover off this slimy thing."

The black canister's complicated multiple dial locking mechanism defied first inspection.

"Any ideas, Linc?"

Bucksaw rolled onto his side, his eyes glazed but alive. "I fix old cars. Never saw anything like this."

Jordon tested a small metal pin. It pushed flush against the cylinder. Something clicked and an access door snapped open to reveal a way to the manipulate the dials. "Found it. Can you hold it?"

"I'll try."

With the little door propped wide, Jordon searched his fuzzy mind for the first eight digits. He spun the wheels until they lined up with tiny arrows. Eight, zero, eight, three, six, five, seven and five. Now the last two.

He prayed the correct series would deactivate the release device. If not, A.J. wouldn't have much time.

"Okay, here goes." He tried zero-zero. *Nothing.*

"Zero-one."

Bucksaw grunted. "This gonna take much time?"

"Zero-two."

"Got one bad headache."

Jordon held his breath. Ninety-nine felt an eternity away.

"Zero-four."

Nothing.

Zero-five. An acid-like odor wafted from the base of the cylinder. Sweat ran into Jordon's eyes. "It's going to drop."

The release cracked like a gunshot.

Jordon closed his eyes and waited for the detonator to fall back into the hole. When he opened them again, he stared into Clifford Foard's face.

"Get. Out." With his hand wedged into the hole, Foard managed to delay the drop of the catalyst. "Take the canister. Go!"

Jordon leaned and gazed into Foard's wide eyes. "Why did you do it, Cliff?"

White spittle formed on his lips. He clenched his teeth. "Needed to flush Dover out. Used you for bait, Chief. Woman not your wife."

"What?" The new information processed through Jordon's mind like an elephant being pushed into a pop bottle. "Kerry's not alive?" The adrenaline, no longer fueled by the emotion of hope, drained away.

"No." Foard's body shook under the strain.

"So, you're not Dover's accomplice?"

"Didn't expect him to shoot me."

Jordon inspected Foard's bloody thigh and sensed the former ball player would never be able to make it down the steps.

"Slipping, Chief!"

"Wrap your arms around the canister, Linc." Jordon tried to scrape away some of the slick goo. "Help me disconnect it from the cable."

Bucksaw wobbled and planted his feet.

When the black cylinder released, it felt light in Jordon's arms and he almost fell backwards. After he'd regained his footing on the slick floor, he glanced down at Foard and watched the life fade from his eyes.

An unceremonious whoosh followed and the detonator dropped back into the hole.

A second later every alarm on the location sounded.

THIRTY-ONE_____

"This is not a test of the emergency broadcast system." Jordon repeated the phrase over and over while he slipped and descended the remainder of the mush covered steps on his backside. His wounded arm held close to his side, he shivered against the cold and wished for a coat. With his hand cupped around his mouth, he squinted in the bright sunlight and turned to yell at Bucksaw over the sound of the klaxon. Abandon ship came to mind. "What are you waiting for? Get down here!"

The old man wobbled on unsteady feet at the top of the landing. Cradled under his arm, the black cylinder stood out against the combination of white snow and paint. "Maybe I..."

The container shot out like a banana ejected from a greasy peel. High into the air it sailed, over the rail and into an ice covered storage container. Jordon worked his way through a drift and stared down at the damage.

Bucksaw, out of breath, arrived at his side. "Everything okay?"

"No." Jordon dropped to his knees and stood the canister on end. A long rupture opened from top to bottom. Inside, a glass cylinder held the answers to a lot of questions.

"That what I think it is?"

Jordon peered into the foggy glass tube at ancient writing. Folded neatly inside, the birth certificate of the nation waited to be rescued. "Your buddy Franklin left one doozy of a time capsule."

The sound of a faint whimper came from several feet away. At first Jordon thought it might be Dover, so he proceeded cautiously until he discovered a mangy, three-legged dog curled next to an overturned fifty-five gallon barrel.

"Limp!" Bucksaw moved toward the animal and knelt in the snow. "It's okay, boy. You hurt?"

The dog yelped at the old man's touch.

Jordon's mental clock continued to tick toward zero. He surveyed the location and noted how Crandell had managed to pull the trailer house away. A crimson spotted trail led to where he assumed Dover made his escape. Tate's vehicle sat near the road, two of four tires flat.

No time, he thought. "Appears we're on foot. All transportation is either gone or disabled." He squinted into the bright sunlight. "Wait a sec. Didn't I see a motorcycle? Had some skis on the front. Parked over by one of the other trailers?"

Bucksaw stood, the wounded dog cradled in his arms. "Yamahammer six-fifty dirt bike. Big mother. How you gonna drive?"

"I'm not." Jordon pulled the canister toward the center of the slushy location. "You are."

Although it didn't appear to have graced a showroom floor in many years, the odd contraption proved ready for action. Bucksaw smoothed out a place in the snow with his boot and lowered the dog gently to the makeshift bed. Satisfied, he hopped on the bike and managed to kick start it on the second attempt.

Jordon straddled the seat behind the old man and tried to figure out a way to attach the canister to the frame. Unable to, he leaned and spoke into Bucksaw's ear. "I'll have to hold it. Open it up wide and stay in A.J.'s tracks. We don't have much time."

Bucksaw pointed at the injured animal on the ground. "What about my dog?"

Sad eyes stared upward. Jordon tossed the canister to the side and dismounted. "Come on, boy. We're going for a wild ride."

The motor revved under Bucksaw's hand. "If we make it out of this alive, you gonna tell 'em what we left behind?"

Jordon slung his leg over the seat and pinned the dog tight between his chest and Bucksaw's back. He forced his boots down hard on the rough sawtooth pegs. "Ain't gonna be no story to tell if you don't light a fire under this thing!"

"This mean my people gonna get the country back?" Bucksaw asked.

Cold, wet slush raced up Jordon's back when the snowchained wheel bit for traction. A moment later, the cycle lay on its side, then righted as it spun a full one eighty donut before the skis centered in one of the ruts. "Now, you're heading in the right direction. Watch the cattle guard."

Bucksaw leaned into the handlebars and wound the motor to full throttle.

In places, Jordon saw where the trailer bottomed out and scraped up huge piles of muck. At times the obstacles sent the bike into wheelies which threatened to throw him off the back of the machine.

With moves too scary for Evil Knievel, Bucksaw maneuvered the cycle around one turn after another. On one side, piles of rubble and rock.

On the other, shear drop-offs of several hundred feet.

The mental clock continued to eat time.

"Any idea where we are?" Jordon felt the dog's muzzle squeeze into his armpit.

Bucksaw applied too much pressure to the brake. His response splintered into unintelligible verbal fragments and scattered into the cold wind.

The climbs and curves continued to test the limits of the bike and every gear got a chance to pull its weight through the course which looked to Jordon like an Olympic bobsled run designed by a miniature golf enthusiast. He thought of the truck, somewhere ahead. "I hope A.J. knows where he's going."

The bike careened around the next corner and a huge object lay across the road a few dozen feet ahead.

Jordon recognized it immediately. The top of the trailer house, which lay on its side. The truck, atop what appeared to be a Jeep, blazed in the trees to his right. Beyond the wreckage, almost hidden in the midst of snow covered evergreens, a traditional cabin stood like an advertisement for maple syrup.

Bucksaw stood on the brake, but the forward momentum carried them toward the overturned trailer. Jordon released his grip on the dog and wrapped his arm around Bucksaw's neck. "GET OFF NOW!" He leaned and pulled both man and animal backward into the slushy road.

The riderless ski-cycle continued forward like a torpedo, kicked upward and crashed through the roof.

Bucksaw and the dog still on top of him, Jordon screamed from the almost unbearable pain in his shoulder. He slid feet first into the metal top of the trailer a yard away from the jagged hole.

The mental clock hit zero.

In his mind, visions of the rig riding high above a mushroom cloud like a SATURN V rocket mingled amid fears of his friends ceasing to be when the mysterious bomb exploded and vaporized everything.

THIRTY-TWO_____

B ig wet sloppy kisses bathed Jordon's face. *If this is heaven,* he thought, *I'm glad I came.*

"Hey, Limp! Give the guy some air!" A female's voice echoed in the darkness.

"Good grief. Cut the dog some slack, Gina. Tough love never hurt anybody."

"Ox, if I didn't feel so glad to be alive..."

"Coo! Ah knowed one tang. Ah vary glad dat Fee Folay stay outside dis cabin!"

"Where am I?" Jordon remembered the snow. The road. Many hands.

"Not sure. I was hoping you might know." Tate Smullins' familiar voice whispered in his ear. "I show up at that rig and the next thing - I'm dragging myself out of an overturned trailer house."

"We all got a headache."

Jordon forced his eyes open and tried to protect his face from the grateful mutt. "Caesar Hamilton? You here?"

"We're all here. Ox, Gina, Miguel, the old storekeeper, Marcel, Linc, the truck driver and a half a dozen guards from the rig. Odd thing is, half of us don't remember a whole lot."

Jordon's shoulder felt like lead, but he tried to sit. "Where is 'here'?"

Theo Shay came into focus across the musty room. "'Bout a hundred feet under Miss Jacks' cabin. Bomb shelter. Maybe she knew all along."

A skinny woman with pigtails paced back and forth. "Didn't think she'd let us in, but I guess a pack of wild eyed geologists don't come running out of the woods every day."

"Where is she?" Jordon let his friend Smullins help him from the floor to a chair. An aroma of chicken soup filled the air.

A very old, but somehow ageless, woman entered the room, steaming bowls balanced on a tray before her. "Now, drink this young man and you'll feel much better." A Norman Rockwell painting of the quintessential grandmother.

Jordon, unsure of the last time he'd eaten, accepted the bowl from her frail hands. Waiting for the soup to cool, he told the group about the contents of the canister.

✗ ✗ ✗

"Same blast pattern. It's *Tunguska* all over again," said Smullins. "Trees flattened for miles. Prime location for a toothpick factory. Wanna go partners?"

Jordon turned his head to see the damage. From the medivac stretcher he surveyed the devastation to the far hills. The cabin, scared with wooden splinters and black smoke, stood minus its porch in defiance to the carnage. "Or St. Helens."

"Yeah, forgot about that one." Smullins unsleeved a toothpick from a cellophane wrap and pointed to several vans parked near where the twisted trailer rested on its side in the road. "They say there's no radiation. Nobody can explain the blast. Shay told me the bomb may have been a prototype."

A commotion broke out near the covey of ambulances. "You will let me see him! I demand it!"

"Cax always knew how to make an entrance." Jordon smiled at the big man, battered and bruised, who bullied his way past the National Guardsmen and slogged through the mud. A woman, her face familiar, followed and stopped a few feet away.

"Kerry?"

She shook her head. "No, my name is Lana. It's a long story."

Uncanny. She does resemble Kerry a little. A lifetime of sadness filled his soul. "Dover said--"

She took his hand and caressed it. "Dover's a liar. Foard used me to flush him out."

"Mitch! Are you all right?" Despite the cold, Grant wiped sweat from his brow as he edged the woman aside.

"Still alive..." Jordon watched her take a few steps backward and disappear into the crowd of responders. "Maybe she is still alive..."

Grant fumbled for his words. Look, Mitch... I know we've aired our differences..."

Jordon pictured the man buried in the rubble of what had once been Wildwood, Oklahoma. Tate told him of the trip to the Philippines, of his search for Kerry. "We've got a lot to discuss, Cax. Later."

"Absolutely." Grant pursed his lips and changed subjects. "Dover?"

His shoulder felt like molten lava, but Jordon managed a shrug. "Don't know. Got away? Tell the chopper pilots to search for a man with his eyebrows singed off."

"So what was so all fired important at the bottom of the well? That blasted Winston woman has been on every news channel since the explosion."

Jordon petitioned Smullins for support.

His friend pointed back. "Hey, you're the guy who tossed it aside to save the dog."

"What?" Grant sputtered with incredulity. "What did you do!"

Jordon tried mock seriousness. "I hate to tell you this, Cax. I held it in my hands, but this three-legged dog..."

"It? What it?" The big man's face flushed red. "The contents of the canister? Tell me or I'll personally see Veronda Winston assigned as your lifetime nurse!"

"You're not going to believe it."

"Try me."

"The Declaration of Independence."

The big man's eyes lost focus and rolled up into his head. With the force of a giant oak, he fell backwards into the cold mud.

Smullins winked. "When he wakes up, you going to tell him it was a fake?"

"I might."

EPILOGUE_____

July 4

"When in the Course of human events..."

The sea of red, white and blue spilled along Constitution Avenue, across the Mall beyond and into the Potomac. Gathered in front of the National Archives to witness history, citizens of every description stood in silent awe while General Antony Stone adjusted his eye patch and read from the historic document.

An elbow away, Smullins leaned to whisper. "Can you believe this crowd? There's more TV cameras here than politicians."

Jordon scanned the first row below the podium to find A.J. and the others, each decorated with their shiny new Presidential Medal of Freedom. "I'd call it an even draw. You ever shake so many hands?"

Smullins cracked his knuckles and slipped a fresh toothpick between his teeth. "Never. How's the shoulder holding up today?"

"No rain in the forecast, so pretty good."

"Hey, we're up."

General Stone introduced the nation's heroes in turn to thunderous applause. He then motioned for Lincoln Bucksaw to stand, went down the line, and concluded with a spunky redhead in a wheelchair. "...and Meg Mordel. To each, our thanks. God bless you all."

When the cheers subsided, a commotion drew Jordon's attention to the steps at the far end of the platform.

"But I'm a personal friend of the President. I should be at his side, not that pompous Grant. I don't care if he did rescind his resignation. Unhand me."

Three secret service men wrestled Veronda Winston to the ground. She bit one and kicked a second in the leg. A moment later reinforcements managed to drag her away leaving one designer high heel shoe at the curb.

Either unaware of the fracas or not wanting to draw attention from the matters at hand, the General spoke on. "Along with the Constitution, the Declaration has traveled an interesting road to this day. Let's examine the path for a moment."

He cleared his throat and changed the stance of his cane. "Most know of the British plot to destroy the Declaration during the War of 1812. Saved from the fiery fate, they housed it in the Patent Office Building for many years. Next, in Philadelphia, came an open exhibition during the Centennial Celebration. You'll be surprised to know that afterward, someone with more patriotism than common sense displayed this fragile document in the State Department library. In a cigar smoking room - near a fireplace, no less. When they came to their senses, they locked the Declaration in a safe, where it remained for a quarter of a century, until it moved to Fort Knox during World War II." The General paused and consulted his notes. "Or so we thought."

"Boy, your father-in-law sure is long winded." Smullins tugged at his collar. "If I don't get out of this suit and into some jeans..."

Jordon shushed him and listened to the end of the speech. When the document had been moved back into the archives by thirteen spit and polished military men, accompanied by drum and fife, he mopped the sweat from his brow and moved toward the steps.

"A moment, Mr. Jordon."

"Of course, Mr. President. Tate, I'll catch up with you later."

"It's a done deal. Mr. President, if you'll excuse me."

Jamison Franklin Wester stood a good four inches taller. Jordon sensed the soft spoken, former Texas senator couldn't have asked for a better gift prior to the November elections. "I've cleared mah schedule for the shuttle dedication down in Florida way next month," he said.

Jordon brought to mind the new spacecraft named in his honor. "I look forward to it, sir. *Prospector* has a nice ring to it, don't you think?"

The President laughed his trademark guffaw, mugged a handshake for the cameras and moved on to speak to Grant. Jordon took the opportunity to make his way to the steps. With the aide of a couple of Secret Service men, he managed to pass through the crowd along Indiana Avenue.

"Thanks, boys. I can handle it from here."

They disappeared into the throng as a white work van with heavily tinted windows screeched to a halt next to the curve.

A tall, leggy Asian woman with a perfect smile and dark sunglasses bailed out of the side door and stuck a microphone in Jordon's face. "Astronaut Mitch Jordon. Paige Tanokara, Video News International. I'd like to ask you a few questions."

Uncomfortable, Jordon eyed the shaggy cameraman who somehow managed to emerge from both the front seat and a sixties rock concert at the same time. The mike in his face and the retro hippy to his back, he nodded. "Sure. Why not?"

People waved flags and wandered by. Some stopped and tried to wave into the camera.

The reporter took her stance, propped her shades on top of her head and addressed the cameraman. "Okay, Sam. On my mark. Three, two, one..." A bright light flashed on in conjunction with her smile. "I'm standing next to the famous space explorer, Mitch Jordon. Please explain how you knew the so-called first 'Oklahoma Declaration' to be a fake and the second one to be authentic."

Jordon held up a palm. He'd answered this question a thousand times along with how the real documents had been hidden in a subterranean vault under Miss Jacks' cabin. "I'm afraid if you don't have anything new to ask..."

She pressed forward. "For the international audience. Please."

Jordon wondered why the cameraman stood behind and filmed the back of his head. He took a deep breath, turned and grinned at the 'international audience' somewhere behind the lens. "When I saw the old document folded inside the canister, I knew it wasn't authentic."

"You took quite a chance." The woman's voice held a smoky quality.

"Maybe, but a gut feeling told me they'd have rolled the real thing up before placing it in the tube." Suddenly he understood the cameraman's proximity as what felt to be the barrel of a small pistol worked into his backbone.

"Interesting." The reporter stepped close and leaned in with the microphone. "Please keep smiling, Mr. Jordon. Get into the van. I think you've taken enough bullets for your country."

Gawkers, unaware of his situation, continued to crowd in and mug for the lens.

"What?" He glanced over his shoulder at the cameraman. "What is this?"

"Quite simple, Mr. Jordon. You're being kidnapped."

To be continued...

Made in the USA
Charleston, SC
04 November 2016